Books by April Wilson

McIntyre Security Bodyguard Series:

Vulnerable

Fearless

Shane (a novella)

Broken

Shattered

Imperfect

Ruined

Hostage

Redeemed

Marry Me (a novella)

Snowbound (a novella)

Regret

With This Ring (a novella)

Collateral Damage

Special Delivery

The Tyler Jamison Series:

Somebody to Love

Somebody to Hold

The British Billionaire Romance Series:

Charmed

For a list of my audiobooks, visit my website:

www.aprilwilsonauthor.com/audiobooks

Ruined

McIntyre Security Bodyguard Series
Book 6

by

April Wilson

Wilson Publishing LLC
P.O. Box 292913
Dayton, OH 45429
www.aprilwilsonauthor.com

Visit www.aprilwilsonauthor.com to sign up for the author's e-mail newsletter to be notified about upcoming releases.

ISBN-13: 978-1985018105
ISBN-10: 1985018101

Published in the United States of America
First Printing April 2018

Dedication

To my dear friend Becky Morean,
for finding Sam for me.

1

Sam

Sixty-two... sixty-three... sixty-four.... keep going, Sam! You're so close, man! You can do this!"

My phone beeps the two-minute mark, and I fall back on the mat, defeated. "Damn it!"

My abs are on fire and my thighs are cramping like a bitch. As I stare up at the ceiling lights high overhead, I rub my left leg, which aches bone deep. I guess I shouldn't complain, though. I managed sixty-four sit-ups in two minutes. Not bad. But unfortunately, not good enough.

"You were so close!" Craig says, patting me on my leg as he sits down beside me. He hands me a towel to wipe the sweat from my face. "Don't be so hard on yourself. You're making great progress."

I frown. "I failed."

"Oh, come on! I don't know anyone who can do eighty sit-ups in two minutes. That's insane."

"I do. And I can't go back to work unless I can too, not to mention eighty push-ups in two minutes, fifteen pull-ups, and run a mile-and-a-half in under ten minutes." I blow out a heavy breath and brush back some hair that escaped my topknot. "I've still got a way to go."

Craig frowns at me. "You don't have to go back there, you know," he says, lowering his voice.

This isn't the first time he's hinted at me staying in Dayton permanently. But no matter how angry I am at Cooper, I can't just give up on him. I honestly can't see myself with anyone else. It's Cooper for me. But, damn it, he needs to meet me halfway. He needs to at least try. I know we grew up in very different eras—he grew up in a time when you just didn't come out. A lot of guys hid their true identities behind marriages of convenience. But times have changed, and he needs to change with them. Or at least make an effort. I'm not asking for a lot. Just a little.

It's late, and the fitness center is already closed for the night. The customers are long gone, and most of the employees have gone home. I'm pretty sure it's just the two of us here now, and that's probably not a good idea. I don't want to give Craig the wrong idea.

"You have a job here if you want it," he says. "I'd hire you in a heartbeat. You'd make an awesome personal trainer."

I glance at my training coach and frown. *God, he's beautiful.* Blond hair, blue eyes, a body like Adonis. He's smart, he's funny, and best of all, he's comfortable in his own skin.

Craig lays his hand against bearded cheek. "Just think about it, okay?"

"Craig—"

Craig shoots to his feet, cutting me off before I can shoot down his proposal—again—and offers me a hand up. "Don't say anything right now. Just think about it."

I reach for his hand, and he hauls me to my feet. When he releases me, I test my balance to make sure I'm not going to fall on my ass. My left leg aches, but it's holding up. I got the cast off six weeks ago, and I've been out of the walking brace for two weeks. I'm definitely on the mend. Now, I just have to get back to fighting strength so I can go back to work. And as far as Cooper goes...well, I'll deal with him when the time comes. Cause right now, I got nothin'. We're trapped—or at least *I'm* trapped—in limbo. I can't go on being his closet boyfriend forever—his dirty little secret. But what will happen to us if he won't at least try? I can't live with the status quo. To be honest, though, I also can't lose him.

I guess leaving him back in December—shortly after my accident—was my way of forcing the issue. I should have gotten a T-shirt that says: I *got hit by a car, and all I got was this lousy T-shirt, a fractured skull, and a broken leg.* But I don't think they make shirts like that.

Craig smiles at me, forcing my thoughts back to him and the present. "Hey, you hungry?" he says. "Do you wanna grab a late-night dinner?"

I frown as I get a whiff of myself. "It's late, and I need to shower. I stink to high heaven."

Craig laughs. "Okay, so go shower. Then how about some dinner? I'll take you to your favorite burger joint, my treat. How about it? I'll even buy you a beer."

As he makes the offer, he reaches out and touches my arm. It's just a casual touch, nothing overtly sexual, but the invitation is there in his eyes. I figure it's not a good idea to mix the way I'm feeling right now—decidedly lonely—with alcohol and a hot guy. The hopeful expression on his face tells me it's definitely a bad idea.

I scrub my hand across my face, thinking I need to trim my beard. Damn it! Why is this happening to me now? The guy I've always dreamed of is standing right here in front of me, practically offering himself to me on a silver platter. He's everything I've always wanted. And he's *out*—he's *so* out. I swallow hard. "It's getting late, Craig. I should just shower and head home."

"Sam." He reaches for my hand, his long fingers intertwining with mine. "Please. I'll get down on my knees right now and beg if that'll make a difference."

I laugh, just as he intended me to. Craig knows the score—I've been up front with him from the beginning. He knows how I feel about Cooper. And damn, Cooper's ruined me for other men. He can reduce me to mush with just one look. With just one word!

"Thanks, but I'd better not." I smile at Craig, hoping to soften the rejection.

He smiles back, but it's a sad smile. "All right. I'll see you tomorrow then. You can let yourself out?"

"Yeah. Thanks."

I watch Craig head for the exit and wonder, just for a second, what it would be like to say yes to him. To be with a guy who doesn't feel he needs to hide me from the world—hide *us*. To be with a guy who's open about his sexuality. But wondering is useless because I know I won't act on it. As fantastic as Craig is, I just can't bring myself to give up on Cooper, no matter how badly I'm hurting right now.

I head for the men's locker room and grab a clean towel and my shampoo and soap. I've got the place to myself, so I take my time and zone out beneath the spray of hot water, close my eyes, and let my mind wander and my body relax.

Now that the pain in my left leg has subsided, my body's coming back online... along with a lot of pent-up physical need. I've been dreaming a lot about Cooper lately and waking up in the middle of the night with a raging hard-on. My body aches for release. The stupid thing is... I haven't done anything about it.

I *could* do something about it. I could jerk off right here in the shower and no one would know. I could close my eyes and pretend it's Cooper getting me off, pretend it's his hand gripping my erection. Or, hell, all I have to do is say the word and Craig would be on his knees sucking me off like there's no tomorrow. I know this because he's offered on more than one occasion.

Instead, I wrap up my shower in record time and put my street clothes back on, which isn't easy when you're packing an erection that just won't quit.

It's late when I make it to my pick-up truck—a loaner from my mom. I open the driver's door and climb inside, then lean back in the seat and close my eyes. I'm lonely and I'm horny, and it's my own damn fault. If I hadn't left Chicago—left Cooper—I'd be home in bed with him right now.

Before I'm even tempted to do something stupid, like call Craig, I start the engine and peel out of the parking lot. It's time to head home to my empty bed.

* * *

When I arrive at my mom's house—a modest, white Cape on a quiet tree-lined street—I see she left a light on for me in the kitchen. I'm sure she's in bed already. She works first shift as a nurse, and she's up and gone by six. She left a note for me on the kitchen table. *Sam—leftovers in the fridge, sweetie. Love you, Mom.*

I nuke the pot roast and veggies and eat standing at the kitchen counter, chasing the food down with a cold beer.

I made good progress today. Sixty-four sit-ups. I should reach my goal of eighty in a couple more weeks. But I still have to tackle the push-ups, pull-ups, and the mile-and-a-half run before I can even think about going home. I won't go back if I'm not fit to work.

The house is dark and quiet, so I go upstairs to my old bedroom to watch a movie in bed until I'm ready to sleep. In the morning, I'll eat breakfast, and then head back to the gym to keep conditioning. That's all I do these days, eat, work out, sleep, rinse and repeat.

I glance around a bedroom that hasn't changed since I left home right after high school to join the Army. I had my heart set on becoming an Army Ranger—just like my Uncle Matt—and I worked my ass off until I qualified. And once I was in, I loved every grueling minute of it... until the day my chute failed to open on a routine training jump. I broke nearly every bone in my body, and that ended my military career.

This time, all it took was one compound fracture to knock me off my feet. But this time it's different. This time I'm going back.

I surf YouTube for a while, catching up on some of my favorite channels. There's this gay couple I watch religiously, and right now they're planning their wedding. I envy them so much, for having each other, for being so open about their relationship with their family and friends. Watching them gives me hope that one day I can have a relationship like that.

For the millionth time, I wonder if I'm asking too much of Cooper. I can't even get him to hold my hand in public, let alone think about marriage. Illinois recognizes same-sex marriage, but it's not doing me any good.

It still hurts to think back to Shane and Beth's wedding reception. I'd worked so hard to get out of my wheelchair and hobble across the great room on my crutches to ask Cooper to dance. Instead of being proud of me for getting on my feet ahead of schedule, he scolded me in front of a room full of people and told me, "Sit your ass back down before you fall down."

I know Cooper's not comfortable out of the closet. Still, these were our closest friends that day. Every single one of them would have applauded us for dancing. There had been absolutely nothing to fear, and still, he wouldn't stand up with me. He couldn't do the one thing I needed from him—to stand up in front of God and witnesses and say, "Sam's mine."

That had been the last straw. I hopped a plane out of Chicago the next morning and came home to Dayton to hide out in my mother's house while I continued to recuperate.

"Fuck my life," I say, blinking back tears. "And fuck you, too, Cooper."

I watch a few more minutes of YouTube, but it just makes me miss my BFF, Beth—we usually watch this channel together—so I turn it off and lie there in the dark.

I toy with the idea of making a quick call to Beth, just to hear her voice, but it's midnight here, which means it's eleven in Chicago. She's probably asleep by now. If I wake her up, Shane will have my balls in a sling. Beth says he's unbearable now that she's pregnant... that if anyone even looks at her wrong, he's all over them. When she says that, I can hear the smile in her voice. She's not fooling anyone. She loves it when he gets all bossy and overprotective.

I shift in my bed, trying to get comfortable. My erection is tenting the sheet, and my poor, neglected balls ache. I shove the bedding aside and wrap my fingers around the base of my cock, gripping it firmly. God, it feels good. As I lie there, staring at the flushed head, Cooper's voice rings in my head. "That's my cock, Sam. You need an orgasm, you come to me."

When he uses that tone of voice with me, I melt.

And yeah, Cooper's the boss of me, at least in bed. I accepted that a long time ago. Maybe that's why I can't move on. It's too late for that—he owns me.

* * *

The next day, I'm right back at it, this time doing push-ups on the mat. Craig is beside me, being all supportive and sweet—everything Cooper's not—when I hear the door open.

As Craig looks up to see who it is, his eyes widen in appreciation as color sweeps across his cheeks. "Can I help you, sir?" he says, his tone uncharacteristically deferential.

"Thanks, but no. I found what I'm looking for."

Oh, shit. I know that deep, slightly-gruff voice. I close my eyes and continue with my push-ups, mentally counting for myself now that Craig has clammed up. *Forty-seven, forty-eight...* oh, who am I kidding? *To hell with it!*

When I open my eyes, I see a pair of polished black loafers not three feet from my head. Giving up, I roll to a sitting position and drape my arms over my bent knees and crane my head up to gaze into a pair of electric blue eyes.

"Hello, Sam," Shane says, crossing his arms over his chest as he stares down at me. He's wearing a dark gray suit with a white shirt and black tie—he must have come straight from the office.

I swallow hard, trying not to feel like I've been called to the principal's office. "Hey, Shane."

Craig jumps to his feet and faces off with Shane, which I find rather funny. They're about the same height, but I know Shane could wipe the floor with Craig before Craig even knew what hit him.

"Excuse me," Craig says, getting in Shane's face. "Can I help you?"

Shane looks at Craig for a second, then his gaze drifts back down to me. "You know why I'm here," he says, his voice clipped. He's definitely not in a good mood, probably because he had to fly down here when he'd rather be back in Chicago with his pregnant wife.

"Yeah, I do. But Shane, I'm not back to full strength yet."

He shrugs. "Doesn't matter. It's been long enough, and Beth wants you home. So, are we going to do this the easy way, or the hard way?"

I sigh, knowing it's useless to argue with him. "The easy way."

He gives me a tight smile. "Good. Make whatever arrangements you need to make and say your good-byes. Our flight leaves at seven sharp. Will you be at your mother's house?"

"Yeah. I want to say good-bye to her and to Rachel."

Shane nods. "Fine. I'll pick you up at six. Be ready."

"All right."

Shane leaves as quietly as he arrived. No fuss, no fanfare. He's just here to keep a promise he made to his wife.

"Who the hell was that guy?" Craig says, sounding a bit flummoxed.

I can't blame him. Shane has that effect on people. "That was my boss."

"What the fuck? He can't just come in here and order you around like that."

I laugh. "Yes, he can." I climb awkwardly to my feet, cursing my weak leg as I limp toward the locker room to change. It looks like I'm heading back to Chicago—and to Cooper—sooner than I expected.

2

Sam

Craig follows me into the locker room and hovers as I strip out of my workout shorts and into a pair of jeans. I pull off my sweaty muscle shirt and use it to wipe my damp underarms. I need to shower, but I'll wait until I get to my mom's house. I'm running short on time.

"Are you sure you have to go back?" he says, his gaze skimming my bare chest for a split second before he looks away and pretends he wasn't staring at my nipple piercings.

I pull on a clean T-shirt. "I promised Beth I'd come back, and it's been three months. I guess my time is up."

"Just because some spoiled, rich bitch—"

"Whoa—stop. You don't even know Beth. She's one of the kindest people I've ever met."

Craig waves his hand dismissively. "Okay, fine! But what about Cooper? Are you just going to fall back into his bed and let him use you again, like nothing's happened?"

That stings, mostly because it's not that far from the truth. "He's not *using* me."

Craig grabs my shoulders. "What do you call it when someone takes what they want from you, but they don't give you what you need in return? Hmm? I'd say that's definitely *using* someone."

I jerk out of his hold. "It's more complicated than that."

Craig shakes his head, obviously frustrated. "You could have anyone, Sam. I don't know why you're wasting your time on this guy. You can't teach an old dog new tricks."

Old dog. That makes me laugh, because Cooper is almost twice my age. I slam my locker door shut and sling my gym bag over my shoulder. "I'm sorry, Craig, but I have to go."

He grabs me again. "Remember, you can always come back here. I'd give you a job in a heartbeat. Please don't forget that."

"Thanks." A part of me—a small part—wants to take the easy way out and stay here with Craig. Going home is going to be hard, and seeing Cooper again—well, that will be the hardest thing of all.

* * *

I have dinner with Mom and Rachel and explain to them that it's time for me to head back to Chicago. I can tell they're disappointed that I'm leaving, but they try to hide it for my sake. I think they were hoping I'd stay for good.

I'm packed and ready to go when a black sedan pulls up in front of the house. There's no point in delaying this, so I grab my duffle bag and my backpack and head out to the car. A uniformed driver meets me at the rear of the vehicle and pops the trunk so I can stow my gear. Then I slip into the backseat next to Shane.

"I'm not there yet, physically," I admit to Shane. "I'm close, but I wouldn't be able to pass the physical assessment right now."

Shane shrugs. "That's okay. Just keep working at it—you'll get there. But you need to come home. Beth misses you."

I nod. Beth is my client, but she's also one of my best friends. I miss her. And, she's pregnant. I'm missing out on all of that, too. I smile, thinking she's probably got a little baby bump by now.

"And she's not the only one who misses you," Shane says, eyeing me pointedly. "Cooper's been impossible to live with since you left Chicago. I can't take any more of his moping. You two need to work things out."

"You make it sound so easy." Just hearing Cooper's name makes my heart pound. I can't imagine being in the same room with him again, seeing him for the first time in... Jesus, has it really been three months? "I'm coming back to Chicago, but not to the way things were before. If nothing's changed...."

Shane nods. "I understand. But I have faith in Cooper. He knows what's at stake. I trust him to make things right between the two of you. Give him a chance, okay? He's been through...situations...that you know nothing about. You need to cut him some slack."

My throat tightens. I don't dare let myself think that Cooper's going to change. "I'm not getting my hopes up," I say. I can't afford to.

* * *

Twenty minutes later, we arrive at Dayton International Airport. Our driver pulls up beside a McIntyre Security, Inc. company jet, which is already prepped and ready. Negotiating the steps is a bit of a challenge with my leg, but I manage to get myself and my bags up into the plane.

Once we're inside, the captain greets us personally, as does the flight attendant.

Part of me is happy to be going home, but part of me dreads it. I have no idea how I'll react when I see Cooper. I have no idea how *he'll* react. I figure he'll either be glad to see me, or he'll kick my ass for leaving him. Either way, seeing him again will be tough.

Shane takes a seat at one of the swiveling leather armchairs in the front of the jet, and I move farther back and take a seat on one of the small leather sofas. He pulls a tablet out of a black leather briefcase and switches it on to do some work. He's a bit of a workaholic, but I guess that's to be expected when you're the CEO of a multi-million-dollar company.

I strap in, get comfortable, and pull out my earbuds to listen to music. It's a quick flight back to Chicago. We'll be home before we know it.

Once we're airborne, the flight attendant comes by and asks us if we want anything to drink. Shane opts for a shot of whisky. That sounds good to me, so I ask for one too, along with a beer chaser. The prospect of seeing Cooper this evening has me on edge, and I could use a little liquid reinforcement.

The flight is quiet and uneventful. Just before we land, Shane makes a quick call to Beth to let her know we're back in Chicago. I bite back a smile. The poor guy can't even go an hour without hearing her voice.

There's a car waiting for us at the airport. After stowing our gear in the trunk, we head to the apartment building. Shane and Beth live on the penthouse floor, along with Cooper. I have my own apartment two floors down from them.

When our driver drops us off in front of the elevators in the underground parking garage, Shane says, "Come up to the penthouse and say hello to Beth. She won't sleep tonight until she's seen you."

My stomach drops at his suggestion because Cooper lives there too. "All right."

Craig's right. I can't let Cooper simply pick up where we left off. I can't do that to myself. I took a stand when I left, and I have to stick to my guns. If he can't meet me halfway, if he can't even make an effort, we're doomed. I'm not asking for much—hell, I'll settle for him holding my hand in public once in a while. He doesn't have to make some big declaration—he just has to stop treating me like I'm his dirty little secret.

* * *

I'm a nervous wreck as I ride with Shane in the private elevator up to the penthouse floor. Shane already texted Beth to let her know we're on our way up, so she's expecting us. It's March already, and the baby's due in early July, so she must be showing by now.

The elevator doors ping as they glide open. Beth is waiting for us in the foyer, and her face lights up when she sees us. Shane steps out of the car first and takes his wife into his arms. Jesus, the way he's kissing her, you'd think he'd been out of town for a week, not an afternoon. I step out quietly, setting my bags on the floor, and try not to stare at them as they lose themselves in each other. But I can't help noticing how he cradles the back of her head with one hand, while his other hand slides down to cup her little baby bump.

He may be a domineering bastard at times, but no one can fault him for how he loves Beth.

I feel like such a voyeur.

"Feeling okay, sweetheart?" he asks her.

She beams up at him with teary eyes. "Yes. I'm so glad you're back. And thank you for bringing Sam home."

"My pleasure, honey." He releases her, and a moment later she's in my arms, squeezing the daylights out of me, and we're both laughing like idiots.

"Oh, thank God, you're home," she breathes. When she releases me, she looks me over from head to toe. The last time she saw me—at Christmas—I still had a cast on my leg, and I couldn't walk without crutches. She squeezes my hands. "You look amazing. How do you feel?"

I shake my head at her. "You are such a liar, princess. I look like shit warmed over, but I'm not complaining. I'm standing on my own two feet again."

Shane's youngest sister, Lia, nicknamed Beth *princess*, and the name stuck. She's got long, pale blond hair, currently pulled up in a sloppy ponytail, and blue-green eyes the color of the Caribbean. She tears up all over again as she looks at me, and I know where her brain is going. The reason I was injured in the first place was because I pushed her out of the way of an oncoming car and took the direct hit myself. I can tell myself I was just doing my job—after all, I'm her bodyguard, or at least I was at the time. But the truth is, I'd do anything for her. I'd take a bullet for her without a second thought. She's like family to me.

Beth glances at Shane with a hopeful expression on her face. "Can he come back to work?"

Shane shakes his head, and I know it kills him to disappoint her.

"I'm sorry, sweetheart, no," he says. "Not until he can pass the physical assessment. Miguel will continue as your bodyguard until Sam can come back."

My gaze keeps turning to the open foyer doors that lead into the apartment. I can see part of the great room and a bit of the kitchen through the open doorway. My heart is pounding at the thought of seeing Cooper again, and I'd be lying to myself if I said I wasn't looking for him to walk through those doors any second. He has to know I'm back.

"He's not here, Sam," Beth says.

Her words hit me like a sucker punch to the gut, and I don't know how to feel. Relief that I don't have to face him for the first time in front of an audience? Hurt that he's not here to see me? Panic? What if he doesn't even want to see me? "Where is he?"

Beth shrugs, looking apologetic. "I don't know. He left a half-hour ago, and he didn't say where he was going. I'm so sorry."

I try not to let them see how much this hurts. "I guess it's for the best." Right now I just need to get out of here and be alone. I pick up my bags and walk back into the elevator. "It's late, and I'm tired. I'd better unpack and crash for the night."

"Will I see you tomorrow?" Beth says, eyeing me hopefully. "How about having dinner with us?"

"Sure," I say, although my heart's not in it at the moment. Right now I just feel numb knowing he left on purpose. "I'll come over after you get home from work. We can catch up then. I want to hear all about little baby boy McIntyre."

* * *

I take the private elevator down to the main lobby where I can catch an elevator that goes to my floor. There's an amorous young couple behind me in the car as I ride up to my apartment. I keep my eyes glued to the doors, trying to ignore the sounds of their furtive kisses and quick breaths, his moans, her quiet giggles. God, I envy them. They can hold hands and kiss and be playful with each other in public without drawing unwanted attention. Just my luck I had to be born queer.

I get off at my floor and haul my bags to my door, setting them on the floor so I can fish my key out of my pocket. Once I manage to get the door unlocked and open, I drop my bags inside and close the door behind me. My heart is still pounding and my adrenalin level is through the roof, but all that worry about seeing Cooper again was pointless. In all my mental preparation, I never considered the possibility he wouldn't even be there.

And yeah, that stings like a bitch. He's avoiding me. For the first time since I left Chicago, I wonder if I did irreparable damage to our relationship by leaving him like that. The thought makes me feel sick.

I have to admit, it's good to be back in my own apartment. Even though the place has been closed up for months, and the air is slightly stale, it's home. I flip on the living room light, and my heart slams against my ribcage when I see Cooper standing across the room. "Jesus!"

Steely blue eyes crinkle at the corners as he gives me a lopsided, hesitant grin. "Sorry, darlin'. I didn't mean to scare you."

The sound of his rough voice sends shivers down my spine, and I simply stare at him, my gaze eating him up. I didn't realize how starved I was for the sight of him.

We stand eye-to-eye, both of us the same height, six feet, although he's more muscular than I am, his shoulders broader. He looks a bit haggard, with faint shadows under his eyes, like he does when he's not sleeping well. Maybe the nightmares have been bad lately. I've lost count of the number of times he's awakened me in the middle of the night, struggling against invisible bonds in his sleep.

He's lost weight. Not as much as I have, but he looks leaner and meaner somehow. He's still bigger than me. He'll always be a bit of a bruiser. His gray hair is cut short, a holdover from his years in the Marines, and he's got three days' worth of salt-and-pepper stubble on his cheeks. But that little bit of beard can't hide his jawline, which looks like it's cut from stone. Damn, he looks good.

Aching need hits me low in the gut, and I find it difficult to breathe.

"You could have warned me," I say, grasping for something to say. Anything. My mind is reeling. He's here...right in front of me. He didn't leave the penthouse simply to avoid me. My pulse is through the roof, and the roar of blood rushing through my skull is deafening. "You scared the hell outta me."

He stalks toward me, and I automatically take a step back, coming into contact with the door.

"I couldn't do this with an audience," he says, his voice gruff.

I swallow hard, feeling wary, and excited, and pissed off, all at the same time. "Do what?"

His voice drops. "See you again."

He steps in front of me, just inches away, and I can feel the heat rolling off him in waves. The faint scent of his cologne hits me like a sledgehammer, knocking the breath out of me. Memories of him come crashing back, swamping me, making my heart pound. His scent, the feel of his body draped over mine, his touch. My belly clenches in anticipation, and my balls start tingling. *I can't do this!* I can't just roll over for him like nothing happened.

Anger replaces my initial shock at seeing him again. "Well, now you've seen me." I jab my thumb at the door behind me. "You can go now."

He looms closer, his hard gaze going to my mouth. *Oh, shit. He's going to kiss me.* I raise my hands to hold him off. "No, Cooper. We're not going to just pick up where we left off. If that's what you came here for, you'd better go."

He keeps coming as if he didn't hear a word I said. When he's right in front of me, he moves fast as lightning, grabbing my wrists and pinning them to the door above my head. I could pull free if I wanted to, but the truth is, part of me doesn't want to. Part of me wants to just give in to him. But the stronger part of me knows I can't do that. I have to stand my ground. "Don't!"

"Don't what?" He makes it sound like a dare.

"Don't kiss me."

"Who said I was going to kiss you?"

He's so close now, I can feel his warm breath on my face, and I can see the short stubble of his five o'clock shadow. With a shock, I realize he's been drinking. Not beer, but the hard stuff. Suddenly, it feels like all the air has been sucked out of the room, and I can't catch my breath. I sag against the door. "Cooper, please don't."

He's still staring at my mouth. "Why not?" He glances crudely at the front of my jeans. "Looks like you want me to."

I shake my head. "No, I don't. I can't keep doing this. Not unless something changes."

His eyes narrow, and he shakes his head. His easy dismissal of my feelings cuts me deeply. He's killing me. And the sad part is, I want him so badly I can barely think straight. It's been so long.

His jaws tighten, making a muscle jump in his cheek. "What we have together is good, damn it! Why can't you be happy with that?"

"Because I'm sick and tired of being your God-damned dirty little secret! If you don't want me enough to man up—"

The next thing I know, his mouth is on me, his lips grinding mercilessly into mine, his breath hot and heavy, spiced with whisky. I taste blood, but I don't know if it's his or mine. I guess it doesn't matter. Either one of us would gladly bleed for the other. That's what makes this so hard. He's fucking *everything* to me, but if I don't stand my ground now and force the issue, we're doomed. Resentment will eat me alive, and eventually I'll grow to hate him, and that will destroy us both.

He transfers my wrists to one hand and grips my jaw tightly with the other, stroking my short beard as he holds me pinned to the door.

"I fucking love you, and you know it," he says, sounding resentful, as if the words are being forced out of him.

The vibration from his voice travels down my spine and straight to my ballsac, zapping me. My balls tingle as my traitorous dick begins to swell, filling the tight confines of my briefs. I make a pained sound and have to shift my stance to make room for a quickly growing erection.

When he skims his mouth lower and play-bites the edge of my jaw, I gasp. Then he spins me so that I'm facing the door. The hard ridge of his erection presses against my ass, reminding me of what I've been missing for these past several months.

"You think I don't want you?" he hisses in my ear, furious. "Do you feel *that*, you little prick? That's me, wanting you. I want you so badly I can barely fucking breathe! I love you, and you left me! *You little shit!*"

I only have a moment to register the unmistakable pain in his voice before he thrusts against my backside, grinding himself into me and short-circuiting my brain. Even through our jeans I can feel the thick ridge of his big cock pressing between my ass cheeks. It feels so damn good, I groan loudly and push back against him. My knees go weak, and the butterflies in my belly make me dizzy.

I sag against the door as my resolve crumbles. "Cooper, please." *Please what? Please don't do this to me? Please fuck me?*

I'm panting with arousal so intense it hurts. My left leg buckles, and he catches me with a strong arm around my waist.

"Do you feel this?" he grates, grinding his cock into me. "Do you?"

"Yes!"

"Does this feel like I don't want you?"

"No!" My eyes are burning now, from the mix of salt and tears, and from the searing realization that no matter how tempted I am to simply give in, I can't.

Cooper grips the back of my neck and marches me toward the bedroom. I stumble in the dark, dizzy from the mix of arousal and exhilaration rioting inside me. Blood is surging into my dick, and I'm hard as a pike. This is what I get for going without him for so long.

Cooper pushes me face down on the bed, bending over me as he presses the side of my face into the bed. I've never seen him so angry.

"You are fucking *mine*, do you hear me?" he hisses in my ear.

"Yes!" I squeeze my eyes shut. How did I ever think I could leave him? How did I ever think I had any control in this relationship? I have none, because he fucking owns me, and we both know it. "Cooper, *please*."

"Please what?" He takes a deep breath, and his voice drops to a low rumble. "Tell me what you want, Sam."

"I can't do this right now." We both know if he forces the issue, I'll cave.

For a moment, I think he didn't hear me. The room is silent—too silent. The only sound I hear is the rush of blood through my skull. Abruptly, he releases his grip on my neck and pushes himself away from me, leaving me suddenly alone and feeling bereft. I roll into a sitting position and stare at the floor, at his scuffed black boots, too shaken to face him. I've never denied him anything before. *Never.*

"Do you want me to go?" he says, his voice hollow. Jesus, he sounds *hurt.*

I gaze up at him, desperate for him to understand. "No! I don't want you to go." *Please don't go.*

At the moment, with his hands propped on his lean hips, he looks very much like the Marine drill sergeant he once was. "You don't want me, but you don't want me to leave either. What the hell do you want?"

I grab one of his hands and squeeze it, grateful for the contact. Then I rise and stand before him, steeling myself for the possibility of rejection. "Stay with me tonight. No sex, just sleep with me. I've spent the past three months alone in my bed, missing you. Needing you. Stay with me tonight. Please."

His expression tightens. "You're the one who left."

Left me. I can hear his unspoken accusation. I did hurt him.

"I know, and I'm sorry. I had to." I reach up with both hands and touch his face, brushing my thumbs along his sharp cheekbones. "I love you, Cooper. It killed me to leave, but when you refused to dance with me at Beth's wedding…it was the last straw. We were in a safe place, surrounded by family and friends. I knew if you couldn't stand up with me there, you never would. And I need you to do that. I need you to stand up with me, claim me, claim us. I need you to be my *boyfriend*, not just my fuck-buddy. Not in front of the whole world, but at least in front of the people who love us. People we trust. You say you love me. I need you to act like it."

His expression is fixed, hard as stone, not giving me any indication of what's going through his mind. But his eyes—his eyes aren't quite so stoic. I see a flash of panic in their depths, and if I didn't know better, I'd think he was scared. But that's impossible. Nothing scares Cooper. He's a force of nature.

He paces, running his fingers through his hair, and for a moment, I'm afraid he's going to walk out. But then he stops and returns to stand in front of me. His hands frame my face, and his voice softens. "All right, I'll stay. Have you eaten?"

"No," I say, nearly dizzy with relief.

Some strands of my hair have fallen loose from my topknot, and he tucks them behind my ear. "You need to eat," he says. "Let's order in, and we'll watch a movie or see if there's a game on tonight. How does that sound?"

My throat works as I swallow hard, then nod. "That sounds great."

Cooper pulls me into his arms and kisses me gently, his touch both soothing and familiar. "Welcome home, Sam."

I feel as if a great weight has been lifted from my chest, and I can finally breathe again. "It's good to be home."

ᶜᴼ 3

Sam

We order in pizza and hot wings, and I've got plenty of beer in the fridge. We end up watching a Chicago Bulls versus Knicks game on TV. I'm not really into sports, but I know he is. I'm more of a sci-fi and aliens nerd. But right now, I'm just happy to be sitting beside him on the sofa, both of us propping our feet on the coffee table. I lean into him, melding my body against his, and he lays his hand on my thigh. Every once in a while, he squeezes my leg, but other than that, he doesn't try to touch me. At least not sexually.

It feels good to be with him again. If only he'd take a couple steps to meet me partway, we'd be okay. Am I asking too much? Am I being too much of a drama queen?

I notice that the apartment is dark—Cooper must have turned off the light. The glow from the television is the only light in the room, except for a bit of ambient city night light coming through the partly open drapes. It's been a long day and, with a full belly and two beers in me, I can't keep my eyes open. My eyelids grow heavier and heavier until keeping them open becomes impossible.

I awake sometime later when Cooper gently nudges me. "Come on, kid," he says. "You're tuckered out." He sounds a lot more relaxed now, more like his usual self. "Let's get you to bed."

He stands and pulls me to my feet, and I follow him into the bedroom. While he pulls down the bedding, I head for the bathroom to take a piss and brush my teeth. When I come out wearing only my boxer briefs, he's sitting at the foot of my bed, looking pensive. He catches sight of me, and his gaze darkens hungrily as it skims my torso.

He stands, pointing at the bed. "In you go."

I grab his arm. "You're going to stay, right? You said you would."

For a minute, I think he's going to refuse, but then he nods. "I'll stay."

I climb into bed and get comfortable while he goes into the bathroom. Cooper usually sleeps here with me, instead of upstairs in the penthouse. We have our routine. He sleeps here with me, and then he's usually gone before I awake, to head upstairs before Shane leaves for work. I think he and Shane have an unspoken agreement between them that Beth will never be left unprotected...not after everything she's been through—not just one attempt on her life, but two. Later, I would head upstairs and have breakfast with Beth before escorting her to work, and then I'd shadow her all day as her bodyguard. I get to hang out with my best friend all day—what better job could there be? Or, at least I did before the botched hit-and-run accident.

Cooper turns off the light in the bathroom and heads for the bed, climbing in beside me. He stretches out on his back, pulling me into his arms, and sighs with pleasure. I know the feeling. I lay my head on his lightly-furred chest and drape my arm across his washboard waist.

He pulls the covers up over us, then slips his hand beneath the bedding to rub slow circles on my bare back, making my nerve endings tingle. I muffle a groan and press my face into his shoulder. The familiar, slightly musky scent of his skin both comforts and arouses me, and my dick stirs. I can sense him stirring beneath the bedding too.

At first, I can't sleep for thinking about how we're not having sex. It's been so long, and I know we both want to. But I just can't. It would negate everything I tried to accomplish by leaving if we just fall right back into our old patterns. But eventually, the feel of his hand rubbing my back relaxes me, and I become drowsy.

He kisses my forehead. "Sleep, baby. Your body needs sleep to heal."

The next thing I know, he rolls me to my side and spoons behind me, draping his arm securely around my waist. Neither one of us comments on his erection, which prods insistently against my ass. I smile, reassured by the blatant evidence that he still wants me, and finally allow myself to doze off.

Sometime in the night I awake to the feel of his lips in my hair, as he whispers to me. "I'm going to make this right for you, baby. You just gotta trust me."

His words are so cryptic. What is he not telling me?

I roll over to face him, my brain only half awake. "Of course I trust you."

"Good." He kisses me, long and slow, and I melt inside. "Please don't leave me again," he says. "You have no idea what that did to me."

My throat closes, and all I can do is tighten my arms around him. I do know, because leaving him nearly killed me.

* * *

When I wake the next morning, I'm alone in my bed, and Cooper's spot is cold. I know without checking that he's gone. Still, I sit up and call his name, just in case he's still here. But there's no answer.

I'm not surprised. It's seven-thirty. He'll be upstairs making breakfast for Beth and seeing her off to work. Part of me wants to go up there and see her before she leaves, but I really don't want to run into Miguel Rodriquez right now. I have nothing against the guy—he's a great guy, and a more than competent bodyguard—but I know I'll be bitten by the green-eyed monster. I hate that I'm back, and yet not fit to return to work. I hate that I'm not the one who will be keeping Beth company at work, and more importantly keeping her safe. There's a baby to consider now, too. It should be me.

Damn, I miss hanging with that girl. She totally gets me, and she never judges.

I shower and dress, killing time until I know Beth and Miguel have left for Clancy's Bookshop, where Beth reigns supreme as CEO and commander-in-chief-extraordinaire. At nine o'clock, I head up to the penthouse floor, crossing through the foyer and into the sprawling apartment. "Cooper?"

"In the kitchen."

As soon as I take a seat at the breakfast bar, he sets a plate of warm food in front of me. He was expecting me, of course, and that makes me smile. Maybe there's hope for us.

"Eat," he says, pointing at the mountain of food on my plate. "You've lost weight and muscle tone. You need both to get your strength back."

"Yes, sir," I say, saluting him as I reach for a fork.

He steps close, wraps his hand around the back of my head, and pulls me close for a long kiss, fairly eating at my mouth. "Don't get smart with me," he murmurs against my lips. Then he pulls back and points at my plate. "Eat. If you want more, I'll make more."

I dig into my food, realizing how much I've missed his cooking. He's gone all out—eggs, bacon, hash brown potatoes, toast, coffee. Luckily for me, Cooper's an awesome cook. We have an agreement— he does the cooking and I do the dishes. It's a win-win for me.

"How's Miguel working out?" I say, after swallowing a mouthful of food.

"Fine. He and Beth are close, and Miguel's a good guy. He's quiet, but he's dedicated. She's in good hands with him. They both are."

And by *they*, I know he means the baby boy she's carrying. "How's she doing with the pregnancy? Is everything okay with the baby?"

"She still has morning sickness from time to time, but a little dry toast and weak tea gets her through that. The baby's doing fine. He's growing right on schedule."

Cooper pours me a second cup of black coffee. "When do you think you'll be able to pass the fitness assessment?"

I take a sip of coffee. "I'm about three-quarters of the way there. In another two or three weeks, I should be good."

He nods. "Good. As much as Beth likes Miguel, I know she wants you back. You can train in the fitness room here, or you can go train at the office. Just get busy and get yourself back into fighting shape."

I spread butter on my toast and take a bite, saluting him. "Sir, yes, sir!"

"You keep that up, wise guy, and see what happens."

That shuts me up quick. Right now, I'm physically no match for Cooper. He could kick my ass in the boxing ring right now, if he was so inclined. It wouldn't be the first time, and I'm not anxious for a repeat. A guy's got his pride, you know.

He walks around the counter and steps between my legs, his big hands coming up to cup my face. I close my eyes and lean into his touch. God, it feels good to be with him. How did I survive three months without this?

His lips are warm and gentle on mine as he gives me a chaste kiss. Then he slides his lips down to my throat and gives me a sucking kiss, which I'm sure will leave a mark. The sucking sensation reminds me of other sucking activities, and my dick hardens so fast it takes my breath away.

I make a sound deep in my throat, part pleasure, part pain, and he chuckles. When his hand slides down my torso to the bulge in my jeans, he presses his palm firmly against my erection. I groan.

He chuckles, holding my gaze as he rubs me through my clothing. "You could have gotten fucked last night if you hadn't been such a pain in the ass. We've got a lot to make up for, haven't we?"

I nod, not trusting myself to speak. His touch feels too damn good, and I'm afraid I'll start blathering like an idiot or, worse yet, begging.

He brushes his thumb across my lower lip and smiles at me, knowing exactly what his touch does to me.

When the elevator chimes, we both turn to see Jake McIntyre walk through the foyer doors. Looking like the angel of death, he's dressed in all black, as usual. His leather jacket is hanging open, and I can see the handle of a Glock peeking out of the gun holster strapped to his chest. He's here for work.

"Hey, Sam," Jake says, giving me a nod. "Welcome back."

I return the gesture. "Thanks. It's good to be back."

Jake turns his attention to Cooper, who doesn't seem at all surprised to see him here this morning. "You ready to go?"

Cooper nods. "Yeah. I just need to grab my bags."

"Go?" I stare at Cooper, not even bothering to hide my surprise. *He's leaving?* "Where are you going?"

He lays his hand on my shoulder and squeezes it. "Relax, kid. I've got some business out of town. I won't be gone long."

He still didn't answer my question. I grab his wrist. "Where are you going?"

Cooper studies me for a moment, then glances back at Jake. "Maybe you should wait for me downstairs," he tells Jake.

My heart starts pounding, and all I can see are red flags. Jake is an enforcer—he's muscle. He's surveillance. He's an extra gun. The only reason he'd be going anywhere with Cooper is to provide serious back-up. Something's going on.

"Sure thing," Jake says, and he heads back to the elevator.

Cooper turns to face me. "I have business to take care of out of town, and Jake's coming along for the ride. It's no big deal."

"That's bullshit! Jake's *protection*. Where in the hell are you going that *you* need protection?"

Cooper takes my face in his hands and gazes into my eyes, his thumbs brushing my cheeks. "Calm down, darlin'. You're blowing this all out of proportion."

I grab both of his wrists and glare at him. He's flat out lying to me. I take a steadying breath. "Cooper, tell me what the hell's going on."

He frowns, looking conflicted. "I promised you I'd make everything right, didn't I? Well, that's what I'm doing. But first, I've got to take care of some business. When I get back, I'll be able to give you what you want."

I shake my head, my brow furrowing. "I'm coming with you."

"Not a chance. You stay here in Chicago and work on regaining your strength. I'll be back before you know it, I promise."

Some emotion I can't pinpoint flashes across his face, and then it's gone, leaving his expression stone cold. My heart slams in my chest as he pulls free of my grasp and walks away, heading down the hall toward his suite.

Something's going on—something big. I can't believe he dismissed me like that. I abandon what's left of my breakfast and head back to my apartment. My duffle bag and backpack are still where I left them, on the floor inside the door to my apartment. The clothes in it are clean—thanks, Mom—but wrinkled. Oh, well. They'll have to do. It's a good thing I didn't bother to unpack last night.

I head straight for the gun safe in my bedroom closet and pull out my Beretta. Since I don't know where we're going, I'd better be prepared for anything. I strap on my chest holster and slip the gun into the cradle, then pull on a jacket to conceal the weapon. Then I stash a back-up firearm and as much extra ammo as I can fit into my backpack. I grab my phone, my charger, and my external battery, and head straight down to the underground parking garage as fast as my leg will allow, hoping I'll beat Cooper. If I don't, I'm screwed, because they'll be gone, and I have no idea where they're going.

When I step out of the garage elevator, I breathe a sigh of relief because there's no sign of Cooper.

Jake, who's leaning against the side of his black Tahoe, frowns when he sees me. "What do you think you're doing?"

I open the Tahoe's back hatch and lay my duffle bag and backpack inside. "I'm coming with you."

Jake looks skeptical. "Did Cooper okay this?"

I open the rear passenger door and slide in. "It doesn't matter. I'm coming."

Jake reaches inside the vehicle and pulls back one side of my jacket, exposing my holstered gun. "Sam."

I knock his hand aside and close the vehicle door. "I'm coming."

A moment later, the penthouse elevator doors open and Cooper steps out. His gaze locks on me with laser precision, and I can tell he's pissed. He heads right for me, but Jake intercepts him. The two of them have a heated conversation, Cooper shaking his head adamantly. But Jake gets in his face, and Cooper stands down. I'm not sure what Jake said to him, but it had an impact.

Cooper deposits his one large duffle bag into the back of the SUV, and then he comes to the rear passenger door, opens it, and says, "Move over."

I slide to the other seat and latch my seatbelt, as Cooper gets in the back with me. Jake hops into the driver's seat, and we're off.

I look from Cooper to Jake, neither one of them offering up any info. "Can you at least tell me where we're going?"

Jake pulls onto the highway, heading west. "To O'Hare."

"We're flying? To where?"

Cooper glares at me, clearly still mad. "Don't ask questions."

He surprises me, though, when he reaches for my hand and squeezes it. He's such a contradiction—he's a strong, hard-headed man, and yet he's also nurturing. He lays our joined hands on his thigh and rubs the back of my hand with his thumb. His touch gentles as his anger dissipates, and I can finally relax.

Jake catches Cooper's gaze in the rearview mirror. "You have to tell him everything, Cooper. For his own safety."

$\mathcal{CO}$ 4

Cooper

I'm so fucking mad at Sam I could throttle him. *The little hothead.* He shouldn't be coming with me—it's not safe. There's too much risk, too much unknown. Where we're headed, I'm about to stir up a helluva hornet's nest. Shane insisted that Jake come along to watch my back, but now we've both got to watch Sam's back. He'll be the one at greatest risk, not me. And, he's coming off a serious injury—he's not fully capable of defending himself right now. Hell, a strong wind could knock him over.

When we reach the airport executive terminal, Jake parks the SUV beside a McIntyre Security, Inc. company jet that is prepped and ready to go. We climb out of the vehicle and grab our bags. I fall in behind Sam so I can assess how well he's moving. He's limping pretty badly and definitely favoring his left leg as he climbs the stairs—yeah, he's in no shape to protect himself.

As usual, Jake takes up the rear.

I'm going to have it out with Sam once we're in the air—he needs to know the score. Jake's already been briefed by Shane. He knows what we're walking into, but Sam doesn't. *Jesus!* I'm not looking forward to having this conversation with him. I was hoping he'd never have to know.

Once we're inside the jet, I point at one of the forward-facing seats and tell Sam, "Strap in."

Jake takes a seat at the rear of the plane, sticks a pair of earbuds in his ears, and tunes us out. Smart guy.

Sam glances back at me with disapproval plastered all over his face when I take a seat in the middle of the plane. Damn. I'm so used to protecting his privacy that it just didn't occur to me to sit with him. I know that's what he wants from me—what he *needs*. But I've spent forty years hiding my sexual orientation from the world—protecting my lovers—it's going to take time for me to change my ways.

The flight attendant greets us, collects our bags, and carries them to the rear of the plane to deposit them in the bedroom. He checks to see that we're all strapped in, then he radios to the pilot that we're ready for take-off. The pilot greets us over the intercom system, makes a couple of mandatory announcements, and then we're rolling down the runway.

As soon as we reach cruising altitude, I unbuckle my seatbelt and stand in the center aisle. "Sam." I motion for him to follow.

He unbuckles his seatbelt and rises to his feet a little unsteadily—more evidence that he's not fully recovered from his broken leg. He looks a bit wary now, as if he's not sure what he's gotten himself into. But it's a little late for second thoughts now—we're in the air.

I point to the rear of the plane, and as he passes me, he gives me what I can only describe as an evil eye. He's pissed at me. Too bad. He's the one who pushed the issue. I fall into step behind him, dreading the conversation that's about to happen. We pass Jake, who's doing a lousy job of pretending to ignore us, and continue to the rear of the plane. I open the bedroom door and motion for Sam to proceed me inside. When he does, I follow him in and close the door behind me.

"I could throttle you right now," I tell him through gritted teeth. "You have no idea what you've gotten yourself into."

⤷ 5

Sam

I face Cooper with my hands on my hips, tired of all the cloak-and-dagger bullshit. "What the hell is your problem? If this trip is so risky that you need back-up, then I should be here. It should be *me* who's watching your back."

Cooper laughs. But his amusement quickly morphs into anger as he gets right up in my face. "Shit, Sam, you couldn't fight off a ninety-pound weakling in your condition right now. You're a fucking liability for me where we're going. Not only do I have to take care of business, but now I've got to babysit your ass, too."

He's right—I'm not up to par right now—and his words sting. I shove him back a step, my face heating up. "I may not be at my best right now, but I can sure as hell take care of myself. I don't need you to babysit me."

Cooper's expression hardens, and he crowds me, pushing me until the back of my legs hit the mattress. He's been pissed at me plenty of times before, sure. But I've never seen him like this. I can feel the waves of frustration rolling off him.

He grabs the back of my head, digging his fingers into my hair with such force that I can't help wincing. I don't think he meant to hurt me, because he immediately relaxes his hold. But he's still holding me to him, nose-to-nose, and he's breathing so heavily his nostrils are flaring. He's so fucking magnificent.

In an effort to derail his anger, I press my lips to his and drink in his every breath, every frustrated sound he makes. He freezes for a moment, as if he's caught off guard. Then he kisses me back, hungrily. He devours my mouth, eating at me and I can feel his hand on the back of my head, holding me, caressing me. When he releases me, we're both trying to catch our breaths.

"Sit down, Sam."

I take a seat at the foot of the bed as Cooper starts pacing like a caged tiger. He seems bigger than life in the tight confines of this small room, and I can't help but be mesmerized as I watch him.

"There's no easy way to say this," he says, running his fingers through his hair, "so I'm just going to come out with it. I realized I was gay when I was about twelve, thirteen years old. Where I grew up, back in the seventies, being gay was a good way to end up face-down in a ditch, you know what I mean? It just wasn't acceptable, period."

He glares at me, as if daring me to contradict him. I nod, unsure where this is going.

"I never acted on my feelings," he says, "because I knew it would be dangerous. I'd seen other boys beaten just because they were *suspected* of being gay. The summer before I started high school—I was fifteen—I spent my days roaming the woods behind my house, alone, wrestling with my identity, tryin' to understand why God made me this way. That summer I found an old, abandoned hunting cabin, and I fixed it up myself, patched the holes in the walls and reinforced the sagging roof. It was just a one-room shack, a real dump, but it was my haven. My safe place. I could hang out at that cabin all day long and contemplate my fucked-up life."

"One day, another kid showed up in the woods. He was my age, and I recognized him from school. He lived about a mile down the road from where I lived with my folks."

Suddenly Cooper stops talking, and I can see the muscles in his throat working hard. His gaze is a little fixed, as if he's lost somewhere in his memories. His hands are balled into fists, and his chest is heaving. He looks haunted, tortured. My heart hurts for him, but I'm not sure how to help him.

"His name was Cody Martin. He was pretty lost, like me, pretty fucked up and lonely. To make a long story short, we became friends that summer. Good friends."

Cooper gives me a pointed look. "*Real good friends,* you hear me?"

I nod. "He was gay."

"Yeah. It was like God answered a prayer, you know? I wasn't alone any more. I had someone in my life who understood me. We had each other. By the end of the summer, we were crazy in love. We were each other's first. We fumbled through it together, figuring it out as we went, and it was exhilarating. We planned to run away, to find a place where we'd be safe, where we could be together. We both knew it wasn't safe for either of us in Sweetwater."

"One evening, just before dusk, we started for home, like we always did. We both had strict curfews and had to be home before dark if we knew what was good for us. When we reached the road, they were waiting for us. Three older boys, high school seniors. I knew these bullies—they were mean."

He continues pacing, relaying the story dispassionately, as if by rote.

"They beat us with baseball bats until we couldn't stand any longer, yelling slurs at us, callin' us fags and sissies and unnatural. And when we were too weak to fight back, they tied our hands in front of us with ropes. They threw us in the back of a pick-up truck and drove us to the Sweetwater River bridge."

I have a sick feeling in my gut as his story unfolds. I know where this is going, but I can't wrap my mind around it. Dear God, surely they didn't do what I think they did.

He keeps pacing, like an animal in a cage, trapped and desperate. His voice is rough, raw, as he forces the words out. "The river was high and fast because of the summer rains. And it's a long drop from the bridge to the water—at least thirty feet. I knew what was coming, and I steeled myself for the inevitable. I was a strong swimmer, so I wasn't too afraid for myself. But Cody...." Cooper shakes his head, his gaze wracked with pain. "Cody couldn't swim." His words hang in the air between us, as the horror of it all sinks in. The poor kid never stood a chance. "I don't think he even registered what was about to happen— I think he'd blocked it all out.

"They threw us both over the railing, with our hands tied, and left us to die. I struggled to make it to the surface and swim to the muddy river bank, finally crawling out of the freezing water. Using the sharp edge of a rock, I sawed through the rope and freed myself.

"I combed the river looking for Cody. I yelled and screamed and cried his name for hours, until I was hoarse, but I heard nothin' but the sound of rushing water. I searched for him all night, on both sides of the river, but I couldn't find him. The next morning, a little after dawn, I found his body tangled up in the branches of a downed tree. He'd gotten snagged on a branch, and he drowned just two feet from the surface of the water.

"I pulled him out and carried him up to the road, where I left his lifeless body in the middle of the bridge, where he'd be found. And then, like a fucking coward, I ran. I didn't go home. I didn't stop for anything. I hitchhiked north to my dad's sister in Illinois because I knew she'd take me in.

"The night I arrived at her place, she called my folks. News of Cody's murder had spread through the small town like wildfire. Even from where I was standing halfway across the room, I could hear my dad screamin' through the phone. He said I'd better stay up there with my aunt, cause if he ever saw me again, he'd kill me himself. I don't know if he thought I killed Cody, or if it was just because he suspected I was gay. I never saw my parents again. My aunt went to court to adopt me, and the day I graduated from high school, I joined the Marines."

He stops to face me, his hands on his hips as he glares at me. "I learned the hard way, Sam. *Don't ask, don't tell.* I learned that lesson so damn hard, I've never been able to unlearn it."

I swallow hard and take a deep breath in an effort to maintain my control. My head is reeling from his story, and I'm absolutely horrified that anyone could treat other human beings this way. To think that he's held this inside himself for so many years. My heart breaks for him. "Why didn't you tell me this before now?"

His face screws up in agony, and his voice breaks. "Are you kidding me? You wonder why I didn't want to tell you what a fucking coward I am? How I got some poor innocent kid murdered? Do you think I wanted you to know that?"

Pain rolls off him like heat boiling off the sun. *Oh, my God, he's serious.* He thinks it was his fault. "You were just a kid, Cooper! You are not responsible for what happened to that boy."

"Bullshit!" he yells, loud enough to rattle the thin wall separating the bedroom from the passenger cabin. "That boy drowned because of *me!* If I'd had more willpower—if I'd stayed away from him—if I'd been *stronger*, he wouldn't have died!"

I shake my head, swamped with sadness for him. He's been carrying this guilt with him for decades. My eyes tear up. "It wasn't your fault."

"The hell it wasn't! I couldn't save him, Sam! He drowned because I couldn't save him!"

He's so choked with guilt and remorse he can barely breathe, his chest heaving and his nostrils flaring as he tries to suck in air. "Do you think I wanted *you*—the love of my life—to know I was a coward?"

I hurt for him, just as bad as he's hurting himself. I jump to my feet and intercept him, laying my hands on his face. "Shh, shh, shh," I croon, stroking his face, desperate to calm him down before he has a stroke. "Look at me, Cooper." His gaze locks on mine. Now that I've got his attention, I give him a crooked smile, hoping to coax him out of his downward spiral. "The love of your life? Really?"

He looks ashamed. "Have I been so damned closed-off that you don't realize what you are to me? You're the love of my life, Sam Harrison. You're *everything*." He squeezes his eyes shut, and tears leak out of the corners and roll down his taut cheeks. He pulls me close so that our foreheads are touching. "I don't deserve you."

"It wasn't your fault, Cooper. Do you hear me? Repeat after me.... It. Wasn't. Your. Fault."

I press my lips gently to his and lay my hand on his chest, right over his heart, which is pounding like a jackhammer. "What happened to the assholes who attacked you?"

"Nothing, as far as I know. The case was never solved, and I never stepped foot in Sweetwater again."

"You didn't tell anyone what happened?"

He shakes his head, his eyes haunted with guilt. "No."

I can see the shame he harbors. He was too afraid, too traumatized to speak up. But he's no coward now. That, I know. And now I realize where we're headed, and why Shane thinks Cooper needs back-up. He's going after those murdering assholes. It's no wonder he's mad at me for tagging along uninvited. I'm his Cody all over again.

It's hard for me to reconcile the man he is at this moment with the strong, domineering man I know him to be. The man I *love*.

I was raised by a mom and sister who adored me. I came out to them when I was five years old, and they never once questioned my sexuality. I guess I was lucky. I've never experienced any of the hate and bigotry he has—and from his own father.

"Come here," I say, taking Cooper's hand and leading him to the bed. "Lie down with me."

He does as I ask, uncharacteristically docile. He's wiped out, gutted. I lie down behind him, spooning against his back. The room is deathly quiet now. "You are not a coward," I murmur into his ear. "And it's not your fault Cody died. That's on them—those three assholes—not you."

When I kiss the back of his neck, he makes a low, pained noise deep in his throat. "You're the strongest, bravest man I know," I tell him. I lay my hand over his heart, feeling the pounding against his ribcage. "That's one of the things I love about you."

We both jump at the sound of a discrete knock, as Jake's muffled voice comes through the door. "Guys? Is everything all right in there?"

I chuckle, realizing all that Jake must have overheard. But then, I'm sure he's already been briefed by Shane and Cooper on where we're going, and why. I tighten my arm around Cooper. "Yes, everything's fine."

Cooper thinks he has to protect me, but I'll be damned if I'd ever let anyone hurt him.

* * *

I've never seen Cooper so rattled in my life. Watching him fall apart really threw me. He's such a strong man. That's what attracted me to him in the first place—his indomitable strength, his domineering personality—he's like a force all his own. I've never seen him shaken before.

He's always taking care of me; now it's my turn to take care of him. "How much time do we have until we land?"

"Two hours, tops." He sounds exhausted.

"Good. You just rest, and don't worry about a thing."

He reaches for my hand and holds it tightly to his chest. "Jesus, if anything happens to you."

"Don't think that way. I'll be fine."

"I'm about to stir up a nest of vipers, darlin'. And they won't come after *me*—they'll go after *you*. You're my weakness. That's why you shouldn't be here. I should send you right back to Chicago the minute we land."

I laugh. "As if you could! There are three of us. We have nothing to worry about. Now, close your eyes and relax. We have a couple of hours before we land. You need the rest."

"Hell, I can't relax." He shifts restlessly. And ten minutes later, he's snoring lightly.

I smile as I press my nose to the back of his neck and breathe him in, taking pleasure and comfort from his familiar scent. I lay my head against his and close my eyes. Whatever we're about to face, we'll get through it together.

6

Sam

Jake knocks on the bedroom door, waking us from our impromptu catnap. I didn't mean to fall asleep, too, but cuddling up to his warm body pulled me right under.

"We're on final approach," Jake says. "You need to get back in your seats."

"We're coming," Cooper says, running his fingers through his hair. He groans. "I can't believe I fell asleep."

"You needed it."

I watch him sit up and swing his legs over the side of the bed. He stands and stretches, his T-shirt riding up to expose his abdomen, which is lean, ribbed with muscle, and dusted with dark hair. My belly tightens at the sight of that sexy hair that converges in a line and disappears beneath the waistband of his briefs.

He glances down at me, grinning when he realizes I'm staring. "Come on. We'd better get seated. You can look your fill later."

My stoic Cooper is back, and I confess I'm relieved. Seeing him so shaken was a bit unsettling.

We leave the bedroom and head up the aisle toward our seats. When Cooper reaches the sofa he'd been sitting on earlier, he catches my hand and pulls me down beside him. "Sit with me."

I try not to smile like a fool as I strap myself in for landing. Cooper asking me to sit with him may be a small thing to others, but it's a big step for him. I glance over at Jake, who's watching us, not bothering to hide his amusement.

Cooper looks at him. "What are you looking at?"

Jake shrugs, biting back a smile as he goes through the motions of putting his earbuds away. "Nothing."

When Cooper frowns, I lay my hand on his thigh, giving it a squeeze. His hand comes down over mine, and instead of brushing my hand away like I expected, he interlocks our fingers and holds my hand. He glares at Jake, as if daring him to say something. Jake turns his attention to his phone, keying something in.

"See, that's not so hard, is it?" I whisper to Cooper. It's a stupidly silly thing, but he's holding my hand in front of someone, and it feels pretty damn good.

* * *

"We still have a two-hour drive," Cooper says, as we retrieve our bags from the bedroom.

When we exit the plane, we're met with temperatures in the

mid-seventies, which is a vast improvement over the frigid temps we left behind in Chicago. A shiny, black Escalade is waiting for us—presumably a rental from an executive car service. Jake shakes hands with the uniformed driver and accepts two sets of keys from him. He hands the spare set to Cooper.

After we load our gear into the vehicle, I climb into the back seat, and to my surprise, Cooper joins me. I expected him to sit up front with Jake. It's a small concession on his part, but the fact that he chose to sit with me means a lot. I shoot him a glance as we buckle up, and he gives me a small smile. Then he reaches over and lays his hand on my knee, giving it a little squeeze. Jesus, he's... *trying*. A knot forms in my throat, and I have to look away.

As we're driving along the highway, Cooper gives us both the rundown on the small town where we're headed. Sweetwater—population 15,000. It's out in the boondocks, far from any metropolitan area. Out here there's nothing but wide-open farmland, crops, pastures, horses, and cattle.

Our first sign of civilization is a surprisingly modern-looking high school with a first-rate football stadium. Apparently, they take their football seriously here. A couple miles later, we enter the city limits, and it's like stepping back in time.

"Not much has changed," Cooper muses, staring out his window as we pass several blocks of quaint, one- and two-story houses with white picket fences in the front yards and detached garages in the rear. "The high school is certainly new, but everything else looks pretty much like it did when I was a kid."

After another ten blocks of houses, with the occasional church, we hit the little downtown area, which looks like it hasn't changed much since the 1950s. There's an old movie theatre with an elaborate neon marque, a few clothing shops, a consignment shop, a hardware store, a second-hand bookstore, and several restaurants and bars.

We drive through the downtown section, all five blocks of it, and keep going out the other side, where we pass some decent looking motels, until farther out we come across one of those ancient motels that dates back way more than half-a-century. Back in its heyday, this one-story motel had been painted mint green with white trim—now it's just a mass of faded and peeling paint. The parking lot, which is long overdue for repaving, is practically empty, so I doubt we'll have any trouble getting accommodations.

Jake parks the Escalade in front of the office and shuts off the engine. "I'll get us a room."

He returns a few minutes later with several sets of keys, and he relocates the Escalade down toward the end of the building.

"Here we are," he says, shutting off the engine.

We grab our stuff and follow him into Unit 36 to take a look around. It's a small, barren room with thread-bare, olive green carpet, one of those big, bulky TVs that dates back to the previous century, and a small round table with two rickety chairs. The room looks clean enough, I suppose, but the air is stale, and it smells like cigarette smoke.

At the back of the room, there's a door that leads to a small bathroom with a shower, toilet, and a pedestal sink. The mirror hanging over the sink has a crack that's been covered with clear packing tape. Nothing but the best.

Jake hands both me and Cooper keys. "This is your room." Then he points at an adjoining door. "My room is through there. Tonight, after dark, I'll set up surveillance cameras in the front and rear of the building so there aren't any surprises."

Jake and Cooper share a pointed look, and Cooper nods at Jake. "Thanks."

I have a feeling it was Jake's idea to get separate rooms. If it had just been the two of them, they would have shared a room without a second thought—it would have been far safer that way. But now that I'm here... Jake is giving us some much-needed space. I'm grateful. Cooper and I need some privacy. Just the thought of spending time alone with him raises all kinds of possibilities.

Jake leaves us to check out his own room, which presumably is a carbon copy of ours. Cooper dumps our bags on the bed closest to the front window.

"We'll sleep on that bed," he says, pointing to the second bed, the one farthest from the door.

We. I smile. I guess we're sharing a bed tonight. The thought makes me flush with heat, and my belly flutters. It's been so long. I stuck to my guns as long as I could, but now that we're here—now that he seems to be trying—I don't think I can deny him or myself any longer. Besides, I *need* him.

I sit on the bed to test the mattress. It's not bad. It's old, and a little soft, but not horrible. "It was nice of Jake to give us our own room."

Cooper gives me a heated look, and I know exactly what's on his mind. "Jake's not an idiot." Then he points at me. "*You're* getting fucked tonight, pal," he says, daring me to contradict him.

My face heats up, and I'm sure I'm beet red. With my red hair and fair complexion, I can't hide a thing from him.

"Have you got a problem with that?" he says.

"Nope."

"Good. Plan on it." He pulls me to my feet and draws me close, grinning. "Are you going to show me some pity tonight and end my misery?" he says in a low, teasing voice. His gaze is hungry as it searches mine. He just barely touches his lips to mine, giving me the gentlest of kisses. Then he threads his fingers through my close-cropped undercut. "Are you going to let me have you tonight?" he says, his voice low and teasing. His mouth opens on mine as he slides his hands down my back side to clutch my butt cheeks, squeezing them, making me moan. "Are you?" he breathes against my lips.

"Yes." My pulse is racing, and I'm finding it difficult to breathe. His scent, so warm and tantalizing, so male, stirs up butterflies in my belly. *Jesus, yes!* I want him so badly.

He runs the pad of his thumb along my bottom lip. "It's been a while for us, you know. Your ass is gonna be so tight. it'll be like starting all over."

Just the thought makes me moan. "God, yes."

He brushes his lips against mine, teasing. "Are you going to let me kiss you?"

I swallow, loving this playful side of him. "Yes."

He smiles. "How about right now?"

I groan in anticipation, and he kisses me, nudging my lips apart. It's a hungry kiss, his tongue dancing with mine. He sucks on my lower lip, biting it gently. I press my aching erection against his, reveling in the feel of his long, thick length straining behind the zipper of his jeans. He's as hard as I am. I'm dying to unzip his pants, right now, and drop to my knees and—there's a sharp rap on the adjoining door, and we both jump. Cooper shakes his head as he releases me to go unlock the door and open it wide.

Jake walks in. "I suggest we scope out the town while we still have the light. We should pick up some basic provisions—bottled water, protein bars. And we need to eat. I'm starving. We passed a decent-looking diner downtown. How about it?"

Cooper nods. "Watch your backs here, guys. I'm about to piss off some potentially very dangerous people. Don't go running off alone."

Of course, he's looking at me as he says that last part. I roll my eyes. "I wasn't born yesterday, you know."

"Hey, don't roll your eyes at me. You're still recovering from some pretty serious injuries. No dumb-ass heroics, got it?"

"Yes, sir!" I love it when he goes all Marine-sergeant on me. Bossy Cooper is damn hot. I have this fantasy where I'm back in basic training, and he's my drill sergeant, and he makes me drop and give him—.

"I mean it, Sam." He glares at me, far from amused. "This is not a pleasure trip."

"I know. I heard you."

Cooper opens his duffle bag to retrieve his chest holster, slipping it on, and his Glock. He loads a magazine into the Glock and tucks it into the holster and pockets an extra magazine. Then he slips on a black jacket, concealing the gun. "We shouldn't go anywhere un-armed," he says, still addressing me. "At least one of us should be carrying at all times. When this shit-storm hits the fan, there's no telling what will happen. This is a small town, Sam. The sheriff here is a big fish in a small pond. He rules this town. You got it?"

"Yes, I get it. Are you expecting trouble from the sheriff?"

Cooper frowns. "He's asshole number one on my shit list, so yeah, I'm expecting trouble from the sheriff."

"Shit. Who else?"

"A local circuit judge and the high school football coach."

I whistle long and low. "Well, damn."

"Let's go," Cooper says, heading for the door. "It's time to wreak havoc."

* * *

We drive around town to get a feel for the place. It doesn't take long—it's not that big. We locate the sheriff's office, which is at the center of downtown, right next door to the courthouse. The high school we already passed on our way into town.

As we're driving down Main Street, Cooper says, "Stop here."

Jake parks in front of the office of the *Sweetwater Daily Gazette*.

"A newspaper?" I say.

Cooper nods. "This is how we get the shit storm started."

The three of us walk inside the front office of the newspaper, where a receptionist sits behind an old wooden desk. Behind her desk is a wooden railing separating the waiting area from the employees' desks. In the back of the office is a row of glassed-in private offices.

The middle-aged woman seated at the reception desk glances up at us, and with a heavy sigh, she puts down a dog-eared romance novel. "Can I help you gentlemen?" she says, her voice thick with the local accent.

Cooper nods at one of the private offices at the back of the room. "I need to see Jenny Murphy."

The receptionist—Patricia, according to her nameplate—glances back at the middle-aged woman seated behind a glass door with the words JENNIFER MURPHY, EDITOR-in-CHIEF emblazoned across it in white lettering. The woman—presumably Jenny—is on the phone. "She's on the phone right now."

"I can see that," Cooper says. "When she's free, will you tell her Daniel Cooper is here to see her."

The woman's wrinkled brow furrows. "Is she expecting you?"

"No, ma'am. But I'm pretty sure she'll want to hear what I have to say."

It might be just my imagination, but it sure seems like Cooper's southern drawl has suddenly gotten a lot stronger.

Patricia points to a row of orange plastic chairs in the waiting area. "Have a seat. I'll let her know you're here."

We take our seats as the receptionist goes back to reading. It's not long before the blonde appears at the wooden gate, her hands clutching the top railing. She's staring at Cooper like she's seen a ghost. "Danny Cooper?"

Cooper stands, his hands in his pockets. "Hello, Jenny."

The editor-in-chief looks like she's in shock. "Damn. I never thought I'd see your face again."

She looks at me, at Jake, and then back at Cooper. "And these guys are with you?"

"Yeah. Can I speak with you?"

She nods, swinging open the gate and waving for us to follow her. "Sure, come on back. You and your friends."

I follow Cooper, who's following the editor. Jake's right behind me.

Once in her office, Jenny sits at her desk. Cooper and I take the two chairs facing her, and Jake closes the door before he goes to stand in the corner, leaning against the wall.

Cooper doesn't waste any time. "Do you remember Cody Martin?"

The woman nods as the blood drains from her face. "The boy who was drowned—murdered—back when we were in school? Yes, of course I remember him. His murder was never solved."

"I'm here to solve it."

Her eyes widen. "You know what happened to Cody? You know who killed him?"

Cooper nods, his expression grim. He looks very much like a haunted man. "I was there the night Cody was murdered. They tried to kill me, too."

"Holy shit." Jenny pulls a digital recorder out of her desk drawer and turns it on. "Tell me everything."

* * *

Cooper repeats his story, exactly as he told it to me on the flight down. Jenny Murphy sits there looking stunned, tearing up as she hangs on his every word.

"I remember Cody well," she says after he finishes. "He was such a quiet kid. He never hurt a soul." She closes her eyes and takes a deep breath, obviously shaken.

When she looks at us again, her blue eyes are hard. "What are you going to do? Are you going to the police?"

Cooper shakes his head. "No."

She looks confused. "Why the hell not?"

"Because your sheriff is one of the killers. I'm here to take him down."

"Sheriff Monroe?" She pales. "Danny, do you have any idea what you're getting yourself into? Billy Monroe runs this town, and most of the deputies are his buddies. They're practically in his back pocket."

"I know. I've been keeping tabs on these three. I'm here for a reckoning. I'm going to make sure they pay for what they did to Cody. Their lives as they knew them are over."

"Who else?" she says. "Besides Billy Monroe?"

"Judd Franklin and Roger Stevens."

"Oh, my God. Judd Franklin is a circuit court judge with connections all across the state. And as for Roger Stevens—well, he's dangerous in his own right. Our illustrious football coach is an alcoholic with a history of domestic violence. When he's drunk, which is most of the time, he's out of control."

Cooper stands. "Will you run the story?"

Jenny looks him in the eye. "You'll give an affidavit?"

"Yes."

"Then yes. It'll be the leading story on the front page of tomorrow's paper. But Danny, you've got to be careful." She looks at the three of us. "All of you have to be careful."

Cooper's expression darkens. "I'm not a fifteen-year-old kid anymore, Jenny. If they come after us, we'll handle it. It won't be a problem."

7

Cooper

Where to next?" Jake says, eyeing me in the rear-view mirror of the SUV.

I check my watch. "Let's get something to eat. Then we'll pick up supplies and fortify the motel rooms."

Jake nods as he puts the vehicle in gear. I glance at Sam, who's sitting beside me, messing with something on his phone.

"I'm texting Beth," he says, when he catches me watching him. "She invited me to dinner tonight. I'm telling her I can't make it."

I watch Sam finish his text and send it. He's so damn beautiful, it makes my chest hurt. His body is lean and muscular, and I know damn well what's beneath his clothes—tattoos, piercings, a gor-

geous cock, and a damn fine ass. His face is beautiful, like that of
a fallen angel, and his red hair reminds me of a flame that burns as
hotly as his emotions. Sam doesn't do anything half-heartedly. He
goes all-in. Whether you're his friend... or his lover, he gives you his
all. I honestly don't know why he wastes time with me.

Beth told me there was someone in Dayton who tried his best to
woo Sam away from me. Craig somebody, someone his own age, a
personal trainer at the gym where he worked out. Apparently, this
guy offered Sam the moon. And according to Beth, Sam turned him
down repeatedly. But Jesus, what if Sam had said yes? I could have
lost him so easily. He might never have come back to Chicago. He
might have decided I wasn't worth all the effort.

My pulse skyrockets, and I feel hot all over, my stomach in knots.
I can't imagine my life without him. In the two years we've been
together, he's become everything to me. The three months he was
gone nearly did me in. I came so close to going after him and dragging him back by his hair. I'm *not* going to lose him. No matter what
it takes—I *won't* lose him.

His words are burned into my memories. "*I need you to be my boyfriend, not just my fuck-buddy.*"

I reach for his hand, linking our fingers together, and rest it on
my thigh. When I squeeze his hand, he gives me a smile that tears
right through me.

Hell no, I'm not going to lose him. And tonight, once we're settled
in for the night, I'm going to show him he's not just my fuck-buddy.
Far from it.

* * *

Like much of this town, Rosie's Diner is stuck in a time warp.

Nothing's really changed since I sat in this restaurant forty years ago. The same black-and-white checkered floor, the same red Formica table tops and red vinyl chairs, the same red vinyl barstools along the counter. I recognize several of the older gals waiting tables as girls I went to school with. And I'll bet the youngsters waiting on tables are daughters of my old classmates.

I ask the hostess, to seat us at a booth at the front of the restaurant. We want a window seat so we have an unobstructed view of the street. It's a little early to worry about trouble—the shit won't hit the fan until tomorrow morning, when the paper comes out—but it never hurts to be prepared. There's no guarantee that Jenny Murphy isn't loyal to Billy Monroe.

Jake takes one side of the booth, and I slide in beside Sam on the other. The hostess—June, according to her name tag—hands us menus and says our waitress will be out shortly. I catch her watching me out of the corner of her eye and have to wonder if she recognizes me. I remember her. She's a lot older than me, but I went to school with her younger brother, Phil. Sure, I look different than I did forty years ago. Back then, I was a tall, skinny kid with a head full of wavy, dark hair. I'm no longer skinny, and my hair is cut short and all but gray now. Still, I recognize her easily, even with her silvery-blonde hair swept up in a beehive. I guess we don't change as much over the decades as we think we do.

She looks at me quizzically. "Danny?"

I nod. "Hi, June."

"I remember you. You were in Phil's class. I haven't seen you in... ages."

"I haven't been back here in ages."

"Well, welcome home. Missy will be right over to take your orders."

Jake's attention appears to be focused on the menu, but I know better. Just like me, he's scoping out the place and watching the activity on the street. I glance at Sam as he looks over the menu, taking a moment to admire the breadth of his chest and his taut arms. My gaze fixates on his long, tanned fingers as he holds his menu. I'm damn grateful Jake got us separate rooms, because it would have been sheer torture to sleep in a bed with Sam and not be able to touch him. I honestly don't think I could have done it. Jake's a smart man.

A teenager with strawberry blonde hair and freckles walks up to our table with a big smile on her face. "Hi, fellas. I'm Missy. I'll be your server."

She gives me a polite, perfunctory smile, then immediately dismisses me when she catches sight of Sam. Her cute, freckled cheeks flush bright pink as she gives him a blinding smile.

Sorry, honey, but you're wasting your time. He doesn't play for your team. He plays for mine. Besides, he's taken. I feel an odd tightness in my chest as she checks out my lover. I should be used to this by now. Sam attracts attention wherever we go, from both men and women. I asked him shortly after we met if he was at all attracted to women—if he was bi. He said he wasn't, and frankly he never pays girls much attention, other than having a few as friends. But that doesn't stop the girls from checking him out, propositioning him, sometimes right in front of me when they don't realize we're together. He gets a kick out of it—thinks it's funny. I don't. And that's why he has taken to wearing T-shirts with gay slogans on them. He calls them public service announcements designed to educate the ladies on his status.

"Will it be separate checks, gentlemen?" Missy asks, smiling coyly at Sam as she makes a little notation on her order pad. She's probably drawing hearts and flowers.

Maybe Sam should take his jacket off so she can read the public service announcement on his shirt—*Gay Men Suck*.

"Two checks, please," I say.

She glances at me, momentarily confused.

I point at Sam. "He's with me."

Her brow furrows as she tries to work it out, and she's probably wondering if he's my son. It sure wouldn't be the first time someone came to that conclusion. Meanwhile, Sam is biting back a chuckle.

For some reason, I'm feeling awfully territorial this evening, which is why I slip my hand under the table and squeeze Sam's knee. He rewards me with a wide-eyed smile, and honest to God, he's blushing.

Touching his knee in public... it's such a small gesture, and yet it obviously means a lot to him. I don't know what possesses me to do it, but I release his knee, stretch my arms above my head, then casually let my right arm fall along the back of the booth, behind him. It's the classic high school cliché. I lay my arm against his back and let the fingertips of my right hand graze the top of his right shoulder. The gesture isn't lost on him. He looks at me like I've just hung the moon especially for him.

"What?" I say, shrugging it off, as if it's no big deal.

None of this is lost on Jake. He's grinning at us from across the table, pretending to ignore us as he places his order for a burger and fries.

Sam's gaze is still on me, and I can see the blatant hunger in his eyes. I'm filled with anticipation, too. It'll be just the two of us tonight, alone in our hotel room, reconnecting for the first time in several months. I can't wait.

When our server finishes with Jake's order, she turns to us. Her sharp gaze goes right to my fingertips as they graze Sam's shoulder.

When I brush the side of his neck with my index finger, she blushes and diverts her gaze, finally getting the message.

"And what can I get for you fellas?" she says, keeping her eyes on her little ordering pad.

I order the burger and fries platter, while Sam orders a grilled chicken salad. Then our little server races off to the order counter.

I stroke Sam's shoulder. "It looks like you have an admirer."

He shrugs off my comment, blushing, and a moment later, I feel his hand on my thigh. He turns to look out the window at the sidewalk traffic, seemingly ignoring me, as his hand burns a hole through my jeans. I harden instantly and have to shift my position to make room in my jeans for an erection that just won't quit.

Yeah, I'm looking forward to getting him back to our hotel room.

* * *

After we finish our meals and pay the bills—I pick up the tab for Sam's meal—we head back to the motel, stopping briefly at a convenience store to pick up water bottles, protein bars, snacks, and a case of beer. Sam grabs two packages of Skittles and a couple chocolate bars to feed his sweet tooth.

The evening is still young, but this early in the year it's already dark by the time we arrive back at the motel. Jake parks right in front of our rooms.

"You want any help setting up the cameras?" I ask as we exit the vehicle.

He shakes his head. "Thanks, but I've got it. You guys relax tonight while you can. Tomorrow's going to be hell."

I nod. He's got that right. "Let me know if you need anything."

As Sam unlocks the door to our room, I scan the parking lot, partly out of habit, and partly just being prudent. I doubt word has gotten out yet about why I'm back in town, but if, by some chance, Jenny Murphy leaked my story, it's entirely possible we could find ourselves with unexpected company.

I follow Sam into our room and lock the door behind me. He switches on the lamp on the nightstand between the two beds and sits on the bed we'll be sleeping on. His hands are clasped in his lap, and his gaze is focused everywhere except on me. I guess it's not surprising that he's a bit nervous, after all it's been a while, so we'll have to take it slowly tonight. He hardly picked at his meal—in fact I don't think he ate much of anything—and that's not like him.

There's a sharp rap on the adjoining door that connects our room to Jake's. I unlock it and open the door.

Jake pops his head through the opening. "Hey, guys. Keep this door unlocked at all times in case I need to get to you quickly."

I nod. "Will do." Then I close the door.

"I'm going to take a shower," I say, unzipping my duffle bag and pulling out a pair of gray sweats and my small toiletries case. I can feel Sam's eyes on me as I cross the room and enter the small, bare-bones bathroom.

The bathroom is small, but at least it's clean. After turning on the water in the shower to let it heat up, I strip off my clothes, hang them from a hook on the back of the bathroom door, then take a leak. Just as I'm about to step into the shower, the door creaks open and in walks Sam, wearing nothing but a pair of black boxer briefs.

Damn! His body is a work of art...lean muscles and black tribal tattoos winding down his arms and across his abdomen, snaking down his hips to his thighs. Hell, just looking at him makes my pulse race.

And his piercings! Everyone can see the small black plugs in his ear lobes and the industrial hardware threaded through the cartilage in his left ear. But the rest of his piercings... no one sees those but me. Both of his nipples are pierced through their flat dusky pink bases with tiny platinum barbells, and there's a curved barbell threaded through the hollow of his belly button. No one sees these piercings—no one *touches* these piercings—but *me*. These parts of him belong to me. Unless...

I realize we've never spoken about Craig. "Did you let him fuck you?"

Sam's eyes widen, and he looks blind-sided. "What? Who? Did I let who fuck me?"

"Don't play games with me, Sam. I know all about Craig. It was all I could do not to go down there to Dayton myself and wipe the floor with his face. Did you let him fuck you?"

"No!"

I stare him down, but he holds his ground. Sam's no liar, and he's no coward. If he'd fucked the guy, he'd admit it.

He reaches up to remove the hairband holding his hair in a top-knot, letting the red strands fall to his shoulders. I have to wonder who's been trimming his undercut for the past three months, because it sure as hell wasn't me. He can't do it himself worth shit, so someone had to have been doing it for him.

"Who's been trimming your undercut?" I ask. "Was it that fucker, Craig?"

"No, my sister did it. Rachel."

I narrow my eyes at him, as if challenging his assertion.

"Craig never touched me, I swear. Not like that."

"But he wanted to, didn't he?"

Reluctantly Sam nods, and I know he feels some small measure of guilt, even if he never encouraged the guy.

"I don't share, Sam."

"He didn't touch me, I swear it! We never fucked. He never even kissed me."

He's looking at me intently, and I know something's on his mind. "What do you want?" I say.

He glances at the shower, which is starting to steam up the room nicely. "Nothing. I just want to shower with you."

I take a step toward him, wrapping one hand behind his head and palming the bulge in his briefs with the other. He's hard as a rock. Good. He wants this as badly as I do.

* * *

Sam steps into the shower after me and pulls the curtain closed. His brown eyes glitter with anticipation as he grabs the shampoo bottle out of my hand and squirts some of the liquid into his palm. Then he sets the bottle down and rubs his hands together, creating a lather. "Turn around."

I turn to face the spray, ducking my head beneath the water to wet my hair. I'm curious to see what he's going to do.

When his fingers sink into my hair, digging into my scalp as he gives me a firm massage, I groan. I glance down at my erection, which is straining in the air, the head flushed dark.

He scrubs my scalp, and when the lather runs down my back, his hands follow, massaging my neck first, then my shoulders, and finally my back, down to my hips. I moan at the feel of his strong fingers on me, and my erection defies gravity as it bobs in the spray of water.

He turns me under the water so I can rinse my hair and back. While I'm doing that, he grabs the bar of soap I brought with me and lathers up. I watch him run his soapy hands over my pecs, then lower to my abs. He dawdles there, taking his sweet time as he traces the ridges of muscles.

When he strokes my cock with wet hands, I reach out to tug lightly on the barbells that run through the base of his nipples. He cries out, throwing his head back, straining the muscles and tendons in his neck. I know how sensitive the piercings make his nipples. The rough, needy sound he makes as I play with them goes straight to my dick.

My balls are hot and aching, and I've had enough of this teasing. I grab the shampoo bottle and quickly lather his hair, scrubbing his scalp hard because I love how that makes him groan. After rinsing his hair, I grab the bar of soap and turn him away from me, pressing up against his backside, letting my erection tease his crack. Now it's my turn to torture him.

I reach around him with soapy hands, starting at his collar bone, and work my way down. I run my hands across his smooth chest, lingering at his nipples, where I tease the little barbells, tweaking them and tugging gently. He arches his back, leaning against me, and the more he squirms, the tighter I restrain him. And the tighter I restrain him, the quicker he melts.

I run my hands down his abdomen, tracing his ridged muscles, to his belly button, where I tease the piercing there.

My hands move lower still, following the path of his thin happy trail as it leads to the wiry nest of auburn hair at the base of his big cock. He's rock hard, his cock straining, turning a deep, ruddy shade as it thickens. His erection bucks in my hand, and when I stroke the length of him, from base to tip, he sags against me, breathing hard.

He rests his head back on my shoulder, his voice dropping to a raspy plea. "Cooper, please."

I run my fist along the length of him, from root to tip, then brush my thumb over the head, spreading his slick pre-come over the crown. "Please what?"

He groans. "Take me to bed. God, please."

I turn him so that he's standing beneath the spray of water and rinse him off. When I release him, he sways on his feet, and I have to steady him. I could kick myself for forgetting about his leg. "Finish up in here, then come to bed when you're ready."

I step out of the shower and dry myself, then leave him to finish up. I wait for him in the bedroom, where I check my phone for messages and kill time by hanging my clothes in the closet and setting my toiletry kit on the nightstand within easy reach. I pull the covers back and grab a hand towel from the closet, where extra linens and towels are stored. Everything's ready.

After that, the only thing I can do is pace the room and resist the urge to hurry him up. The anticipation is killing me, but I figure he's a wreck too.

The bathroom door opens, and there he is, his skin flushed from the hot shower. His hair is damp, but the long strands are back in his signature topknot. I like the manbun—it makes for a nice hand hold. He's standing in the open doorway, naked, with a body that makes my knees weak. Despite the effects of his injuries and slow recovery from the accident, he's still lean and fit, his muscles chiseled. He's a feast for hungry eyes, and I can't look away.

His tight expression tells me he's just as affected as I am. I meet him halfway and run my finger up his arm, tracing the curve of his bicep. He's breathing hard, his chest rising and falling, and that tells me everything I need to know. He wants this, just as much as I do.

I step up to him and touch my mouth to his, just a gentle kiss, letting my lips cling to his for a moment. He's hard already, and I run a hand along his shaft, squeezing lightly and loving how his breath catches.

He exhales a shaky breath and smiles when I take his hand and lead him to the bed, urging him to lie down on his belly, presenting me with a view of his perfect ass. His butt cheeks clench, and he starts to squirm, pressing his erection into the bed. He's in such a submissive position, his ass in the air as he waits for me to mount him and cover him with my body. I run my hands over his two round globes, giving him time to anticipate what's coming. The longer he thinks about it, the more jacked up he'll be, the harder he'll be. I want him so aroused he can't think straight. I'm going to remind him what he's been missing, and just who the hell he belongs to.

$$8$$

Sam

My heart is pounding so hard I think I might crack a rib. God, I need this. I need him. My stomach is in knots, and I feel like a virgin all over again.

He's taken me every which way imaginable, but this is my favorite position—his too, I think. I love feeling him behind me, draped over my back as he thrusts deeply inside me. And I know he likes pinning me down. I like it, too—I'm not ashamed to admit that to myself. His strength is such a turn-on. Craig asked me once why I was 'wasting' my time with an 'old' man—his words, not mine—who was stuck in his ways. It's this! It's his indomitable strength, not to mention the fact that he's sexy as fuck. In my line of work, I have to be strong, fearless—I have to be ready and willing to run into danger, not away from it. But when I'm with Cooper like this, just the two of us alone, I can relax for a change, because I know he's got me. Nothing gets past him. Sometimes I just want to feel protected.

Cooper's a born protector—it's in his nature. I think that's why Cody's death hit him so hard—he failed to protect someone he cared about when it really mattered. But he was just a kid himself back then; he couldn't have saved Cody.

I hear Cooper unzip his toiletry kit on the nightstand, undoubtedly getting the lube. I think he's intentionally giving me a few minutes to calm down and get in the right head-space. There's no question about who's dominant in bed. Occasionally I take the lead and top him, but that's rare. Our relationship works so well because we both get what we need.

"Sam?"

"Hmm?"

"Is there any reason I should use a condom?"

His deceptively simple question hangs in the air between us as I work through what he's really asking me. *Have you slept with anyone since we were last together?* We used condoms when we first met, for about the first six months of our relationship. After that, we committed ourselves to being monogamous, and since we were both free of STDs—we even went to the clinic and got checked out together—we stopped using condoms. Now, what he's really asking me is, *Are we still monogamous?* "No. No need for a condom."

"All right then."

And that's that. Anticipation leaves me quaking inside, my heart pounding, my chest tight. With him, it's more than just sex. I can have sex with anyone. What Cooper gives me is something much more—a feeling of being consumed, of being cherished. He's not in it solely for his own pleasure. He always makes sure I get mine, in spades. When he's done with me, I'll be completely wrung out, little more than a puddle of sensation.

A slender shaft of light coming from the bathroom illuminates the dark bedroom, and I can feel the warm, humid air wafting into the room. Even with my face pressed into the pillow, I can hear him getting prepared. Part of the excitement for me is the anticipation... waiting for that moment when he first lays his hands on me, wondering what he's going to do. Will it be slow and sweet? Or will it be fast and rough?

Tonight's different, though. It's been months since we were together, so he'll have to take his time preparing me. He's a big man to take to begin with. Tonight, it'll be like starting all over again, and that sends shivers down my spine.

My heart rate picks up when he tosses a brand-new bottle of lube on the bed. Then the mattress dips as he kneels beside me. His big hands are still warm from his shower, and they feel good as they skim over my back and hips. He strokes my skin lightly, teasing my nerve endings and reducing me to a puddle of need.

"God, I've missed you," he murmurs, his voice low. "You have no idea, Sam."

My throat tightens painfully, and I feel a surge of remorse for leaving him high and dry at the wedding reception. But I did what I had to do at the time, no matter how painful it was. We're here now, aren't we, in Sweetwater, dealing with his past? Dealing with the demons that have kept him so closed up.

I turn my head so I'm facing him, my head propped on a pillow. "I missed you, too." The words themselves are woefully inadequate, but the pain in my voice speaks volumes, and I think he realizes that.

He bends down and kisses my temple tenderly. "I'm sorry." Then his lips settle over mine. "It was my fault—I drove you away. I might have been angry at you for leaving, but I never blamed you."

He skims his lips down my neck. "I'm going to take you like it's the first time all over again. We start fresh tonight, okay?"

I shiver when his lips slide down to a spot at the base of my neck, where he sucks on my skin. I know he'll leave his mark there, below the collar of my T-shirt—where no one can see it. But he knows it's there, and I know it's there. We'll both know he marked me, and that's sexy as hell.

He trails kisses down my spine, making my nerves tingle. His hands slide down my sides to my hips, then to my ass. He grasps each one of my butt cheeks, giving them a little squeeze, and then a sharp little bite, which makes me gasp.

Then he comes back up the bed to press a kiss behind my ear. "You're going to be so tight, aren't you, baby?"

I'm wound so tightly I can barely speak. "Yes."

"I'm going to get you ready to take me again, and then I'm going to remind you who you belong to. When I fuck you tonight, you'll be screaming my name. You got me?"

"Yes!" *Jesus!* These walls are paper thin. Jake's going to get an earful, I'm sure. "What about Jake?"

Cooper chuckles, seemingly unconcerned. "I'm sure he's heard worse." Then he kisses his way down the small of my back, and I can feel the five-o'clock stubble on his chin. He kisses each of my butt cheeks reverently before gently squeezing them. "Turn over."

He rolls me to my back, exposing my body to his hungry gaze. Crawling forward, crouching like a tiger on the prowl, he lowers his mouth to mine. He grips my jaw, coaxing my lips apart with his own, and slips his tongue inside. He eats at me, drawing out every breath and moan. He grabs my hands, linking our fingers together, and pins my hands firmly to the mattress.

His kiss finally softens, and he makes love to my mouth, sipping at me, stroking my tongue, drinking in every sound I make. My cock is straining, flushed and thick, and my balls are already so tight I wonder how long I'll last. I swear he could make me come just from kissing me.

"You are so fucking beautiful," he says, his voice low and rough. He trails kisses down my throat. "Every sound you make, every cry. Every time you tremble in my arms, you slay me."

His lips trek down to my pecs, and when he flicks his tongue against one of my nipples, I cry out, arching my back. But he's still holding my hands pinned to the bed, restraining me, which drives my desire even higher. He tongues and nibbles on my nipples, licking me and teasing my piercings. I strain against his hold, raising my hips, pressing my cock against his abs. He grinds himself against me, gritting his teeth in pleasure.

With a growl, he releases my hands and scoots down the bed to rub his face in the hair at the base of my cock, breathing in my scent with a low groan. Then he runs the flat of his tongue along my erection, making me gasp. With one hand, he cups my balls, gently massaging them, while his other hand grips the base of my cock.

"Who do you belong to?" he says, his voice rough and low.

I can barely breathe, he's got me wound so tightly already. "You."

His grip slides to the tip of my cock and his thumb collects the wetness there, spreading it over the head. Then he leans down and licks the slit, which he knows drives me crazy. My back bows off the mattress. "Fuck!"

He makes a pleased sound, a low rumble deep in his chest, as he licks the head of my cock again, drawing out the sensations, wracking my body with searing pleasure. When he finally stops teasing me and takes my dick into his mouth, all the way to the back of his throat, I start making incomprehensible noises and throw my head back into the pillow.

Cooper goes down on me like nobody's business, sucking and licking, stroking me with his tight fist as he draws me to the back of his throat. I fist the sheets, panting and squirming as he works my cock, driving me toward climax. But when I get close—when fire rips down my spine and into my balls, drawing them up even tighter—when my throbbing dick pulses in his mouth, he backs off, letting me come back down to Earth. He tortures me like this, over and over, until finally he lifts up. He won't let me come, at least not yet. We'll come together. After he's shot his load inside me, he'll jerk me off.

Cooper rolls me back onto my belly, which is difficult given how hard I am. My cock is trapped between my body and the mattress, and then by his, as he settles over me. He covers my back with his body, and I shiver when I feel his lips behind my ear, murmuring hot, needy words. I give a low, drawn-out moan, and he chuckles.

I'm barely aware of what he's doing when he reaches for the lube and sits back on his haunches. I close my eyes, focusing on the exquisite pleasure still coursing through me. He pulls one of my butt cheeks to the side and dribbles that cool slipperiness down my crack and right over my hole. Then his finger is there, spreading the lube and testing my readiness. When he presses the tip of his finger inside me, I tense automatically, my muscles drawing tight.

"God, you're tight," he says. His lubed finger is a little more insistent now as it slides in, then out, over and over, sinking a little deeper each time as he spreads the lubricant. "Relax, baby. Just breathe."

I exhale a long, shaky breath, and his slick finger sinks easily inside. I groan loudly when he curls his finger and grazes my prostate.

Oh, my God, it's been so long. How did I survive three months without this? Without his touch? He knows exactly how to make me shiver and squirm. I start moving my hips, lifting to meet his thrusting finger, all the while craving a thicker penetration.

He kisses me as he finger-fucks me, rubbing and stroking me inside where my nerve endings are rioting with pleasure. Then he withdraws his finger to apply more lube, and this time he works two fingers into me, stretching me slowly.

His long fingers stroke me deep inside, brushing against my prostate with each pass, tormenting me with what's still to come. When he finally thinks I'm ready, he withdraws his fingers and moves to kneel between my spread thighs, leaning down to cover me with his big body. He's heavy, but I like the way he pins me down. His thighs nudge mine farther apart, and he moves in closer. He taps his erection between my ass cheeks, letting me feel how hard he is, how heavy. As he lubes his dick, my belly and ass clench in anticipation.

We both groan as he teases my opening with the blunt head of his cock, rubbing against me, pressing lightly against my tight opening. Gradually, he increases the pressure as he presses forward, becoming more insistent that I let him in. Our bodies play this exquisite dance, where he seeks entrance, but mine tightens until gradually the promise of pleasure overrules me, and I open for him, softening. He presses steadily inside, filling me inch by inch, advancing slowly as he waits for me to adjust, until finally we're both gasping with pleasure. I feel the inevitable little bite of pain and breathe out, a long, slow exhalation to help me relax.

"That's it, baby," he murmurs, clutching my hip with his free hand. I can picture his other hand wrapped around his thick cock as he guides himself into me. "Just relax and breathe."

Cooper's a big man, with an equally big cock. It's thick and long, and it takes some time for me to take all that gloriousness inside me.

He rocks forward, sinking a little further into me each time. And once he's fully seated, he pauses, giving me time to adjust. He's hot and throbbing inside me, and we both groan loudly. When he finally starts to move, slowly at first, I clutch my pillow, gritting my teeth to keep from crying out in pleasure. Every time he strokes inside me, the heat and pressure of him tease my sensitive nerves, lighting me up inside. The pleasure swells until I'm groaning shamelessly into my pillow, pushing back against his hips to drive him even deeper inside me.

He takes his time, working over me, until he gradually picks up speed. I press my hot face into the soft material to muffle my cries. I'm a loud fuck—I always have been. And Jake's right on the other side of that thin wall. I guess I'm enough of an exhibitionist to get off knowing he might be listening to us.

Cooper groans each time he sinks inside me. And once my body is open to him, he gradually speeds up his movements, thrusting long and deep, driving us both insane. His voice and his breath are harsh as he grunts with increasing exertion, moving faster and faster. My body lights up inside when he hits my prostate, sending jolts of pleasure along my spine to my balls.

When we're both close, he hauls me up onto my knees so that I'm kneeling in front of him, my back is pressed against his scorching hot front. At this angle, he's destroying me, hitting my pleasure spot with each stroke, making me gasp. One arm crosses over my chest, holding me to him, and with his free hand, he reaches down to grip my cock with a lubed palm, stroking me firmly, just as I like it. My chest is heaving. My belly is clenched, and my balls are drawn up tightly. I can barely catch my breath as he jerks me off, spreading my pre-come over my length.

I grit my teeth, holding out as long as I can, until his rough shout fills the quiet room. With a hoarse cry, he bucks into me, over and over, filling me with scalding heat, pressing in deeply as he growls into my neck. Gradually, his movements slow as his climax wanes. He's so slick inside me now. His grip on my cock tightens, and he gets serious about bringing me to climax, murmuring hot words of encouragement into the back of my neck. With a loud cry, I come so hard I see stars, spurting my load on the sheet.

When it's clear I'm ready to collapse, he releases me gradually, slipping out of me as I fall forward to lie in my own jizz. I'm far too exhausted and boneless to move a muscle. Cooper disappears into the bathroom for a moment, where I can hear the water running as he cleans himself up.

He returns a few moments later with a warm washcloth and a clean towel. "Roll over."

I roll onto my side, groaning at the exertion.

He lays a towel over my spunk, then cleans me up with the washcloth. "Okay, lie back down."

After another quick trip to the bathroom, Cooper turns off the light and sets his Glock on the floor beside the bed, where he can easily reach it, then climbs into bed beside me.

I'm absolutely wiped, both body and mind sated for the first time in months. My ass is sore and throbbing from being stretched, but it feels so good. And I can still feel the blinding pleasure of my climax echoing through me.

Cooper pulls me to him and kisses my forehead. "Get some sleep, baby. Tomorrow's going to be a real bitch."

I groan in response, too wiped out to reply.

As I lay my arm over his muscular torso, running my fingers through his chest hair, I melt into his embrace, soothed by the scent of his warm skin and the steady beat of his heart.

God, I don't ever want to be separated from him again.

9

Sam

When I awake the next morning, I am blissfully content. Cooper's warm body is pressed up against my back, and his arm is around my waist, tucking me in close to him. His hand is splayed possessively over my belly. I'm surprised—but happy—that he's still in bed with me. He's usually such an early riser.

I stretch and groan.

"Rise and shine, sleepyhead," he murmurs against the back of my head as he strokes my hair, latching onto my topknot and giving it a firm tug, which makes me groan. "We've got work to do. Jake's already up."

I crack my eyes open and reach for my phone to check the time.

It's eight o'clock. I'm surprised he let me sleep this long. "Is the paper out yet?"

"Yeah. It comes out at six-thirty am. Let's get a move on."

I shudder to think of what the reaction's going to be to Cooper's story now that it's out—assuming Jenny Murphy kept her word and printed the story. I suppose a lot of people in this town simply won't believe him. He's essentially an outsider now, and he's pointing the finger at three very prominent men in this small community—accusing them of murder.

Cooper slides his hand down to caress my right butt cheek. Then he gives it a light squeeze. "How do you feel?"

"Fantastic."

"Are you sore? Was I too rough last night?"

"I'm a little sore, yes. And no, you weren't too rough. I needed that, badly."

He chuckles as he kisses my shoulder. "I did too."

He smacks my thigh lightly as he sits up. "I've got to take a piss, clean up, and then speak to Jake for a minute. You get ready. We'll be heading out soon."

"Where to, exactly?"

"Probably back to the diner for breakfast, and to gauge the town's reaction. Trust me, that diner is the main pulse point of this town. If there's trouble, we'll hear about it there."

Cooper hops out of bed and heads to the bathroom. I lie in bed for a few indulgent moments and listen to the sounds of him getting ready. The flushing of the toilet is followed by the sound of water running. When I finally haul my ass out of bed, I stand in the open bathroom doorway and watch him brush his teeth. I like this little bit of domesticity. He's usually long gone from my apartment by the time I wake up, so watching him do something as simple as getting ready in the morning is a rare treat.

He meets me in the bathroom doorway, dressed in jeans and a plain navy blue T-shirt that emphasizes his muscular chest. The fabric strains over his biceps and pecs, sending a wave of longing through me. The man is built like a fucking boss, and I'm ready for round two.

"You didn't shave," I say, reaching up to stroke his two-day stubble. "I like it." Some days he's clean-shaven, some days he lets his beard grow. I like how it feels on my skin when he kisses me.

"I think I'll let it grow a while." He pauses just long enough to give me a minty kiss. "Get dressed while I check in with Jake. I won't be gone long."

I watch him head for the adjoining door, admiring the way he moves, with just a hint of swagger. He looks like a man on a mission. Once he's through the door and out of sight, I grab clean clothes from my duffle bag and my toiletries kit and head into the bathroom.

He walks into the bathroom just as I'm running a brush through my hair. Without saying a word, he reads the slogan on my T-shirt, *My Boyfriend Is More Badass Than Yours*, shakes his head, then takes the brush from me and brushes my hair, drawing it up into a high ponytail. Then he takes the hair band from me and expertly twists my hair into a topknot. "Ready to go?"

"Almost. What did you talk to Jake about?"

He shrugs. "Oh, just a logistical consideration. Nothing you need to worry about."

I frown at his reflection in the cracked bathroom mirror. "Let me guess...I'm your logistical consideration."

His expression hardens, and he reaches out to comb his fingers through my undercut. "I'll trim this for you in a couple days. It'll be ready then."

"You didn't answer my question."

His gaze meets mine in the mirror. "I already told you. You're my weakness. They'll go after you, not me."

"What did you tell Jake?"

"I told him your safety comes first. If things go south, he's to get you out of here and back to Chicago. I can take care of myself."

I turn to face him, livid. "Bullshit! We're not leaving you here alone!"

He smiles, gently cupping my face in his hands. "Sweetheart, it won't be your call. It'll be Jake's. And trust me...Jake will hogtie you if necessary and physically remove you from danger." He drops a sweet kiss on my lips, then turns and walks out of the bathroom, leaving me fuming.

My stomach drops like a stone as I stare at his retreating back. He's dead serious. He would expect me to leave him here if the shit hit the fan. There's no fucking way.

I finish up quickly and grab my chest holster, check my weapon, and suit up as well before joining Cooper standing by the motel door. He's got his jacket on, which means he's armed too. "I suppose I don't need to ask," I say, "but you've checked on the concealed carry laws here? We have reciprocity?"

He nods. "We do."

I follow him outside, and he locks the door behind us. Outside on the sidewalk, I glance up at the wooden soffit above our door and spot a tiny surveillance camera. You'd never notice it if you weren't looking for it. Jake's got cameras on all our doors and windows, front and back of the building, all feeding into the standalone WIFI network he set up in his room.

The door to Jake's room opens, and he walks out, dressed as usual in unrelenting black, his black hair freshly trimmed short. He looks like he's ready to rumble.

He meets us at the SUV with a huge grin on his face. "I trust you both slept well last night."

Oh, shit. He heard us. As I slide into the back seat beside Cooper, my face heats up. "I told you he could hear us," I hiss. "The walls are paper thin."

Cooper shrugs. "I told you, I'm sure he's heard worse."

Jake slides behind the driver's wheel. "Yes, I've heard a lot worse. So, where to?" he says as he guns the engine.

"To the diner," Cooper says. "Let's get some breakfast and see what the morning paper has to say."

* * *

Cooper was right about the diner—it's the main pulse point of this town. When we step inside, the place is packed this morning, and the noise level is so high it's hard to hear anything. There are morning papers strewn across the counter and the tables, and groups of diners are all talking over each other, some of them arguing.

Cooper leads the way, me behind him, and Jake last. We take our place at the back of the line of folks waiting to be seated. Immediately, a hush falls over the place as everyone—even the servers—stops what they're doing to turn and stare at us. *Shit.*

The hostess from yesterday—June—approaches us with a stack of menus cradled in her arms. "It might be best if you find somewhere else to eat today," she says to Cooper in a hushed voice. She glances back nervously at the seated diners who are blatantly watching us. "Everyone's talking about the article in the paper, and there's a lot of speculation going on, none of it good."

"I figured as much," he says. "Thanks for the warnin', but we'll stay."

Cooper's southern drawl has resurfaced again. I've noticed it comes and goes, depending on the situation. Right now, it's back in full force.

June shakes her head in dismay, letting us know what she thinks about the decision. "You'll have to wait for a table."

"That's fine," he says.

While we're waiting to be seated, I surreptitiously scan the dining room, noticing how many people are on their phones, keying in text messages as they pretend not to look at us. More than a few phones are pointed in our direction, and I'm sure they're taking pictures. We'll probably end up plastered all over social media.

June finally returns about fifteen minutes later when we're first in line. "I've got a table open, over there. If you want a booth, you'll have to wait."

"The table's fine," Cooper says.

We follow her across the dining room to our designated table at the far side of the room. On the way, Jake snags a discarded copy of the morning's paper and begins reading, a scowl on his face.

June lays three menus on the table. "Your server will be out in a minute."

As she heads back to the hostess's station, Cooper and Jake stake out their seats, each with a strategic view of the restaurant, the door, and the street. They both sit with their backs to the wall, facing the diners and the front door. I'm left taking either of the two remaining chairs, neither of which offers me a very good vantage point. Apparently, I'm ceding to the old guys today. I choose the chair across from Cooper, the one that faces the kitchen. It might come in handy if the cook tries to throw waffles at us.

A middle-aged brunette hurries to our table carrying three glasses of ice water, which she sets down rather hard, sloshing water over the rims. "Sorry." She tosses three straws onto the table. "Do ya'll know what you want?"

We each order the breakfast special and coffee, and she practically races back to the kitchen.

Cooper seems perfectly relaxed, and Jake's still reading the front page of the newspaper. I can just make out the giant headline sprawled across the top of the page.

40-YEAR-OLD MURDER
FINALLY SOLVED?

Damn. She really did it. The editor printed Cooper's story. I never doubted his story for a second, but I'm kind of surprised the editor wasn't a little more skeptical. Cooper made some very damning accusations about prominent men in this town. That's not going to go over easy. They're not just going to roll over and confess to the authorities.

After he finishes reading the article, Jake hands the paper to Cooper. "It's all there, verbatim."

Cooper skims the article, then hands it to me.

Sure enough, she printed Cooper's story practically word-for-word, just as he told it to her. Thank goodness for digital recorders. The few parts she added, mostly related to the impact of his story on this town, were well thought-out. She clearly took him seriously, which I think was rather gutsy on her part.

Our server brings a pot of coffee to our table and pours three cups. "There's cream and sugar on the table, fellas."

"Thanks," Cooper says, as the woman scurries away.

The once-hushed diners have all gone back to their conversations, and every once in a while, I catch Cooper's name, or the names of the three men he's accused of murder.

I can feel their eyes on the back of my head, burning into me. There's a lot of skepticism in this room. Hell, there's a lot of thinly veiled hostility in this room—I can see it on their faces. They're probably wondering who the hell this Daniel Cooper is, to be coming into their community and stirring up shit. All it would take is a spark to set them off.

As I glance around the room, I notice several of the men speaking furtively into their phones. I'm afraid it's only a matter of time now before things get truly uncomfortable.

A woman Cooper's age—mid-fifties—walks up to our table, looking right at him. "Danny Cooper, is that you?" She sounds incredulous.

"Yeah, it's me." He studies her for a moment, his brow furrowing. "You're Dana, right?"

She nods. "Dana Martinez. I went to school with Cody—we were friends." Nervously, she twists her hands. "We always sat beside each other in homeroom. Is the story in the paper true? Did those men kill Cody?"

Cooper nods. "Yes, ma'am. They did."

"What's going to happen to them now?"

Cooper shrugs. "I guess that's up to the authorities. I'm curious to find that out myself."

She frowns. "But Billy Monroe is the sheriff here. And Judd's a judge. How can there possibly be a fair investigation?"

Our food arrives then, and the woman leaves us alone to eat. Cooper and Jake are both hyper-vigilant, as if they're expecting trouble.

I can tell the instant Cooper goes on high alert. His gaze snaps to attention at a spot somewhere behind me, toward the entrance.

A moment later, the door to the diner crashes open, and the folks standing near the door scatter. I turn to look and there's a man scanning the dining room. When he spots Cooper, he comes barreling right for us. His face is flushed a deep red—unnaturally so—and his eyes, which are locked on Cooper, are overly bright and hard as diamonds.

Cooper stands, his hands on his hips, looking implacable, and the locomotive comes to a screeching halt.

"You!" the red-faced man yells, jabbing his finger in Cooper's direction. "How dare you fucking come into our town and spew your filthy lies?"

Jake rises to his imposing height, making as if to move toward Cooper, but Cooper raises a hand and holds him off.

This guy is trashed. Damn, it's not even nine o'clock in the morning, and he's hammered. I can smell the liquor rolling off him. Well, that answers that question. I was wondering if this was the sheriff, the judge, or the alcoholic football coach. I'm going with the alcoholic.

The coach—Stevens, I think is his name—spins around in a wobbly circle to address everyone in the diner. "Lies! God-damned filthy lies!" he rages. Then he turns back, getting right up in Cooper's face. "No one's going to listen to your filthy lies, you damned pervert! Get the hell out of this town and go back to whatever rock you were living under!"

Cooper stares at Stevens, not moving a muscle. Jake looks like he's more than ready to take this drunken fool out—he's just waiting for a signal from Cooper. But Cooper stands his ground, glaring at Stevens.

"Are you proud of yourself, Roger?" Cooper says. "For beating a harmless teenage boy senseless and throwing him in the Sweetwater

River to drown?"

Stevens's flushed face screws up and his mouth opens, but all he can do is sputter. A sudden hush falls over the room as the occupants wait to hear what he has to say. Even the kitchen staff has stopped what they're doing to crowd around the counter for a front-row view.

Stevens glances briefly at Jake, then he turns his hard gaze on me and smiles with deliberate calculation. I can see the wheels turning in his head as he contemplates his next move. Shit, Cooper was right. I'm Cooper's weakness. Stevens is afraid of the man Cooper is today, so he's turning his sights on me.

"And I suppose this is your newest boy toy?" Stevens points his fat finger at me. His voice is thick, and his words are slurred. He turns to glare at Cooper, swaying on his feet. "You get off on perverting young men, don't you, you filthy animal!"

The coach is average height, with a beer belly that won't quit, and he's wearing a track suit that's a size too small. He looks like he's just coming off a bender, with his dirty blond hair hanging in his face, and his blue eyes bloodshot and slightly unfocused.

Stevens turns back to me. "And you! You're disgusting, letting him defile your body. Someone needs to set you straight, boy."

The instant Stevens takes a step in my direction, Cooper and Jake both act. Jake moves in front of me just as Cooper intercepts Stevens, blocking his path to me. "If you touch one hair on his head, I'll kill you."

Stevens hesitates, clearly recognizing that Cooper's serious. I hear sirens in the distance, and I'm relieved the local authorities are on their way. Cooper doesn't make threats lightly, and the last thing I want is for him to end up in a local jail cell for having committed murder.

"Oh, dear God," says one of the diners, a middle-aged man who jumps to his feet as he reads something on his phone. "Judge Franklin was found dead in his office this morning. He... shot himself."

For a second, everyone goes silent as the news sinks in. But the quiet is shattered by the screech of sirens right outside the diner. The room erupts into chaos, voices raised in unison, when two deputies storm into the restaurant looking like they're ready to crack some skulls.

"Quiet down!" one of them yells as the other one lays his hand on the handle of his holstered firearm.

Everyone in the diner grows quiet, watching in anticipation. I get a bad feeling when the two deputies approach our table, their gazes jumping between Cooper and Stevens. Now both deputies have their hands on their firearms.

"Coach, you need to leave," says one of the deputies, taking me completely by surprise. I'd expected them to target Cooper as he's an outsider. But no, their attention is focused on Stevens. "Otherwise, we'll have to take you in."

The deputies, both of whom look to be in their thirties, are close enough now that I can read their name tags. One of them is Williams, the other Turner. Williams is the one doing the talking.

"Take me in for what?" Stevens says.

"Disorderly conduct."

"Me?" Stevens points at Cooper. "Arrest him for indecency! He's a fucking homo-sexual!" With a wave of his shaky hand, he indicates the three of us. "They're all a bunch of degenerates! Arrest them!"

Stevens lunges for me, trying to by-pass Cooper. Cooper snags him in a choke-hold, forcibly restraining him, and cutting off his airflow in the process.

"Let him go, sir," Deputy Williams says to Cooper. "We'll handle this."

Cooper releases Stevens and hands him over to Deputy Williams, who slaps handcuffs on the coach's wrists.

As the two deputies march Stevens out of the restaurant, Jenny Murphy comes in the diner and heads right for our table. She drops down into the spare chair, breathless. She brushes her blonde hair back as she looks us over. "Are you guys okay?"

"We're fine," I say, when neither Cooper nor Jake responds. At least I hope that's true. Cooper still looks fit to be tied. If those deputies hadn't hauled Stevens off to jail, Cooper would have exacted his own form of justice, which would probably have landed him in jail.

Jenny looks at Cooper, her expression tight. "Judd Franklin committed suicide this morning, not long after the paper came out. He reportedly left a suicide note confessing to his part in the killing of Cody Martin." She leans closer to us, lowering her voice. "Rumor has it, he said he'd been haunted all of his life over what happened to you and Cody, and that he couldn't live with the guilt any longer. He said that, as a judge, he was sworn to uphold justice. He said he was a hypocrite, and he couldn't bear it any longer. Now I haven't seen it for myself, but it sounds like his suicide note corroborates everything you said in your story. He *confessed*, Danny."

Cooper sits motionless. "Even back then, Judd wasn't the instigator. He followed Billy around like a puppy and did whatever Billy said. Billy and Roger were the true bullies."

"Roger won't be in jail for long," Jenny says. "They'll keep him there until he sobers up, and then they'll let him go. It's the same thing every time he goes off the deep end."

Our server brings Jenny a glass of ice water. "Can I get you somethin', Miss Jenny?"

Jenny reaches for the glass and drains half of it in one go. "No.

Nothing for me, thanks." She sets the glass down and faces Cooper. "Roger Stevens was placed on administrative leave this morning at the high school, pending an investigation. So was Billy Monroe. Danny, it's not safe for you to be here. I'm afraid both Roger and Billy will be gunning for you. And in Billy's case, I mean that literally. The man's armed to the teeth."

Cooper's gaze shifts to Jake, and then to me. "We'll leave when we're good and ready," he says. "I appreciate the warning, Jenny, but I know firsthand what these two are capable of. We'll leave when I know justice will be done, and not a minute sooner."

10

Cooper

Just as Jenny leaves to return to the newspaper office to wait for more news, our server brings us our breakfasts. We eat in silence, monitoring the temperature of the room. We're still getting plenty of odd looks, if not downright hostile stares, but no one else approaches us.

Sam's awfully quiet, and I don't blame him. Just as I feared, Stevens focused his ire on Sam, thinking that was the quickest way to get under my skin. Stevens was right.

After we finish eating, Jake settles our bill, and we all head out to the SUV, which is parked a block away from the diner. There's a handwritten note tucked underneath one of the windshield wiper blades. Jake retrieves it, reads it, then hands it to me.

I'm going to fucking kill you.
You should have stayed gone.

Just as I'm about to shove the note into my pocket, Sam grabs it and reads it.

"Any idea who wrote it?" Jake says, as he unlocks the vehicle doors with the key fob.

"I'm pretty sure I can guess," I say, taking the note back from Mr. Hot Head and sticking it in my pocket. We might need it for evidence.

I open the rear door and motion for Sam to get in the vehicle. When I join him in the back seat, he gives me a pleased smile. He wouldn't be so happy, though, if he knew I was seriously thinking about sending him home on a commercial flight. I don't mind risking my own neck to get justice for Cody, but I sure as hell mind risking his.

I know Sam can take care of himself. He's a former Army Ranger, for God's sake. Yes, he's coming off some pretty serious injuries, but he's still capable. He's not Superman, though. He's not invincible, especially if his opponent is armed and dangerous, which we have to assume that Billy Monroe is. Probably Roger Stevens, too. I'm honestly not sure which one of them is worse—Billy or Roger. Maybe Roger, because the alcohol adds a degree of unpredictability. Roger's always been an angry drunk, even back in school. But Billy...he's a snake in the grass.

"Where to?" Jake asks, catching my gaze in the rear-view mirror.

I'm tempted to tell him to take us back to the motel, where we can hunker down and wait this out. I want to know what's going to happen now that the newspaper has run the story. There's no statute of limitations on murder. I'm waiting for murder charges to be brought against Billy and Roger. And now, with Judd's reported death-bed confession, the case against the other two men is bolstered.

"Let's go to the Sweetwater River Bridge and pay our respects," Sam says, reaching for my hand and linking our fingers. He tugs on my hand. "Come on. You need closure."

The thought of returning to that bridge makes me sick. Two young boys were terrorized on that bridge. One of them died there. And I feel guilty for being the one who survived. Maybe Sam's right. Maybe I do need closure.

Jake's watching me patiently through the rearview mirror, waiting for some direction. I nod. "We might as well."

I lay our joined hands on my thigh and look at Sam. His brown eyes are glittering, and he looks ready for a fight. He's fearless, and that's what worries me. He's not invincible, no matter if he thinks he is.

* * *

Fifteen minutes later, Jake parks the Escalade on the shoulder of the road, just a few yards from the bridge. The three of us get out and walk the small incline onto the two-lane bridge, which spans the broad Sweetwater River. As usual, in early spring, the water is high and fast, rushing past downed trees that line the muddy banks. The river is about a hundred yards wide, and it's a challenge to swim on a good day. When the river is swollen like this, fair to bursting at the seams, it's a bear.

We stand at the railing in the middle of the bridge and gaze down at the churning water.

"It's about a thirty-foot drop," I say, watching the water rush by.

"How deep is it here?" Sam asks.

"It's at least twenty feet deep, maybe a little more."

My throat tightens as the memories come flooding back. I guess it's inevitable. The last time I was here, I was facing possible death. I knew I could survive the fall, and I knew I could swim that river, but with my hands tied in front of me, it was anyone's guess.

I knew Cody likely wouldn't make it. I remember looking over at him, seeing his blank stare as he faced straight ahead, not looking down at the water. I don't know where he went in his head, but he wasn't mentally present on that bridge. I think he'd already checked out. Fear can do that to you.

I swallow against the hard knot in my throat, feeling my pulse pick up, along with my breathing. I exhale heavily, trying to rein in the panic and not start hyperventilating. I keep reminding myself I'm not a scared teenager anymore.

"Jesus, Sam! What in the hell do you think you're doing?"

At the sound of Jake's incredulous voice, I whip my gaze over to Sam, who's in the process of stripping down. His boots and socks are lying on the pavement, along with his jacket and gun holster. He pulls his T-shirt over his head and tosses it to the ground.

"What the fuck are you doing, Sam?" I say, my voice sharp.

As his gaze darts to the metal railing, my stomach drops like a stone. I'm afraid I know exactly what he's planning. "Don't you dare."

He lowers the zipper on his jeans and shoves them down and off, leaving him in nothing but his black boxer briefs. "Closure," he says, heading for the railing. "You need closure."

"Sam, no!" Panic overtakes me, bringing back hellacious memories. *Oh, hell no! Not again.*

I move to intercept him before he can reach the railing, but the sudden, ear-splitting shriek of a police siren distracts me. I glance behind me to see a patrol car heading right for us, its lights flashing.

Shit!

When I turn back to Sam, he's standing on the railing, balancing like an acrobat on a four-inch wide piece of steel as he stares down at the rushing water.

He opens his arms wide and yells, "Fuck this river!"

The same two deputies we saw this morning at the diner exit their vehicle. "Freeze! Don't you dare jump!"

Sam laughs. "Sorry, I can't hear you!"

He flips off the cops, then leaps into the air, his arms spread wide. Mid-air, he twists to form a perfect arc as he dives toward the water. I race to the railing and look over just in time to see him curl in on himself, wrapping his arms around his knees, and hitting the water like a cannonball. He disappears beneath the dark surface of the water, and for a second, I can't breathe. Then I shake myself out of it. "Sam!"

I reach for my left boot, intending to strip and go in after him, but Jake lays a calming hand on my shoulder, stilling me. "It's okay." He nods toward the opposite side of the bridge, and I race over there. We all do. And there's Sam, twenty yards downstream, doing the breast stroke as he swims toward us, fighting against the raging current in a river that has to be cold as ice this time of year. If he doesn't drown, he'll surely die of hypothermia.

I shake my head, caught between fury and laughter. Laughter wins out when Sam salutes me from thirty feet below. He's so damn full of himself, grinning like a fool. "See? It's just a river," he yells.

"That little prick," I murmur, and damn if I don't love him so much right now I can hardly stand it.

Jake laughs. "Damn. You have to admit, the guy's got balls."

The two deputies join us at the railing, looking over the side at Sam.

"Jesus Christ," one of them says—Deputy Williams. He looks at me and shakes his head. "He's crazy. Some idiot dies here every year jumping off this damn bridge."

Sam's teeth are chattering as he treads water, and I can tell he's freezing his ass off. The current is strong, and he's moving farther downstream at an alarming rate of speed.

"All right, that's enough!" I yell, waving at him to get out of the water. I'm struggling not to laugh, because I don't want to encourage his impetuous behavior. But God, that was pretty awesome. "Get your ass back up here!"

Jake looks amused as hell—and more than a little impressed—as he watches Sam swim to the bank. *Damn.* I never thought I would stand on this bridge again and laugh. And that's why he did it. To give me something else to remember about this bridge. I'll never forget what happened here forty years ago, but at least now I have another memory to hold onto.

I watch Sam crawl up the bank, slipping and sliding on the wet grass, and then walk up the hill to the road that leads onto the bridge.

He's limping when he reaches us, clearly favoring his left leg, and his lips are blue. "Damn, that water's cold," he says, grinning at me as he shivers uncontrollably. "Why the hell didn't you warn me?"

For a second, I just drink him in. He's so damn fearless, I could fall on my knees. Instead, cognizant of our rapt audience, I hand Sam his clothes. "Let's get you back to the motel to warm you up, before you catch your death."

When Sam's dressed, Deputy Williams hands him a slip of paper.

"What's this?" Sam says, turning it over to read the print on the other side.

Deputy Williams grins. "It's a ticket, you fool." He points at a warning sign clearly posted on the bridge. "There's a hundred dollar fine for jumping off this bridge."

Sam laughs as he pockets the ticket. "Hell, it was worth every penny. I'd do it again, but my balls are frozen solid."

* * *

The minute I get him back to our motel room, I march Sam straight into the bathroom and start the shower. "Take off your clothes."

"Yes, sir," the cocky son-of-a-bitch says, looking way too pleased with himself.

I cross my arms, trying to look stern, but what I really want to do is grab him and kiss him senseless. "You're pretty damn proud of yourself, aren't you?"

He nods as he yanks off his boots and socks, followed by his T-shirt. As he reaches for the fastener on his jeans, I brush his hands aside and unsnap them for him. Then I lower his zipper and tug his jeans down his long legs. I want him so badly that the need is like a knife in my gut. But first, he needs to warm up after his impromptu ice bath.

He removes his briefs and steps into the shower, groaning with pleasure when the warm water hits his ice-cold skin. I close the shower curtain partway, leaving it open just enough that I can stand there and watch him. His nipple piercings glint in the light, and his body is still flushed from the cold.

He leans his head into the spray of hot water and moans, soaking in the heat. "God this feels good. I was serious earlier, when I said my balls were frozen solid. Damn, I couldn't even feel them." He reaches down—the smart ass—to cup his big sac, hefting its weight. "Oh, thank God, they're still attached."

I laugh. "I should beat your ass for what you did. It was reckless and stupid. You could have gotten hurt."

He looks at me, suddenly serious. "I'd do it again in a heartbeat."

"Why? What possessed you to do that?"

Sam shrugs as he grabs the bar of soap I brought and lathers up. "I imagined what you must have felt as a kid, standing on that bridge, looking over the railing. Wondering if those were your last minutes on Earth. Wondering if you were going to die. Hell, as a kid I dived from higher heights than that. I used to drive my mom insane. I jumped to show you that it's just a river, nothing more. It's not scary, it's not the bogeyman. What happened to you and Cody was a heinous crime, a damn tragedy. And honestly, it's a miracle you survived. I kept picturing you, a gawky teen with your hands tied. It gutted me, babe. So I jumped, to show that river it's not the boss of us."

He rinses off, and I hold out a towel for him as he steps out of the shower. I wrap it around him and draw him against me. He's warm and damp in my arms, so strong and sturdy. The heat of him soaks into my T-shirt, and the air in the bathroom is as hot and humid as a sauna. Damn. He takes my breath away.

He also pisses me off to no end, taking a risk like that. I grip his chin and make him look at me, our faces just inches apart. "Don't you ever take a God-damned chance like that again, do you hear me? You took ten years off my life today, and I don't have any to waste. Not if I'm going to keep up with you."

He grins, and I don't think he's taking me seriously. I am serious, though, dead serious. But right now, with him in my arms, feeling his firm, muscular body against mine, all I can think about is how much he means to me. I meet his gaze head on. "I love you, Sam."

He swallows hard, his eyes glittering, so young and cocky and full of life. "I love you, too."

"Come with me." I take his hand and lead him to our bed. I'm so choked with emotion right now that I'm afraid to say anything more. I'm afraid I'll lose it. I pull the towel away from him, leaving him standing butt naked at the foot of the bed, and I drop to my knees to worship him the best way I know how.

He gasps, gripping my shoulders hard as his fingers dig into my muscles. He throws his head back with a guttural cry when I suck his semi-hard dick into my mouth. I stroke him from base to tip, reveling in how quickly he swells in my grip. I lick the swollen, smooth head, and he mutters something completely incomprehensible, which makes me smile. A burst of pre-come hits my tongue, and I groan. His fingers continue to flex on my shoulders, alternately gripping me hard, then gently, until he finally gives up and holds onto me for dear life.

I swallow him deep, taking him all the way to the back of my throat, then smack him on his bare ass, encouraging him to move. He takes my cue and begins to thrust, slowly at first, then faster and faster until he's fucking my mouth with a fervor and exuberance that tells me we're both just happy to be alive.

I bring his hands to my head, encouraging him to use me as he wants. Groaning, he clutches my head and holds me in place to receive his thrusts. His cock slams into my mouth, faster and deeper with each thrust, until I'm forced to relax my throat muscles and breathe shallowly through my nose.

I slip a hand between his legs to cradle his sac and find his big balls drawn up high and tight. He's close to shooting his load, and I want him to give it to me. When he tries to pull out, I grab his ass and hold him in my mouth. With a loud cry, he throws his head back, arching his beautiful, strong neck. His hands clutch my head in desperation as he spews his load down my throat. I swallow pulse after pulse, my tongue gently stroking the underside of his throbbing cock, coaxing him, praising him.

"Oh, Jesus," he gasps when he finally pulls out of my mouth. "God, Cooper."

I stand, still fully dressed, and watch him shivering naked before me. He's still warm from his shower, and after that little workout, I don't think he's cold. I think he's shaken to the core. When I see the glitter of tears forming in his eyes, I know I'm right.

"Get in bed," I tell him, as I quickly strip off my clothes. It's only just after noon, and we have things yet to do today, but right now I don't give a damn. We need some quiet time together, to just hold each other.

I crawl under the blankets with him, drawing him into my arms, and he lays his head on my chest. I rub my hands along his back, down to his hips and ass. He's boneless in my arms, still reeling from the pleasure of his climax. I can feel his heart hammering against my chest.

When he rises up and reaches for the lube on the nightstand, I stop him and pull him back down to me. "No. That was for you."

"But you didn't—"

"That's okay. Right now, I just want to hold you."

When I watched Sam jump off that bridge railing, I had flashbacks of Cody going over the edge that horrific night.

It broke my heart when Cody died.

If I lost Sam, it would destroy me.

"Just rest, baby," I tell him, stroking his back.

My chest feels tight, like it's being squeezed in a vise. Right now, I need a tangible reminder that Sam's okay. When he was hit by a speeding car just a few months ago, it shook me to the core watching him lying in a hospital bed connected to a half-dozen beeping monitors.

Today, I was reminded once again that he's not immortal, even though he sometimes thinks he is.

11

Sam

An hour into cuddle time, my belly growls like a wild beast in
rutting season. How long has it been since we ate breakfast?
Cooper laughs. "Sounds like somebody's hungry." He
slaps my ass. "Let's get dressed, and then we'll go grab something to
eat."

I pull on clean briefs and my best ripped jeans. If we're going to
raise hell in this town, I want to look good doing it. I dig around
in my duffle bag until I locate my favorite "Beyoncé" T-shirt. It's either wear that, or wear my *I'm His* T-shirt, or my *Gay Men Suck* tee,
but Cooper would have a heart attack if I wore either of those last
two out in public. "I need to hang up my clothes—they're getting

wrinkled."

Cooper points at the closet in our room, giving me a *duh* look. His clothes are already hung up, de-wrinkling as we speak. He's much better at adulting than I am, but of course he's had many more years of experience than I have, as I often like to remind him.

As he dresses, I empty the clothes out of my bag, shake out the wrinkles as best I can, and hang them up. I brought two pairs of distressed jeans with me and a half-dozen tees and a couple muscle shirts. Depending on how long we're going to be here, I may need to hit a laundromat. And a gym.

After Cooper finishes in the bathroom, he heads to Jake's room to coordinate our plans for the rest of the day. I put on deodorant and brush my teeth and hair.

I don't know what the plans are for the afternoon, but as long as it involves food, I'm good. Maybe we can do something fun tonight. I wonder if there's a decent nightclub in this small town. I seriously doubt I could talk Cooper into dancing, but I know he'd play pool or shoot darts with me. Jake too.

When I come out of the bathroom, the adjoining door between our two rooms is open. I walk through to Jake's room.

"Whoa." I give a long, low whistle at the sight of Jake's high-tech surveillance center, which he has set up on a small round table. He's got three laptops running video footage. On each screen is a live stream from one of the three cameras he's got positioned: the two cameras outside—one in front of the building, and one in back—plus a camera in his room to protect the equipment while we're out.

Jake pockets his wallet and grabs his keys. "So, what's the plan, guys?"

"I'd like to check in briefly with Jenny Murphy," Cooper says. "She might know what's happening with the investigations into Stevens and Monroe. After that, we should grab some dinner."

Jake opens the door to his room. "Sounds good."

But first, a side trip. Cooper takes the keys and gets behind the driver's seat. Jake sits up front, riding shotgun, and that leaves me in the back seat.

"Where are we going?" I ask, sitting forward and leaning over the back of Cooper's seat. I brush my thumb across the back of his neck and smile when he shivers.

"Since I'm here, I'd like to drive by the house I grew up in."

I lay my hand on his shoulder. "More closure?"

He nods. "Yeah."

I remember Cooper telling me that his mom passed away eight years ago. His father, who has Alzheimer's, lives in an assisted living facility at the edge of town. Their family home was sold years ago to help pay for his father's medical expenses.

Cooper drives for about ten minutes, heading out of the town limits and into the open countryside. We drive for a while on a long, two-lane rural road where we pass large farms on both sides of the road, fenced-in pastures, a few herds of cattle and horses.

He finally slows the vehicle and pulls over to the shoulder, parking in the gravel beside a drainage ditch. We're parked in front of an older single-story house with white clapboard siding. The house is pretty far back from the road, at the end of a long, tree-lined gravel lane. Even from here, we can see a man outside washing his pick-up truck, and two young boys tossing a ball for their dog. Behind the house, it's nothing but woods as far as the eye can see.

"This is where you grew up?" I say.

He nods, staring at the house. "It seemed a lot bigger when I was a kid."

"Is he nearby? Your dad?"

Cooper nods. "It's about fifteen minutes from here."

"Do you want to go see him?"

"No."

"Cooper—"

"I said no."

I lay my arm over his shoulder, my hand resting over his heart. "This may be the last time you'll get to see your dad. I think you should go. Just see him."

"He probably won't even know me."

"That's okay. What matters is that you know him. You should see him, while you still have a chance. You never got to see your mom again. You never got to say good-bye to her. Don't miss that opportunity with your dad."

Cooper sighs heavily as he starts the engine. Then he pulls out onto the rural lane and heads back toward town. I think he's going to ignore my suggestion completely, but suddenly he pulls into the parking lot of a sprawling, one-story resident center. *Sweetwater Manor*, according to the sign out front.

"This is a bad idea," he says, parking and shutting off the engine. He hands the keys to Jake. "Wait here. I won't be long."

"I'm coming with you," I say, hopping out of the vehicle.

Cooper just shrugs, and I take that as an invitation to join him.

We stop in the front office, and Cooper explains who he is, and asks to see his father. The woman who runs the facility—Sherry Miller, the director—recognizes him, and they shake hands.

"He can get pretty agitated, Danny," the woman says, leading us down a hallway past a secured check point. "The facility is secured so that our residents don't go wandering around and get lost."

Once we're through the secured check-point, we follow Ms. Miller down another hallway to a closed door on the right. The name plate beside the door says *Harold Cooper*. Ms. Miller knocks, but there's no answer.

"Let me go in first," she says, turning the door knob. "I'll come back and get you if he's up for visitors."

She leaves the door partly open, and we can hear her talking in a low, soothing voice to someone inside the room. A few moments later, she returns. "He's sitting in his recliner looking out the window," she says. "But he's not very responsive today. He wouldn't look at me or answer any of my questions. Some days he's more lucid than others. Some days he pretty much talks the head off anyone who will listen to him. Today's not that day. I'm sorry."

"Can I see him?" Cooper says.

He's standing ramrod straight, his body radiating tension. I can't even begin to imagine how difficult this must be for him. The last thing he heard his father say was that he—Cooper—should stay in Illinois with his aunt, because if his father saw him again, he'd kill him.

Ms. Miller smiles sadly as she lays her hand on Cooper's shoulder. "Sure. Let's give it a try."

We follow Sherry Miller into Cooper's dad's room. It's a small suite, with a sitting room, a bedroom, and a bathroom. There's a small kitchen area with a sink, small refrigerator, and a table that seats two, but there's no stove or any other cooking appliances. In the sitting room, there's a sofa along one wall with a television set on the opposite wall, next to a bookcase filled with books and family photos.

Cooper stops to look at the photos. Every photo is of the same couple, a middle-aged man and woman—his parents? But I don't see any photos of Cooper.

His father is seated in a recliner beside a large window, looking outside at a collection of bird feeders on a small patio.

"Mr. Cooper?" Sherry says. "You have a visitor."

His dad looks to be in his mid-eighties, I'd guess. His gray hair is cut short, and he's very trim, almost underweight. He's wearing glasses with black plastic frames.

Ms. Miller walks up behind the man's chair and lays her hand on his shoulder, patting him. "Mr. Cooper? Your son's here. Danny's here to see you."

Harold Cooper frowns, looking confused, and shakes his head.

"Would you like to say hello?" the woman says.

"No, no," the man says, shaking his head. His voice is deep and gravelly. "My son's dead."

The conviction in the man's tone breaks my heart. I know Cooper's an only child, so his dad couldn't be talking about anyone else.

Cooper moves to stand in his father's line of sight, staying a few feet back. His expression is neutral. "Dad? It's me, Danny."

The old man lifts his head, his eyes focusing on Cooper. "Danny?"

"Yeah, Dad, it's me."

Then the old man shakes his head, frowning. "No, I don't have a son. My son died years ago."

Then Harold turns his head back to the view out his window, where the multitude of birds flit around on the bird feeders, squawking at each other as they jockey for the best perches.

Ms. Miller smiles at Cooper. "I'm sorry—"

Cooper turns on his heel and heads for the door. Ms. Miller and I follow him out.

The director closes the old man's door quietly and turns to face Cooper. "Danny, I'm so sorry. If you'd like to come back another time, maybe after dinner this evening, he might be more receptive."

Cooper shakes his head. "Forty years ago my dad said he'd kill me if he ever saw me again. I tried talking to him over the years, but he never relented. I was dead to him, as far as he was concerned. I guess that hasn't changed." He takes a shaky breath, his throat muscles working hard as his lips flatten. "Thanks for letting me see him, Sherry. I appreciate it."

Ms. Miller walks us back out of the secured wing and back to the main entrance where we came in. We say our good-byes, and she returns to her office, leaving us to let ourselves out through the double glass doors.

Once we're outside, Cooper stops, standing motionlessly as he stares out across the parking lot.

My chest hurts, and I rub it, not sure how to help him. "Cooper—"

He shakes his head. "Not right now, Sam. Please." He starts toward the Escalade, motioning for me to follow him. Without a word, he slides into the backseat, and I follow him in.

Jake, who's still seated in the front passenger seat, turns and looks at Cooper, then at me.

I shake my head, signaling Jake to give Cooper some space.

Jake hops out of the vehicle and walks around to the driver's side, slipping behind the wheel and starting the engine. "Where to?" he says, eyeing us through the rear-view mirror.

"The newspaper office," Cooper says, his voice deadpan. He buckles his seat belt and leans back in his seat, reaching blindly for my hand.

12

Sam

We head back into town and park in front of the newspaper office. When we walk inside, Patricia, the receptionist, looks up from the book she's reading. When she sees it's us, she points behind her to Jenny's office door. "She's on the phone with the acting sheriff. Have a seat, and I'll let her know you're here."

"Thank you, ma'am," Cooper says, slipping back into his southern manners.

Patricia stares contemplatively at Cooper. "Do I know you? Did you used to live around here?"

Cooper nods. "I lived here in Sweetwater until my freshman year of high school."

"Oh, yeah, I remember you." Her eyes widen. "Danny Cooper, right?"

"Yes, ma'am."

"Oh, hell, you don't need to call me ma'am. I was just two years ahead of you in school, if I remember right. Are you going to be in town long?"

"I doubt it. I'm just here to take care of some business."

Patricia glances behind her at Jenny, who's still on the phone. Then she turns back to Cooper. "I remember you. You were tall for your age, with dark hair. Now you're a silver fox, aren't you?" She smiles, blushing as she tucks her long silver hair behind her ear.

Oh, my God, she's flirting with him. I sneak a peek at Cooper, who meets my gaze. He shrugs innocently.

"Danny, I'm glad you're here."

We both turn just as Jenny Murphy walks up to the wooden bannister. She opens the swinging gate and motions for us to follow her back to her office.

Once we're seated inside, she closes the door. "I just got off the phone with the acting sheriff, Denny Williams. Deputy Williams has taken over while the investigation's on-going. The feds are involved now. A team arrived in town early this afternoon, and they've set up an office in the courthouse."

"Deputy Williams, eh?" Cooper says, chuckling. "We've run into him a couple of times today. Once at the diner, and then later on the Sweetwater River Bridge. He gave Sam a hundred dollar fine for jumping off the bridge."

Jenny's eyes widen as she looks my way. "You jumped off that bridge? Are you insane?"

"Apparently, he is," Cooper says, winking at me.

Jenny shakes her head. "Williams is a good guy—you can trust him. His mother is the town's mayor—you remember Rita Howard? She went to school with us. Well, she's Rita Williams now—Mayor Williams. It's Billy you need to watch. He's not taking this investigation well. He's insisting your story is nothing more than a delusion. He claims you killed Cody."

Cooper goes silent, sitting perfectly still. I glance at him, noting the muscle flexing in his clenched jaw.

"And why would I do that?" he says, his voice deceptively calm.

Jenny frowns. "He claims Cody threatened to tell your father about the two of you—that you were lovers—and that you were so afraid of your father that you would have done anything to shut Cody up. Including murder."

Cooper exhales, but says nothing, and I can only imagine what he's feeling. He's a man of honor, before all things. It must kill him to hear such an accusation.

"Is there any truth to that?" she says.

Cooper sighs as he looks at me, as if he's worried about what I'll think. "Cody and I were lovers, yes. Did I kill him? Hell, no. He was my first boyhood crush. And as for my father—he was a vicious bigot. Yes, I was afraid of him, but not so much that I'd kill over it."

Jenny frowns. "Be on your guard, Danny. As long as Billy's at liberty, he's a threat. Watch your back. I wouldn't put it past him to retaliate."

Cooper nods. "What about Stevens?"

Jenny rolls her eyes. "The last I heard, he's holed up at his house, on a drinking binge. His wife reportedly left him this morning and went to stay with her mother halfway across the state. She'd long been fed up with his drinking, but a murder charge? That was the final straw."

"What about the feds?" Jake says. "What's their angle?"

"They're investigating Cody's death as a hate crime," Jenny says. "That puts his murder under federal jurisdiction—they're citing the *Civil Rights Act of 1968*."

"Who notified the feds?" Cooper says.

Jenny smiles. "I did. I'm sick of how Billy Monroe runs this town. He's as much a bully today as he was forty years ago. He needs to be held accountable. He and Roger, both."

On our way out, Cooper asks Jenny, "Where's a good place for us to grab some dinner and beers?"

"Tucker's. Head east four blocks. You'll see it on the corner, on your right. The food's good, and the prices are decent. It can get a little rowdy in there—it's a bit of a meat market—but I'm sure you boys can hold your own."

* * *

We park on the street within easy walking distance of Tucker's Tavern. Sam and I secure our firearms in a gun safe hidden under the floorboard in the rear of the vehicle, but Jake keeps his. We don't want to be too conspicuous going into this place, but we don't want to be completely unarmed either.

We walk the two blocks, past a hardware store and a florist's shop, to the bar. It's five o'clock and the downtown retail shops are closing up for the night. Only the diner is still open, the movie theater, and the bars.

I stop abruptly at the tavern door, and Cooper nearly runs right into me. He grabs my shoulders to steady us both. "Sam? What's wrong?"

I can't help laughing. "Two gay guys and a hitman walk into a redneck bar. What could possibly go wrong?"

Jake laughs as he reaches around me to open the door and push me inside. "Don't worry. I've got your back."

Tucker's has got to be one of the original fixtures in this town. The wooden door is an antique with a little peep-hole window, and inside the old wood floors have been burnished over the years to the color of fine whisky. The bar runs along the back wall, extending nearly the width of the building. To the left are dining tables and in the back there's a sign indicating restrooms. To the right of the bar are pool tables and dart boards.

The dance floor is currently empty, but most of the seats at the bar are occupied, as are half of the dining tables. It looks like this place is a popular spot for dinner.

A pretty brunette with a perky ponytail hustles by us as she carries a tray laden with empty glasses to the bar. "Take a seat, fellas," she says as she passes us. "I'll be right with ya."

Jake stakes out the corner table and sits with his back to the wall so he'll have a clear view of the room. Cooper takes the other seat facing the room.

"Age before beauty, eh?" I say, taking one of the shitty seats with my back to the room. As usual, I lose out to seniority.

It's warm in the room, so I take off my jacket and hang it over the back of my chair.

Jake takes one look at my T-shirt and rolls his eyes. "Way to fly under the radar screen, pal."

I glance down at my T-shirt—*My Boyfriend Is More Badass Than Yours*—and shrug. "What can I say? It's true."

The juke box is playing some lame country song from the previous century, so I get up and amble over to the machine to cue up something from this century. I luck out with a couple of my favorite Beyoncé songs, a classic Lady Gaga, two Sam Smith's, and an old

Elton John song, *Rocket Man*—my only concession to the last century. Cooper will appreciate the Elton John song—it's old school, like he is.

I don't know about the other guys, but I plan to do some dancing tonight. This town is way too serious and full of drama. It's time we kick back and have some fun. If I'm lucky, I'll meet up with a bunch of girls who will let me dance with them, like I do with Beth and Lia when we go clubbing at home. I prefer dancing with girls, cause they're mostly there to have fun. I get hit on a lot at nightclubs. Cooper wouldn't be upset if he saw girls hitting on me, but if he saw a guy hitting on me—hell. He'd shit a brick. None of us needs *that kind* of drama.

Just as I return to our table, our server—the cute brunette with perky tits—comes to take our orders. She's petite and curvy as hell in all the right places, and she's got her eye on Jake. She's got a twinkling crystal piercing in her left nostril, and her belly button is pierced—that's obvious thanks to her low-cut, crop top, which reveals more than it covers. Her name tag says "Carrie."

"What can I get you, gentlemen?" she says in a charming southern accent. As she writes down our orders, her gaze keeps returning to Jake. Yep, score one for the big guy! Going by the flush in her cheeks and the way she's batting her eyelashes at Jake, I'm pretty sure our server is sending Jake an open invitation. It's a good thing he has his own room—he could get lucky tonight if he wants to.

I opt for something light tonight—just a salad with grilled chicken—because I want to dance and have fun. *And I plan to get lucky tonight with my own big guy.*

Carrie returns to our table twice more, asking if we need any refills. She stands close enough to Jake to give him a front-row view of her bountiful cleavage. "Is there anything else I can do for you, hun?"

she says, giving him a come-hither smile.

"No, thanks, I'm good," he says, making a point to look anywhere but at her tits.

She reaches across him to retrieve his discarded menu, blatantly brushing her breasts against his bicep, but he doesn't respond. Oh, hell, I don't even play on her team, and I can tell she's smoking hot, so I wonder what Jake's problem is. He's not dating anyone. In fact, I can't even recall hearing him ever talk about a girl. He's not gay—my gaydar would have picked up on that a long time ago—so what's his problem?

By the time we're done eating, the bar is packed. Most of the tables are filled, and the dance floor is finally seeing some action. Some slightly inebriated folks across the room are playing pool—very loudly—and shooting darts.

I finished my beer ages ago, and I'm dying of thirst, but ever since Jake gave our server the brush-off, she's been avoiding us. If I want a refill, I guess I'll have to go get it myself. I stand. "I'm gonna get a refill. You guys want anything?"

Jake nods. "I'll take another Coke. Thanks." Right—he's armed tonight. So, no alcohol for him.

I look at Cooper.

"Sure." He holds up his empty beer bottle. "I'll have another."

I skirt around the crowded tables and head up to the bar, which is equally crowded with folks standing two and three deep. The staff behind the bar is hustling to fill orders. As I wait in line to place my order, somebody bumps me from the side. I glance over at a guy in his early twenties, with short black hair and gorgeous dark eyes. He's holding an empty tumbler, and his eyes are a little too bright—I think he's halfway trashed.

"Sorry," I say, smiling apologetically as I give him a little room.

He moves with me. "No need to be sorry," he says, winking at me. Yeah, he's skunked. He reads the slogan on my T-shirt and laughs. "I like your shirt." Then he reaches over and skims his finger down my arm.

Wow, *subtle*. I smile and shake my head. "Sorry, buddy, but I'm not interested. Thanks."

He pouts prettily, and damn if he isn't a little hottie. He's half-a-head shorter than me, with a tight, fit body. I wonder what it's like for him living in this small town. As he doesn't seem to be cowering in fear, I'm hopeful that things have changed around here since Cooper was a kid.

"You're new here," the hottie says, giving me a coy smile. "I would have remembered seeing you before."

I nod, keeping my eyes forward. I don't want to encourage him. "Just visiting from out of town."

He steps closer again, so that our arms are touching, and tips his head back towards our table. "I saw you come in with those two guys. Are you with one of them?"

"Yep."

"Which one? The muscle guy or the old guy?"

I laugh. "The old guy."

Hottie takes another look at my T-shirt and chuckles. "I'll bet," he says, glancing back at Cooper. "There's something to be said for the older guys, right? At least they know what they're doing."

I've had enough of this guy, and it's all I can do not to roll my eyes.

"If you wanna hang out for a few minutes, I'll give you a tour of the place," he says. He nods toward the dimly lit hallway left of the bar, where the restrooms are located. "There's a door back there that leads to the alley."

I get hit on all the time and it usually doesn't bother me—I just smile and slough it off. But for some reason, this guy rubs me the wrong way.

"No thanks."

"Hey, come on. I'll even buy you a beer."

The bartender saves me from having to tell this guy no a second time, when he says, "Hey, son, what can I get you?"

I hold up my empty beer bottle. "Two of these, please, and a Coke."

"Sure thing," he says, rushing off to fill my order.

When my persistent admirer puts his hand on my lower back, I turn to him with a smile on my face. "Get your hand off me, or I'll break it."

13

Cooper

Jake nudges me with his elbow. "Your boy's getting hit on at the bar."

"Yeah, I can see that," I say, tapping my boot on the scuffed floors. I'm about two seconds away from going over there.

"You know, if you glare any harder, you'll hurt yourself."

I take my eyes off Sam just long enough to scowl at Jake, who's enjoying this way too much. "This is why I don't like to go to clubs with him. It's like this constantly. He's a magnet. It's better when he goes out with the girls. They insulate him from a lot of unwanted attention."

Jake chuckles. "You have to admit he's pretty to look at, no matter which way you swing. He's bound to draw attention."

I stiffen in my seat when Sam's current admirer puts his hand on Sam's lower back. "Son of a bitch."

I start to stand, but Jake puts his hand on my arm. "Relax, Cooper. He's fine."

Sam deftly dodges his admirer as he accepts our drinks from the bartender and heads back to the table, juggling two bottles and a glass. Watching heads turn as he winds his way through the maze of tables, I can certainly understand the appeal. With his ripped jeans hanging low on his lean hips and that T-shirt showcasing his chiseled biceps and pecs, he's a damn fine specimen of a man. And that red hair? Hell, it might as well be a flaming torch, because it gets him noticed wherever he goes. And those big brown eyes.... *Damn.*

"I see you made a new friend," Jake says, as Sam hands him his glass of Coke.

Sam frowns as he hands me my beer. "Yeah. He just wouldn't take no for an answer."

"What did he want?" I say, forcing my voice to remain neutral.

Sam rolls his eyes. "To show me the back alley." And we all know what that means. Eyeing me closely, Sam reaches out to squeeze my hand. "Relax, big guy. I told him, 'You see that silver fox over there? My ass belongs to him.'"

Jake chokes on his drink. "Shit man, are you kidding? You really said that?"

Sam grins, looking like a young devil. "Nah. But I did tell him I was with the 'old guy.' His words, not mine." And then he winks at me just before taking a swig of his beer. "Now, I came here to have some fun, dammit. Who wants to play pool? Or darts? Or dance? I'm not picky." He eyes us both expectantly.

"I'm sure as hell not dancing," I say. "But I'll play darts with you."

If it was up to me, we'd leave now and head back to our motel room. Here, I feel like I have to be on guard at all times—I've seen the ugly underbelly of small towns like this. I know what can happen. But Sam has led a sheltered life. He's never experienced blatant hostility just because of who he is.

We cross the bar, skirting around the dance floor, which is swarming now with gyrating bodies, and find an open dart board. We collect our darts and move behind the line of tape stuck to the floor.

Sam nods at me to go first. "Age before beauty, babe."

Smart ass. Shaking my head, I test the balance of the steel-tipped dart poised in my fingers. The dart board is standard issue—black and white with red and green rings. We don't bother playing by the official rules, though. We have our own contest to see who can bury the most darts in the tiny bullseye out of three tries. I'd better win this game. I'm a former sharpshooter in the Marines. If I can't hit the center of a dart board at eight feet, I don't deserve to keep my job.

I throw my first dart and hit the bullseye dead center. Then I retrieve my dart, and Sam steps up to the line to take his shot. He nails the center spot too. So, after round one, we're tied.

Round two. I throw my second dart and hit the bullseye, upping the pressure on Sam.

"Damn," he says. "Not bad for an old guy."

"Very funny." After I retrieve my second dart, he toes the line and throws his second dart—and it's a score. So, we're tied, two and two. I notice we've attracted a bit of a crowd. The pool games have been put on pause, and some slightly flirtatious women have formed a lose circle around us, giggling and whispering to each other.

"Your turn, babe," Sam says, prompting some snickers from the onlookers.

Just before I throw my third and final dart, Sam leans close and whispers in my ear. "If you win, I'll give you a blow job when we get back to the motel. And if I win...." He pauses for effect. "If I win, you have to let me top you tonight."

Holy shit. He's not kidding.

Well, hell, if that's not enough to make me lose my concentration, nothing is. It wouldn't be the first time he's topped me, and it certainly won't be the last, but the thought definitely messes with my concentration.

Just as I'm poised to throw my final dart, hoping like hell for a third bullseye—at least a tie—I hear a glass-shattering crash and a loud cry as a server drops her tray. My dart goes wide, just missing the board, and ends up buried in the wall.

"What the fuck are *you* doing in here?"

I know before looking who that deep, bellicose voice belongs to. Billy Monroe has aged a hell of a lot since I last saw him standing on the Sweetwater River Bridge, but he hasn't really changed much. He's still a loud, obnoxious ass. The big difference this time, though, is I'm not a scared teenage boy.

Monroe is dressed in filthy jeans, equally filthy work boots, and beneath his leather jacket, he's got on a blue flannel shirt that is straining to hold in his gut. And he's not alone. He's flanked by two younger men who look to be in their mid-thirties. Based on their regulation haircuts, I suspect they're off-duty deputies.

"Get out of here, faggot!" Monroe yells, his face mottled with varying shades of red. "We don't want your kind in here."

It's been a long time since anyone has dared to call me that to my face. I can feel my blood pressure spiking, but I do my best to ignore him as I retrieve my dart from the wall. I glance at Sam, who is clearly on alert and watching me closely, taking his cues from me. I can see that Jake is calmly making his way over here. *Three against three.*

It's been a long time since I've been in the middle of a bar brawl.

"You don't want to mess with me tonight, Billy," I say, keeping my voice level. "I'm not in the mood."

Billy Monroe looks like he's about to pop a blood vessel. It's too warm in the bar to be wearing a heavy jacket like he is, so he must be carrying. His two pals are similarly dressed, and I have to assume they're all armed.

"So, this is what a homophobic child-killer looks like," Sam says, drawing out the words as he scowls at Monroe. Sam moves in beside me, shoulder to shoulder.

Monroe's complexion turns a darker red. "I did not kill that boy!" He jabs his fat index finger in my direction. "You killed him, to shut him up, because that boy was going to expose you as the depraved monster you are. And now you're back here in Sweetwater trying to ruin the reputations of three innocent, God-fearing men. Hell, Judd's dead because of you!"

"Billy, you need to get outta my bar, right now!" The bartender points to the exit with a tire iron clenched in his fist. "All three of you boys, get out before I call the cops."

"I am the cops, you idiot!" Monroe growls at the bartender.

The bartender shakes his head. "Not right now, you're not. You're out on leave. Now, get out!"

"What's the matter with you, Frank?" Monroe says, taunting the guy. "Are you a homo lover too?"

The bartender bristles at Monroe's slur, just as Jake moves in, pressing the muzzle of his gun to the back of Monroe's head. "You heard the man," Jake says in a low voice. "Get out."

The room goes quiet—someone even mutes the sound system— as Monroe stands there fuming. Then the silence is broken by the distant wail of police sirens.

The fingers on Billy's right hand begin to twitch, and I'm afraid he's going to draw his gun. I step in front of Sam, to shield him.

"Don't even think about it," Jake warns, shoving his gun against the back of Billy's skull.

One of Billy's guys breaks the tension. "Come on, Billy," he says, grabbing Billy's arm and tugging him toward the exit. "The cops are coming. Let's go."

Billy pulls free of his friend's grasp and heads toward the exit, motioning for his buddies to follow. Jake lowers his gun as he watches them leave.

We return to our table just as the deputies come inside. One of them we recognize—Deputy Williams. The other is a female deputy we haven't seen before. Frank, the bartender, greets them and gives them an update.

Deputy Williams and his partner come to our table. "Everything all right?" Williams says, his hands propped on his waist just above his gun belt.

"So far," I say.

Williams nods. "We'll try to keep an eye on Billy. He's pretty angry right now. I'm sure you can understand why."

I nod. "What's going on with the investigation?"

"The feds are here. Have they been by to see you yet?"

"Not yet," I say.

"They will. Judd Franklin's suicide note corroborates your story, Mr. Cooper, but they'll need to interview you themselves. The feds are looking at murder charges. I think Billy's worried. I know Roger is."

"They should be," I say.

* * *

When we arrive back at the motel, there's a black sedan with darkly tinted windows parked in front of our rooms.

"Looks like the feds are here," Jake says, parking the Escalade beside the sedan.

I wish I could keep the ugliness from my past out of Sam's life, but unfortunately, I can't. "I'll go talk to them." I look at Sam. "I want you to wait in Jake's room."

ᥱ 14

Sam

The waiting is driving me crazy. I pace Jake's motel room, restless and antsy, listening to Sam Hunt through my ear buds. Cooper's been sequestered in our room with the feds for over an hour, and we've had no word. "This is driving me nuts!"

"Would you please sit down and stop pacing?" Jake says, glaring at me from over the top of his laptop. "You're driving me nuts."

Jake is seated at a little table in front of three laptops—his own little command center. He points at the empty chair on the other side of the table. "Sit down, please."

I sit, then remove my ear buds and observe him for a minute. "Our server sure had the hots for you tonight—the cute brunette.

Why didn't you get her number? She practically threw herself at you. I may not dig girls that way, but even I could tell she was uber hot."

Jake keeps tapping away on his laptop, ignoring me.

In the two years I've known Jake, I don't recall him ever going out on a date. "Are you gay?" I know the question is ridiculous as soon as I ask it. If he were gay, I would know.

He glares at me once more over the laptop screen. "No. I'm not gay."

"Do you like girls?"

More glaring, along with a clenched jaw. "Yes."

"Then why haven't I ever heard about you dating anyone? I mean, come on, you're a good looking guy, with mad skills and a great job. You have a lot to offer, so why aren't you offering?"

Jake leans back in his chair and crosses his arms over his ridiculously muscular chest. "Are you finished?"

"Hey, I'm not trying to be an ass. I'm just curious. What's your deal? You live like a monk."

"*My deal* is that my personal life is none of your business."

"Ouch!" Clearly, I hit a raw nerve. "Sorry, man. I was just making friendly conversation."

His expression softens. "No, I'm sorry. I shouldn't have bitten your head off. It's just—complicated."

"Are you... like... celibate?"

Jake levels his gaze at me, but says nothing.

Yeah, I definitely hit a nerve. "Never mind, man. I shouldn't have said anything."

"No, it's okay." Jake swipes his hand across his face, exhaling heavily. "I—I was engaged once. We were both really young—just out of high school. Too young, I guess. Anyway, her folks thought I was a bad risk for their precious daughter. I had no idea what I was going to do with my life then, no ambition. I thought about going into the military, like Shane and Jamie had, or maybe becoming a firefighter like my dad, or a teacher like my mom." He laughs. "I was all over the map back then. I guess I can't blame them for being concerned. Anyway, her parents talked her out of marrying me. Not only that, but they talked her into marrying someone else—an accountant in her father's firm."

Jake looks at me with hard eyes, and I can see the pain buried deep.

"Shit, man." I feel guilty for bringing up such a painful subject. "I'm sorry. I didn't know."

He shrugs. "It's all right. Her husband's now a partner in the accounting firm, and they've got a huge house in Lincoln Park. They've even got a kid—a little boy, I hear. I guess she made the right choice."

Jake acts very cavalier as he discusses his ex-girlfriend, as if she means nothing to him now, but he's not fooling anyone. "What's her name?"

"Annie Elliot—well, I guess it's Annie Patterson now."

"Do you still love her?"

Jake shoots to his feet, pocketing his phone as he grabs his jacket off the back of his chair. "I'm going out for some air. You stay here or I'll kick your ass, you got me?"

I nod, wishing I'd kept my damn mouth shut. Jake's a pretty private guy. He doesn't share a lot about himself—at least not to my knowledge. I shouldn't have pushed him.

He leaves the motel room, shutting the door behind him with a bit more force than is necessary. I walk to the window, peering through the drapes to see how far he's going. But he doesn't go far. He leans against the SUV, his expression stony as he seems lost in his thoughts. He's got to be hurting. Personally, I think this Annie

Elliot must be an idiot. Who would dump Jake? He's an amazing guy.

I do some quick mental math. Jake's around thirty, so he must have been engaged to this girl about a decade ago. Has he been pining for her all that time? Jesus. He needs to move on. He can't put his life on hold forever because of this girl. She made her choice.

I wonder if she's happy married to some hot-shot accounting partner. With a kid, too. She's probably some spoiled rich bitch now. Jake has done pretty well for himself. He loves his job, and he's damn good at it. Shane counts on him. He may not make as much as an accounting partner, but he certainly makes more than enough to support a family comfortably, even in Chicago. He would have made her a damn fine husband.

The adjoining door opens, and Cooper walks through looking nothing short of haggard. His eyes are rimmed with red.

I meet him halfway, raising my hands to cradle his face, his stubble scratching my palms. "Are you okay, babe?"

He looks at me without saying a word. Then he shakes his head as if trying to clear it. "Rehashing it again was rough. They really dug deep."

"I'm sorry." When I lean in to kiss him gently, his lips cling to mine. Damn, he's really shaken. "Let me tell Jake you're done, and then you and I can crash in our room."

I open the front door and stick my head out, just as the feds pull away. Jake watches them go, then turns to me when they exit the parking lot.

"We'll be in our room," I say.

Jake pushes away from the SUV, nodding. "I'm going for a walk. I won't go far."

* * *

Cooper sits at the foot of our bed, looking a little shell-shocked. I remember seeing guys in the Rangers look like that when they lost a buddy in combat.

"Hey." I drop down beside him and put my arm around him, drawing him close. "It wasn't your fault."

"I didn't kill him, no," he says, his voice wooden. "But maybe if I'd stayed away from him. Maybe if I hadn't acted on my sexual impulses, he'd—"

"Cooper—"

"Cody never got the chance to grow up, because three bullies were afraid of what they didn't understand." He looks me in the eye. "Billy claims I killed Cody to keep him quiet about the nature of our relationship. He's also insinuating that I murdered Judd Franklin."

"That's bullshit! The judge committed suicide. Besides, you were with me all night and all morning. You have an ironclad alibi."

Cooper laughs. "You realize you're not exactly an objective witness, right?"

I shrug. "Jake's video footage is, though. He'll have it on film that you were here in our room all night long."

"The feds said an autopsy is being performed on Judd, but that the initial forensics investigation concluded it was a cut-and-dry case of death by a self-inflicted gunshot wound. They told me not to worry about Billy's attempts to deflect blame. None of his claims hold up to scrutiny." Cooper reaches out to touch my cheek. "I'm sorry I brought you down here. You don't need this."

I reach for his hand, linking our fingers together. "Hey, I wanted to come, remember? In fact, I think I insisted on it."

Cooper shakes his head. "I never wanted you involved in my fucked-up past."

I nudge him with my shoulder. "Shut up. There's nowhere I'd

rather be than by your side, drama or not. I love you." And then I kiss him.

* * *

We stay in for the rest of the evening. An hour later, Jake returns from his walk and proceeds to make enough noise over there to wake the dead, opening and closing doors. I feel bad for dredging up his past.

"What's his problem?" Cooper says.

"I think that's my fault. I asked him about his love life, and he told me about his ex-girlfriend."

"Ah, yes. Anne Elliot."

"Yeah. I shouldn't have pushed him. It put him in a really bad mood. It's been ten years though. The guy needs to move on."

Cooper shrugs. "The heart wants what it wants."

Our conversation is interrupted when Shane calls Cooper to get an update on our status. While Cooper's talking to Shane, I reply to text messages from Beth and Erin. Beth's not happy that I left Chicago so soon after returning. Erin's going on and on about Mack—Jesus, I wish those two would just hook up already and quit dancing around each other. I promise Beth I'll be home soon, and I recommend that Erin buy some low-cut tops and display a bit of cleavage to motivate Mack to take action. So there's a bit of an age gap between them. Who cares? Shane's a lot older than Beth. And hell, look at me and Cooper. He's old enough to be my father.

Erin texts me back:

But I don't have much cleavage to display. : (

Chuckling at Erin's reply, I text her back:

Mack's a red-blooded heterosexual male. Trust me - he

won't be able to resist cleavage, regardless of its size.

Cooper and I eat some snacks while we watch a movie in bed. It's late, and I'm half sleep when Cooper turns off the TV and nudges me. "Time for bed." He gets up and heads to the bathroom.

Just as I get up to follow him, the adjoining door bursts open and Jake comes through the door, gun in hand. "Look alive. We've got company." He peers past the drapes in our room to the parking lot. "We've got three Tangos in the rear of the building. I don't see any-one out front." He scans the room. "Cooper's in the bathroom?"

"Yeah." I grab my gun and tuck it in the back waistband of my jeans, then grab Cooper's gun and head for the bathroom. The door is partly open, so I rap quietly before pushing it open. Cooper's standing shirtless at the sink. I flip off the bathroom light and hand him his gun. "We've got company. Three Tangos out back."

Cooper tucks his gun into the waistband of his jeans, then pulls on his discarded T-shirt.

There's a window in the bathroom, but the glass is frosted, so we can't see out of it. Cooper double-checks the window's lock, and we back out of the bathroom to confer with Jake, who's back in his room consulting the video feeds on the laptop screens.

"We've got three guys in the rear of the building," he says, point-ing at the surprisingly clear black-and-white video feed. Then he hands us each a two-way, wireless communication earbud. "Billy Monroe and the two guys he had with him at the tavern this eve-ning. They're armed with shotguns and wearing Kevlar."

"Then they came to do some damage," Cooper says grimly, as he inserts his ear piece. Then he checks his weapon.

"They're moving around to the front of the building," Jake says, moving to peer out through the drapes in his room. "Stay clear of the windows and door."

We move away from the front wall of Jake's room.

"Do you want to call it in?" Jake asks Cooper, letting him make the call. "Are we going to handle this ourselves or let the police deal with it?"

Cooper considers the question for a minute, then shakes his head. "I'm sure someone will call it in when the bullets start flying. Until then, we'll let them make the first move. Then we can claim self-defense. Let's take out as many of these assholes as we can. After all, they started this."

Not a moment later, the front wall of Jake's room is sprayed with gunfire. The large window shatters inward, sending glass flying into the room. The screens of two of the laptops shatter, and the door is riddled with holes and now resembles a huge block of Swiss cheese. Fortunately, the other room is untouched.

"They don't know we have two rooms," Cooper says, moving back into our room to make sure there's no damage. Then he returns to Jake's room and takes up a position near the base of the shattered window.

I take a spot, too, at the open window, and we return fire on the assholes who are now hunkered down behind an older model pick-up truck.

A sharp cry of pain is the only indication that we hit at least one of them.

"I'm going out the back window so I can come up on their right flank," Jake says, heading for the bathroom. "Keep them occupied."

A couple minutes later, with Jake positioned out front, we're firing at the Tangos from two sides. We hear a second scream, indicating a second Tango has been hit.

The shrieking wail of sirens rents the air, letting us know that some helpful citizen has called 911, and our opportunity to take these guys out is quickly coming to an end.

Jake moves closer to the pick-up, using our rented Escalade as cover. I throw open the damaged door to Jake's room so I can race outside and take shelter behind a large metal trash can. I figure our best bet is for Jake and me to come at them from opposite sides and pin them down behind the pick-up. If we can force them to make a run for it, out into the open, we'll have clear shots at them.

"Sam! Get back inside!" Cooper hisses into the comm system, clearly pissed.

Shit! Now is not the time to let Cooper coddle me. The sirens are getting closer, and we don't have much time. Jake must be on the same wavelength, because he lifts his hand, catching my gaze. At his signal, the two of us lay down a solid wall of fire on both sides, while Cooper fires through the broken window.

Using parked cars as cover, Jake and I work our way farther from the motel and closer to the pick-up. From where I'm crouching behind a rusty old station wagon, I can see one of the men lying flat on the pavement. Another one is sitting propped against the rear of the truck, clutching his belly. The third man, Billy Monroe, is still on his feet, hunkering down behind the pick-up. He appears to be unscathed. The asshole.

Monroe's our primary target. He's the problem we need to solve before the cops arrive.

Just as Jake and I prepare to make another go at them, three police cruisers pull into the motel parking lot, lights flashing and sirens ablaze. Damn it!

Monroe takes advantage of the distraction to jump into the driver's seat of the pick-up and take off, abandoning his two fallen pals. As Monroe tears out of the parking lot, I aim for his tires, but the patrol cars enter my line of sight, and I have to lower my weapon.

Deputy Williams and several other officers exit their patrol cars, guns drawn, shouting at us to lower our weapons and step out into the open.

When he sees us, Williams holsters his revolver. His expression is part annoyed, and part something that looks an awful lot like amusement. "I figured you guys had to be involved. What the hell's going on?"

"Monroe and his buddies opened fire on my motel room," Jake says, stepping out from behind his cover and holstering his gun.

Cooper steps out of Jake's room, his gun tucked into the waistband of his jeans. "Monroe attacked us. We caught everything on the surveillance cameras."

Both of Monroe's buddies are on the ground—one of them alive and wounded badly, the other one prone and showing no sign of life.

Deputy Turner checks the pulse of the second man. "Jesus, Denny," Turner says, glancing up at his partner. "It's Harvey Jackson. He's dead."

"I'll need copies of the surveillance feeds," Williams says to Jake. Then to Turner, he says, "Call the EMTs for Fisher and the coroner's office for Jackson."

Williams turns back to the three of us. "I'll need statements from all of you." He shakes his head as he looks at Cooper. "You sure are stirring up some shit in this town."

* * *

I walk around the leased Escalade, counting the dings in the side and rear panels—at least a dozen. The paint is certainly destroyed, and there are two cracks in the rear window. The vehicle must be armor plated, because none of the bullets pierced the sides. "Who's going to tell Shane he just bought a slightly used Escalade?" I say.

Jake just shakes his head.

It takes an hour for the deputies to finish up documenting the crime scene. One of Jake's laptops survived the hail of bullets, so he was able to collect the video footage from the online server and e-mail it to the police station. After they took our statements, and after the EMTs carted away the injured guy and the coroner took away the dead guy, we were left alone.

Jake's room is, of course, unusable, so he collects his gear and moves into our room. He sets up the remaining laptop on the little round table and configures the video feeds from the surveillance cameras, both of which survived the shoot-out.

"Let's go home," Cooper says. "We've done all we can do here. The rest is up to the local authorities and to the feds. We've given them all the evidence they need."

"I'll call Shane and order an evac," Jake says, pulling out his phone. While he's talking to Shane, at midnight, he dumps his duffle bag at the foot of the other bed and roots around inside.

"Looks like we're sharing a room after all," I say, grinning at the frown on Jake's face as he gives his brother an update.

Jake gives me an annoyed scowl, so I head into the bathroom, where Cooper's double-checking the lock on the back window.

"Hey," I say, walking in. "Jake says the surveillance cameras are still working, and we've got one functioning laptop. We should be okay for the night."

Cooper turns to look at me, his face ashen.

"What's wrong, babe?" I ask him.

"I want you out of here," he says. "Tonight was too close for comfort. You could have gotten hit out there."

"I was just doing my job."

He brushes my hair back. "I know. I just hate to see you in harm's way." He steps close and wraps his hand around the back of my neck to draw me close for a kiss.

At the touch of his lips on mine, I feel a kick of desire low in my belly. "Damn. We have a roommate tonight."

Cooper chuckles. "Just think, by this time tomorrow we'll be home sleeping in our own bed."

When we head back into the room, Jake's seated at the table, keying something into the laptop. "Shane will have the jet down here early tomorrow morning. We have to be at the airport by seven."

"Good," Cooper says. "The sooner the better. I'm ready to go home."

Everyone's in bed—Jake takes the other bed—and the lights are off except for the faint glow of the laptop screen. Any motion in the front or the back of our section of the building will set off alerts.

"No shenanigans, guys," Jake says, as he settles into his bed. "This isn't a frat house."

Cooper laughs. "Don't worry. I'm not an exhibitionist."

"I don't know," I say. "I think I'm okay with a little bit of exhibition." I'm lying on my side, facing Jake's bed, and Cooper's lying behind me, his chest and hips pressed against my backside. He's got briefs on, but I can still feel his erection prodding me from behind. His arm is over my waist, beneath the covers, so that Jake can't tell he's lazily tracing the outline of my rock-hard cock through my briefs.

"Good night, Jake," I say into the darkness.

Jake sighs loudly. "Good night, Sam."

"Good night, Cooper," I say.

Cooper muffles a laugh. "Good night, Sam."

"Now you guys say good night," I say, managing to keep a straight face.

"Honestly, Cooper, how do you put up with him?" Jake says.

Cooper laughs. "He keeps me young."

ℰ 15

Cooper

Long after Sam falls asleep in my arms, I lie awake with a bad feeling I just can't shake. Morning can't get here fast enough. I want Sam on that plane and heading back to Chicago.

The wind soughs through the branches of the trees behind the motel, but instead of creating a soothing backdrop, the sound heightens my nerves. Rationally, I know we're safe. I can see the video feeds from my bed, so I know the cameras are working fine. If we have any more late-night visitors, we'll be alerted in ample time to respond.

I tighten my arm around Sam's waist and press my lips to the back of his bare shoulder, breathing in the natural scent of his skin, mixed with a bit of honest sweat and a faint hint of his deodorant, which is familiar and comforting. When I dwell on how much he means to me—like I'm doing now—I get choked up. I'm an old-school relic, and I don't deserve him. I'm stubborn, stuck in my ways, and a poor excuse for a boyfriend. I don't know why he puts up with me. He could have anyone, someone his own age, like Craig, who's probably better able to meet his needs.

I shudder when I realize how close I might have come to losing him to that personal trainer. Of course, I wouldn't have lost him without a fight. I was more than ready to head down to Dayton if need be, to fight for the love of my life—because that's exactly what he is.

He's dead to the world, and I'm pretty sure Jake is asleep too. I close my eyes and let sleep overtake me.

* * *

Sometimes you know when you're just dreaming, but the dream unfolds anyway and you just can't seem to stop it. And then the dream becomes a nightmare. But still, you're trapped.

I'm standing on the Sweetwater River Bridge beside Cody, only I'm me now—an adult—and Cody's just a boy. The fog is so thick I can't see the three bullies looming behind us, although I can certainly hear their biting taunts.

My hands are tied in front of me with rope, but I'm not afraid for myself. I can survive this fall, and I can get myself to shore, even with my hands tied. But Cody? I look over at him, to see him staring blindly off in the distance, seemingly unaware of what's happening. I think he just shut down.

Rough hands push us both closer to the railing, and when I glance one last time at Cody, my heart in my throat, a raw scream tears out of me. It's not Cody standing beside me, staring numbly out across the rushing river. It's Sam. My Sam. My beautiful, vibrant, brave, hot-headed Sam. And he looks catatonic.

Oh, fucking hell, no! "Sam!" *I scream at him, hoping to shake him out of his stupor.* "Sam!" *He can survive this. He can handle himself in the water, get himself to shore. He can do this.*

"Sam!"

But he just stands there, listless and lost, and my heart climbs up into my throat, choking me, cutting off my air.

"Sam, wake up!" *I try to yell, but nothing comes out.*

Billy Monroe, an old man now, grabs Sam and shoves him over the railing. I peer over the side and stare in horror as Sam falls head first into the water, lifeless. He sinks beneath the murky surface, disappearing from sight.

"Sam! No!"

* * *

"Cooper, God damn it, wake up!"

I open my eyes, gasping and blinking against the bright light coming from the bedside lamp. Sam's sitting beside me, shaking me.

I grab his wrists, trying to orient myself. "What? What is it?"

Jake's sitting upright at the side of his bed, watching me with sympathetic eyes.

My heart pounds as I reach out to touch Sam's face, just reassuring myself that he's here and he's alive. That he's not lying dead at the bottom of that damn river.

"Nightmare?" he asks quietly.

"Yeah." This isn't the first time I've awakened Sam in the middle of the night with a nightmare. "Only this one was different."

He laughs quietly. "So I gathered. You kept yelling my name."

I look up at him, the panic threatening to overwhelm me all over again. "It was you this time, instead of Cody. And you just stood there and let him throw you over. You just...gave up."

Sam brushes his hand over my hair. "Well, that's ridiculous," he says, grinning in an attempt to cajole me out of my stupor. "You know I never give up." He smiles and leans forward to kiss me. "It's okay, babe."

* * *

Somehow, I manage to fall back to sleep, but not until long after Sam turns off the lamp and lies back down beside me. I pull him into my arms, and he lays his head in the crook of my shoulder, his arm draped over my chest. As I lie there, I have to force myself not to think about the image I have of him from my dream, standing there on the bridge. The sense of helplessness and panic I'd felt overwhelm me, even now that I'm fully conscious that it was just a dream. It takes a long time, but I finally manage to calm down to the point that I can sleep.

The next thing I know, the alarm on Sam's phone is going off. It's our five o'clock wake-up call.

"God, I feel like road kill," he mutters, reaching to hit the snooze function on his alarm. "I could sleep 'til noon."

"We'll be back in Chicago long before noon," Jake says, as he heads for the bathroom.

"Hurry, man," Sam says, groaning as he stretches. "I really gotta piss."

The three of us get ready quickly and quietly, happy to put this place behind us. Sam and I pack up our clothes, as Jake goes outside to remove the surveillance cameras from the front and rear of the building. When Jake returns, he packs up the three laptops and his other electronic gear.

As I head into the bathroom to gather up our toiletries, I hear Sam in the other room, saying, "I'll carry our bags out to the Escalade."

After I've packed up the last of our stuff, I strap my gun holster on and slip in my weapon. Jake does the same, and we glance around the room.

"That's all of it," Jake says, reaching for his laptop cases. He freezes and looks at me. "Where's Sam?" There's no mistaking the sudden urgency in his tone.

My stomach drops, and I feel chilled to the bone. I try to gauge how many minutes he's been gone, but it can't be more than a handful. "He carried our bags out to the vehicle," I say, but already I'm moving to the door with my hand instinctively going to the handle of my gun. Jake's right behind me.

It's dark outside, as sunrise is still an hour away, but the lamplight in the parking lot casts a warm circle of light on the Escalade parked outside our room.

We slam to a halt at the sight of Billy Monroe holding Sam in a choke hold, holding a 9 mm handgun to his temple. Sam's hands are gripping Billy's arm, and based on how red his face is, we can tell Monroe's cutting off his air. My heart slams into my ribcage, my adrenalin going on overload. It's fight-or-flight time in my Neanderthal brain, and I'm sure as hell fighting.

Like a well-orchestrated team, Jake and I draw our guns simultaneously, pointing them at Billy, who blanches. I don't think he expected us to do that.

"Drop your weapons," Billy growls, glaring directly at me as he jabs his gun into the side of Sam's head. "Or I swear to God I'll blow his perverted head right off."

I make eye contact with Sam, who's alert and watching me for a cue. As a bodyguard at McIntyre Security, he's trained for this type of hostage scenario a thousand times, and the inevitable response is second nature to him. It's just this time, he's on the other side of the equation. There's no negotiating with a gunman who's holding a weapon to a hostage's head. I give a barely perceptible nod, and Sam drops to the ground, gravity ripping him out of Billy's grasp. Once we have a few inches of clearance, Jake and I fire our guns, simultaneously plugging Billy between the eyes.

As Billy falls, Sam rolls away from him, coming to his feet and kicking Billy's gun away.

"Jesus Christ!" Sam yells, sucking in some badly-needed air as he gazes down at the hole in Billy's forehead. "Damn, you guys are good."

Jake crouches down to verify Billy's condition, but a quick glance down at Billy's lifeless eyes confirms to me that he's dead.

I holster my gun and go to Sam, my hands shaking uncontrollably as I grasp his face. I stare into his eyes for a long moment, then pull him into my arms and hug him maybe a little too hard. His strong arms come around me, and it takes me a minute to realize he's rubbing my back. "It's okay," he murmurs into the side of my head. "I'm okay."

A shudder rips through me as the what-ifs assail my brain. What if I hadn't drawn fast enough? What if Billy had just shot Sam from the outset? What if Jake and I had missed? So many variables, and none of them under our control.

Jake looks at us from where he's crouching beside Billy's body. "You wanna call this one in, or shall I?"

* * *

We don't make our eight o'clock flight after all. Our good friends Deputies Williams and Turner show up, and we have to stick around an hour longer for all three of us to give sworn statements. As it turns out, there was a witness to the shooting—an early morning arrival who was unpacking his vehicle when the trouble started— and he recorded the entire thing on his phone. We get a chance to see the footage, which is rather dark, but not so dark that it's unclear what happened.

Watching Sam drop like that, right on cue, is surreal.

"I think Deputy Williams will be glad to see the last of us," I say, as the patrol cars drive away.

Now that we've been given the go-ahead to leave town, we head for the airport and our ride home.

* * *

The sight of a McIntyre Security, Inc. company jet prepped and ready for take-off is a beautiful thing. Jake parks the slightly damaged Escalade, and we grab our gear and climb up the steps to the plane.

The flight attendant waits for us just inside the cabin and collects our bags to stow them in the back. "Glad you guys could make it," he says. "I heard you had some excitement at the motel this morning."

"A bit," Jake says, moving down the center aisle to the rear of the plane. He sounds as wiped out as I feel.

The flight attendant gives us all a visual once-over as if looking for injuries. Then he picks up our bags and deposits them in the bedroom. He heads for the small galley kitchen near the front of the plane. "I'll bring you some coffee and breakfast once we're in the air."

I grab Sam's hand and lead him to the leather sofa I'd sat on during the flight down. "I'm not letting you out of my sight until further notice." I'm still shaken from what happened this morning—from how close I came to losing him for good. I don't think he minds, though, as he smiles when I pull him down to sit beside me and reach for his hand.

Jake pops in his ear buds to give us the illusion of privacy.

Disregarding our audience, I raise Sam's hand to my lips and kiss the back of it, grateful he's in one piece and glad to be going home. I feel different somehow, as if this trip back home really did exorcise some of the demons from my past. Seeing things from an adult perspective changed a lot for me. I realized what a small, insulated environment I came from. And seeing that guy at the Tavern, hitting on Sam? It pissed me off, sure, but it also made an impression on me. Here was an openly gay man, out in public, hitting on another man. Forty years ago, I never would have dreamed that possible in Sweetwater. I guess times do change. I guess it's past time for me to change too.

I glance at the young man seated beside me, who's currently keying in a text message on his phone. He's probably telling Beth we're on our way home.

"Sir, would you care for some breakfast?"

I glance up at our flight attendant, who's pushing a cart containing three covered dishes. He lifts the lid on one of the plates to show me a hot breakfast.

"Thanks." I accept the plate and a fork from him and hand it to Sam. With all the excitement this morning, we didn't have time to grab any food. I'm sure he's starving.

The flight attendant hands me a plate for myself. "I'll bring you gentlemen some coffee in just a moment," he says, just before he makes his way to the back of the plane with Jake's food.

I watch Sam dig into his food with gusto, happy that he seems rather unaffected by the morning's drama. "I want you to move in with me."

He abruptly stops chewing, then swallows hard and turns to stare at me. "What?"

"You heard me. I want you to move in with me."

His eyes widen. "Into the penthouse?"

I nod, trying not to choke up at the hopeful expression on his face.

He starts to speak, then stops abruptly and simply nods, his eyes eloquently expressing both surprise and pleasure.

I pat his thigh, wishing I could do a hell of a lot more, but that's going to have to wait until we get home. "I told you I'd make it right," I say.

16

Sam

It's amazing the difference a couple of days can make. So much has changed, and I'm reeling as I try to catch up. Despite the hell we went through in Sweetwater, Cooper seems more relaxed about us than I've ever seen him. The fact that he held my hand on the plane—kissed it even, in front of Jake!—is unbelievable.

When we disembark at O'Hare, Shane is waiting for us with our Escalade, and he's not alone. Beth is with him, bundled up in a warm winter coat, boots, hat, and a scarf. Damn, I'd gotten used to those nice mid-seventy degree temperatures down south. I'd forgotten how frigid it still is this time of year in Chicago.

As the three of us trudge down the steps with our gear, Shane

steps behind the SUV to open the back for us. He doesn't say anything as we stow our gear, but I can tell he and Cooper are having
one of their silent conversations. I leave them to it when Beth runs
to me, and I open my arms to catch her, wrapping her up in a careful bear hug.

"Welcome home again!" she says, her voice muffled in my jacket.
"Are you okay? How's your leg?"

"I'm fine. And the leg's doing pretty well all things considered." I
glance over her head at Cooper, who's standing beside Shane. The
two of them are now leaning side-by-side against the SUV. They
both have their arms crossed over their chests, both smiling in-
dulgently at us, and I realize how connected we are. Beth's my best
friend, and Cooper is the closest thing she has to a father. Shane and
Cooper are blood brothers—I guess that means we're all more or less
family. My throat tightens at the thought.

Shane waves Beth over. "Back in the vehicle, sweetheart. It's cold
out here."

She climbs into the backseat, and I follow her in. Cooper slides in
beside me—another unexpected move. He's usually the one behind
the wheel. But this time Shane is driving, and Jake takes the front
passenger seat.

I'm sitting between two people I love dearly, feeling pretty damn
good. And that reminds me...I lean close enough to Beth to whisper,
"I'm moving into the penthouse."

I can tell by her pleased smile that she already knows.

"Is that okay with you?" I say. "And with Shane?"

She bumps me with her shoulder, which is well padded by her
downy coat. "Of course it is, silly. We couldn't be happier."

My mind is reeling as we head for The Gold Coast and the apartment building. I'll be living on the top floor now, with Cooper. Shar-

ing his suite. In the open. And, I'll be sharing a place with Beth. I can just imagine all the trouble she and I can get into if we're living under the same roof. Movies, binge-watching our favorite TV shows...maybe I can even talk her into playing video games with me.

Cooper reaches across me to pat Beth's knee. "How're you doing, kiddo? Feelin' all right?"

She nods, smiling. "Yes. I feel great, and the baby's doing well. I had a check-up yesterday, and the doctor told me he's right on track."

"You've been eating well?" Cooper says.

She laughs. "Well, it wasn't easy with you gone, but I think we managed."

* * *

When we arrive at the apartment building, we head straight up to the penthouse with our bags. Beth whips off her scarf and hat, handing them to Shane to hold while she unzips her coat and shrugs it off. She looks adorable in her short maternity dress, paired with tights and cute little ankle boots. Shane relieves her of the bulky coat and lays it over his arm along with the rest of her outerwear.

"He's so well trained," I whisper to Cooper, who bites back a grin as he nudges me with his elbow.

If you ask me, this elevator—with its mirrored walls, plush burgundy carpet, and fine gold trim and light fixtures—looks more like a fancy boudoir than an elevator. Personally, I find it rather kinky. Cooper and I have had more than a few frantic make-out sessions in this gilded box.

Right now, my gaze keeps going to one of the mirrored panels, to Cooper's reflection. I never get tired of looking at him. I find his trim silver hair downright attractive, and he's absolutely rocking that four-day-old beard. And those shoulders! Damn!

He catches me staring at his reflection, and I smile, totally bust-ed. "What about my stuff in my apartment?" I say, trying to look innocent.

He returns my smile, not fooled one bit. "Let's eat lunch first. Then I'll scrounge up some boxes and help you pack your stuff and move it upstairs. You won't need to bring any furniture, unless you absolutely want to…just your clothes and electronics and personal items."

The elevator car comes to a smooth stop, and the doors glide open with a muted ping. Shane and Beth step out first and head across the foyer to the apartment.

Cooper picks up our bags and steps in front of me, blocking my path.

"What?" I ask.

He smiles at me. "Nothing. Just…welcome home." And then he leans close and kisses me. And it's not just a peck either—it's a deep, luscious, toe-tingling kiss. His hands are full holding our bags, but mine are free. I grab the front of his jacket and pull him against me, nestling my dick against his, which is hardening as we stand here.

He pulls back, a little breathless, and gives me a rueful grin. "Hold that thought, kid. After we get you moved up here, we'll christen the bed."

When we walk into the apartment, there's no sign of Beth and Shane. They've probably disappeared into their private suite. I fol-low Cooper down the hallway to the left, where his private suite is located. He opens the door for me and steps aside, letting me enter first. I almost feel like a bride crossing the threshold. Now if only he'd carry me inside….

"What are you snickering about?" he says, pushing me into the suite.

I've been in here a thousand times, but this time it feels different. Nothing's changed. The focal point of the room is still a king-sized bed that we've made excellent use of. And across from the bed is an impressive entertainment and gaming center—I know because I spent weeks recuperating in that bed right after getting out of the hospital, watching movies and playing video games on the Xbox system he installed just for me. Besides a huge walk-in closet, which is vastly underutilized, there's a sitting area with a sofa, mini-fridge, and wet bar; a fireplace; and a private bathroom with a sunken hot tub that rivals those in any spa. We've made excellent use of the hot tub as well, and the sofa, and the shower.

Cooper sets our bags on the gleaming hardwood floors, just inside the door, then turns to me, taking my hand. "I told you'd I make things right between us, and I meant it. You *are* the love of my life, and I'll do anything to keep you."

I squeeze his hand and smile. "You had me at *love of my life*. That's good enough for me."

We jump apart, a little guiltily, when there's a light rap on the door. The door is partly ajar, and Beth pokes her head through the opening, grinning at us. "Getting settled in?" she says.

"He will be soon," Cooper says. "I'll help him bring his stuff up later. First, we eat lunch."

"Oh, good," Beth says, laying her hand on her slightly protruding bump. "Baby boy and I are starving."

* * *

While Cooper heads to the kitchen to make lunch, Beth sits on the bed as I open my duffle bag and pull out my clothes. She picks up one of my T-shirts and holds it up to read the printing—*That's What He Said*. "Oh, my God," she says, laughing.

She lays the T-shirt down on the bed and smiles at me. "We are going to have so much fun. Just wait until Lia finds out you're living with us now. I'll invite her and Jonah over for dinner tonight. Jamie and Molly, too. Jake and Liam, and Shane's parents. The whole family. I'd better arrange for some catering."

The whole family. I think I've done more than just move in with Cooper. I think I've been officially adopted by the McIntyres.

I hang the couple clean T-shirts I have in Cooper's walk-in closet—which is not even ten percent full, tossing the dirty clothes in the hamper. There are racks on three sides of the spacious room, and his clothes take up a tiny portion of just one side. The rest of the racks are completely bare. I really need to teach my guy the joy of shopping.

When we hear Cooper calling us, we head back down the hall to the great room, where Shane is seated at the dining room table with a copy of *Chicago Tribune* spread out in front of him and a cup of coffee. Cooper is in the kitchen, dishing up a meal into large serving bowls.

"Can we help?" Beth says.

Cooper hands her a casserole dish containing wild rice, veggies, and sausage. He hands me a large bowl of salad and a basket of warm dinner rolls. It looks like my guy has some mad skills in the kitchen, to put something like this together so quickly. "Would you carry that to the table?" he says.

Cooper brings in chilled bottles of beer for us guys and a bottle of water for Beth.

"Let's have a dinner party tonight," Beth says to Shane as she takes her seat beside him. "You know, to celebrate Cooper and Sam coming home. We'll invite all of your family, plus Gabrielle, if she has the evening off. And Tyler, too."

Shane sets the paper down and takes a swig of his beer, nodding. "I'll call Peter to see if he can have something sent over. If Gabrielle's working tonight, maybe she can come oversee the meal. I'm sure Peter won't mind."

Cooper gives Shane and Beth an update on everything that happened in Sweetwater, from meeting with Jenny Murphy and giving her the story, to Judd Franklin's suicide, to our run-in with Roger Stevens and the shoot-out with Billy Monroe and his thugs, and ultimately the final showdown with Monroe, which ended in his death.

Beth looks rather pale as she stares aghast at me. "He held a gun to your head?"

I shrug. "I wasn't worried. Cooper and Jake were both pointing their weapons at him, not five feet away. I knew they'd take him out."

The horrified expression on Beth's face would be comical if I didn't feel so bad for freaking her out. "Yeah, but he held a gun to your *head!*"

Cooper's phone rings, diverting the conversation away from my head. After checking the screen to see who's calling, he picks it up quickly. "Jenny."

I lean toward Beth. "Jenny Murphy's the newspaper editor from Sweetwater. She ran Cooper's story on the front page of the *Sweetwater Daily Gazette*."

"What?" Cooper says, his suddenly sharp voice drawing everyone's attention.

I get a sick feeling in my gut as I watch the color drain from his face.

"Are they sure?" he says. And then, after a couple moments, he says, "All right. Please keep me posted. Thanks."

Cooper ends the call and lays his phone on the table. His expression is wary as he looks at me. "Roger Stevens was arrested and charged with murder for the death of Cody Martin. He was released from jail this morning on bond, but now he's missing. He emptied his bank account and disappeared, along with two handguns and his SUV."

Cooper meets Shane's gaze, and the two men stare at each other in more of their secret silent communication. Then Shane's gaze drifts over to Beth, who is watching both men warily.

"What?" she says to her husband. "Why are you looking at me?"

Cooper scrubs his hand over his stubble. "Fuck."

"That's putting it mildly," Shane says, frowning as he continues to stare at Beth, his expression darkening by the second.

As Cooper and Shane carry on this cryptic conversation, I can pretty much guess what they're thinking. If Stevens follows us to Chicago, looking for Cooper, we'll be leading him right here to Beth's door. No wonder Shane looks fit to be tied. And I don't blame him. He takes his wife's safety very seriously.

"Well, shit," I say.

Beth sighs. "Would someone please say something intelligible?"

Finally, Shane speaks up. "Sweetheart, what do you say to spending a few days at the Kenilworth house?"

"What? Why? What's going on?" When Shane doesn't answer her, she looks at me.

"I think he's worried that Roger Stevens might be heading this way."

"Who's Roger Stevens?" she says.

"One of the guys who tried to kill Cooper years ago. Apparently, the guy skipped out on bail this morning and disappeared."

"And you guys think he's coming here?" she says, laying her hands protectively over her abdomen. She turns to Shane. "You think he's coming after Cooper?"

"It's a possibility," Shane says, leaning back in his chair and doing a great job of appearing calm, when I'm sure he's anything but. "That's why I'd like for you to stay at the Kenilworth house for a while. Just until this gets resolved."

"You and Sam both," Cooper says, looking from Beth to me.

"No!" we both say.

Shane frowns. "Beth—"

"No. You don't know for sure he's coming here. Besides, it's harder for me to get to work from the Kenilworth house."

Shane's brow furrows. "Honey, I don't want you going to work until this is resolved. You'll have to work from home. And you can work from Kenilworth just as easily as you can work from here."

Beth's eyes narrow as she glares at her husband. "I'm not going to be sent away," she says.

"Me neither," I say, trying not to laugh. It looks like princess is developing a backbone. "If Beth's not going, I'm not going."

Now it's Cooper's turn to glare at me. "Don't be a wise ass, pal."

17

Sam

After we finish a rather tense lunch, Shane holes up in his home office to make some phone calls, undoubtedly setting some additional security wheels in action. Beth curls up with a blanket and a book at one end of the sofa facing the fire burning in the hearth. Cooper's in the kitchen, cleaning up after the meal.

"What can I do?" I ask Cooper, as he's washing the casserole dish.

"Grab a towel and start drying."

Our plates and silverware are in the drying rack, already washed. There's an automatic dishwasher at his disposal, of course, but he says he prefers to wash the dishes by hand. I pick up a hand towel and start drying. Cooper shows me where to put the stuff once I've dried it.

"Are you okay with moving in here?" he asks me in a low voice.

His question catches me off guard. "Yes."

He nods as he hands me a bowl. "I didn't want you to feel pressured or anything. If you don't want to—or if you're not ready—and you want more time to think about it—"

"Hey, stop. I said yes. Are you kidding? Of course I want to move in with you."

"All right. You can keep your apartment if you want to. I'm sure Shane wouldn't mind."

I step closer and kiss him, just to shut him up. "What's wrong? Why are you so worried?"

"I'm not worried. I just don't want you to feel pressured, that's all. I sprung the idea on you kind of quickly."

He sets the last dish in the drying rack and turns to face me, leaning against the counter. "And I should have *asked* you to move in with me, not told you." He eyes me for a long moment. Then he takes the plate and the dish towel out of my hand, sets them down on the counter, and takes both my hands in his. "Sam Harrison, will you move in with me? Live with me? Share my bed every single night?"

That knocks the air right out of me, and I can barely speak over the knot in my throat. *Damn.* "Who are you, and what have you done with the Daniel Cooper I know and love?"

He grins. "I guess the past couple of days really taught me what's important, and that's you. I don't want to lose you, Sam."

Ahh, so it's fear that's driving this sudden change in his behavior. I grab his hand. "You're not going to lose me. Even if you don't ask me to move in with you. I'm not expecting some kind of overnight miraculous transformation. I just want you to *try*. And you are trying. I can see that, so relax."

He glances over at Beth, who's snuggled down in the couch, completely out of sight, presumably engrossed in her book. He pulls me into his arms. "I don't want to just *try*, Sam. I want to make you happy." When he kisses me, his lips gentle and coaxing, I feel a surge of heat sweep through me. When our bodies meet, his erection presses against mine, making my knees go weak.

He reaches around and squeezes one of my butt cheeks. "You go visit with Beth for a few minutes while I finish up here. Then I'll scrounge up some boxes, and we'll move your stuff upstairs. All right?"

I cup the back of his head and pull him to me for another kiss. Being able to touch him like this, openly, is life changing. Before, he never would have let me do that. I could get addicted to this.

I head back over to the sofa and sit down at the far end, opposite of Beth, and put her feet in my lap. "Fuzzy pink socks. Cute."

"Thanks."

"Were you eavesdropping on us?"

She grins. "Yes. I didn't look, but I heard you kissing."

"You could hear us kissing? No way! No, you couldn't, could you?"

"Yep. You're a noisy kisser. All that moaning and groaning."

"Oh, stop! We were not that loud."

She grins at me. "Yes, you were."

I hold one of her feet in my hand and threaten to tickle it. "You'd better stop, or I'm tickling."

"No, don't! If you do, I'll wet myself! My bladder is not my own right now. The baby's sitting on it."

"All right. No tickling." I look at her for a minute, turning serious. "Can I touch your baby bump?"

"Sure." She throws her blanket aside, and underneath, she's wearing pink flannel lounging pants and a white top. "Give me your hand."

She takes my hand and brings it to her belly, pressing it down over the little mound, which is surprisingly firm. I get chills thinking there's a tiny little human nestled somewhere in there, just waiting to be born.

"I'll bet Shane's excited," I say.

She nods. "He is. We're both so thrilled. But my God, he's impossible right now. He won't let me lift anything heavier than my iPad."

"He just wants to protect you, Beth. He can't help it." I think of how I felt down in Sweetwater, watching Cooper suffer. I would have done anything to ease his pain, even jump naked into an ice-cold river. I glance back toward the kitchen, but Cooper's already gone to get boxes. "I can relate."

She lays her hand on top of mine. "So, you're moving in with him. That's a good sign, right? Things must be improving."

I smile. "Yeah. He's really trying. That's all I'm asking for, not a miracle. What about you guys? Is everything good in matrimonial land?"

She blushes, which I take as a big fat yes. "We're good. Shane's even more protective now that I'm pregnant, but I don't blame him for that. He doesn't like me working full time now, so I work from home two days a week and go in the other three. Erin manages the store for me on the days I work from home."

"Yeah, well, I imagine Shane's not happy with us right now. Not if we're bringing trouble with us."

"Oh, you mean the guy who skipped bail."

"Yeah."

"Do you think he's really a threat?"

I nod. "It's entirely possible. We had one run-in with him, in a restaurant of all places. He was drunk as a skunk, and I was afraid it was going to turn violent, but the cops showed up before it did, and they arrested him and took him away."

* * *

Cooper drops a stack of empty cardboard boxes in front of the foyer door and calls me over. "Ready to move?" he says.

I pat Beth's leg and leave her to her book. "Yep. Let's do it."

Cooper's passcode allows us to stop at my floor, and we head to my apartment each carrying a stack of boxes. It's dim and cool when we step inside my apartment. I open a couple of windows to bring in some fresh air.

I glance at Cooper. "Do you really think Roger Stevens would come here?"

He frowns. "We have to assume he would. We can't take any chances, especially where Beth is concerned. Shane's already arranging additional security to make sure Stevens can't get in. And, as you know, he wants to move her to Kenilworth until Stevens is apprehended."

I laugh. "And I think she made her opinion on that known today at lunch."

Cooper shrugs. "Shane's going to do what he feels is best to keep her safe, even if that means moving her. And just to be up front with you, I was serious when I suggested that you go with her. You can hang out with Beth at the estate and work on your strength training."

I grab his forearm. "Hell, no, I told you I'm not leaving you, not after what we went through in Sweetwater. I'll see this thing through with you."

His eyes narrow. "You'll do what I think is best, Sam. Besides, you would be good company for Beth."

I know he's worried, so I let his I'm-the-boss-of-you attitude slide for the moment. "Send Lia to Kenilworth, or Erin," I suggest. "Erin would love to go."

Cooper hands me several boxes and points toward my bedroom. "Let's get busy. We've got some packing to do. We'll worry about the rest later."

As I watch him walk away, I now have more sympathy for Beth. She complains about Shane being overprotective, and now I get it. Ever since the accident, Cooper acts like I need to be protected and coddled, too. I don't. I need to get back up to fighting strength and pass my physical assessments so I can go back to work. It's okay for him to boss me around in bed, but not on the job.

* * *

I really don't have a lot of stuff to bring up to Cooper's suite, so we're done with moving in two hours. I bring up my toiletries, clothes, shoes, books, DVDs, and Xbox games. I leave the kitchen-ware and the furniture behind, because the penthouse is already decked out with stuff much nicer than mine. I empty my fridge and cupboards of anything that will spoil and take out the trash.

"I guess that's it," I say to Cooper.

He's got my boxes stacked in the hallway outside my door. After I lock up, it takes us two trips to haul everything upstairs to his suite. We stack the boxes in the closet and I start unpacking.

He clears out half of the drawers in his dresser for me. In the bathroom, there are his-and-his sinks with drawers, so I get my own.

When I leave the bathroom, everything put away, I catch him watching me. His expression darkens, which makes my belly clench deliciously. I know what's on his mind when he looks at me like *that*.

But man, we don't have time right now.

He walks up to me and, without a word, reaches for the hemline of my T-shirt, pulling it up and over my head before tossing it onto the bed.

"People are coming over," I remind him. "We really don't have time."

He shakes his head. "Not until six. We have the next couple of hours all to ourselves, and I've been wanting to put my hands on you all day long."

The entire time he's talking, he fingers my nipple piercings, alternately teasing them and gently tugging, making me squirm and arch my back, moaning in pleasure. When he bends down to lick my nipple, his tongue flirting with the piercing, I gasp and shudder. And while he's busy distracting me with his tongue, his hands are working the fastener on my jeans.

I notice that the door to his—*our*—suite is closed. But is it locked? I really don't want Beth walking in on us and seeing something that might shock her delicate sensibilities. "The door—"

"It's locked," he says, his voice low and rough. He pulls me close and kisses me, teasing my lips with his, sucking lightly on my bottom lip before drawing it into his mouth. "Tonight, after everyone leaves, we're christening this bed, you hear me? Be ready—consider yourself forewarned."

I smile and nod, not trusting myself to speak.

He leads me to the side of the bed and takes a seat, pulling me between his knees. "We've got a little bit of time now, though." He finishes unfastening my jeans, lowering the zipper and tugging them down around my thighs. My erection presses insistently against the fabric of my briefs, begging for attention. He cups me through the soft material, molding his hand to the shape of my cock. And then he traces the outline of it with his index finger, his touch light and teasing, making it increasingly harder for me to breathe.

"Take off your boots and socks, then step out of your jeans," he says in a gruff voice that has me on pins and needles. He sits back to watch me as I comply, looking like a man who expects to be obeyed. Everything is spiking in me now—my pulse, my breathing, my temperature. When I'm done, he tugs my briefs down my legs and off, leaving me standing naked in front of him, while he's still fully dressed. I'm so hard I can barely think straight, and my cock is bobbing in the air in front of him, defying gravity.

The gaze he rakes over my naked body is hot and demanding, and damn, he knows what this does to me. When he turns domineering, like now, my legs turn to jelly. I've got butterflies in my gut, and my dick's rock hard, straining toward him at a ninety-degree angle from my body. He nudges my legs farther apart so he can reach between them to cup my ballsac.

He takes hold of my erection and swipes his tongue over the tip, catching a bit of pre-come on his tongue.

"Gah!" is all I can say. I grab his broad shoulders for support as my legs feel like they're about to give out.

He smears my pre-come across his palm and grips the shaft of my cock, sliding his hand along it. When he draws me into his mouth, I lose the ability to think rationally. All I can do is feel spine-tingling pleasure. My hips start moving on their own, and I thrust deeper into his mouth. He can take me incredibly deep, and the pleasure is mind-numbing. He works me over with his fist and tongue until my balls draw up tight and fire races along my spine, giving me a warning signal. "Oh, God," I say, accompanied by a desperate groan.

He reaches around to my backside to tease me with a slippery finger, the tip of it easily sinking past my tightened sphincter to my happy spot, which he strokes diligently.

"Oh, shit!" I can't hold out long, not with both his mouth and his finger driving me crazy. I'm thrusting fast and hard into his mouth, and he takes it easily, continuing to torment me with both his mouth and his finger.

"I'm gonna come," I gasp, giving him all the warning I'm capable of. I latch onto his broad shoulders and hang on for dear life.

But he doesn't let up, not one bit, and that's all the permission I need to blow my load.

I try to be quiet about it, but damn it, it's hard when it feels this good. I grip his head as I come, crying out, and he swallows my spunk right down. My legs are shaking, and he pulls me down to sit on the bed before I plant my ass on the floor.

"Oh, fuck," I say, panting for breath. I fall back onto the bed, lying there with my legs hanging over the edge. "I'm wiped."

He lays his hand on my chest and chuckles. "I just wanted to give you a preview of what's coming tonight."

Glancing at his crotch, I'm not one bit surprised to see his erection straining the front of his jeans. "What about you?"

When I start to reach for the fastener on his jeans, he catches my hand and brings it to his lips for a kiss. "Don't worry. I'll get mine tonight."

I laugh. I'm sure he will.

✑ 18

Sam

I t takes a while for my brain to come back online after that
explosive orgasm. One thing about my lover, he sure knows how
to work me to a feverish climax. And I know I'll have another
one coming my way tonight, after the post-dinner party dust settles.

I'm looking forward to tonight. The McIntyres definitely know
how to throw a party. They're never dull affairs, and the food is always excellent, not to mention the company. I'm looking forward to
meeting Jamie's girlfriend, Molly. Beth has already regaled me with
stories about Molly Ferguson, who apparently swept Jamie off his
feet. Or maybe it was the other way around. It's a little unclear. Anyway, I've heard they're pretty much inseparable now—literally, as

she functions as his eyes now. I can't wait to meet the woman who stole the heart of that big, stoic former Navy SEAL.

I take a shower and trim my beard. Then Cooper takes the clippers from me and trims my undercut.

"I need to do laundry," I tell him. "Most of my clothes are dirty from our trip."

After I get dressed, Cooper shows me the laundry room which, like everything else in this place, is impressive as hell. There are five washing machines—count them, five!—and five dryers, plus a long folding counter with a granite top, a pressing station, a steaming station, and a small kitchen. There's even a TV in there, in case you need to catch up on your shows during the rinse cycle.

I toss my clothes into one of the fancy glass-front washers, add some detergent, and turn it on. Then I hop up on a long, counter-height table and pull out my phone to kill time while I'm waiting.

"Who in the hell needs five washing machines?" I say to myself, baffled.

I hear soft laughter coming through the open door, and when I look up, there's Beth, dressed in a billowy, pale yellow linen dress and a delicate white sweater. Her blonde hair is pulled up in a pony tail, and she's wearing pink fuzzy slippers. She's holding a fat bunch of red grapes in her palm.

"You can never have too many washing machines, right?" she says, grinning at me as she pops a grape into her mouth.

I shake my head. "I'll never get used to how rich folks live."

She gives me a pointed look. "You do realize that your boyfriend is as rich as Midas, right?"

"What?"

She nods. "He and Shane formed the business together when they got out of the military. Cooper owns half of McIntyre Security.

He just prefers to be a silent partner."

"Holy shit. I had no idea."

Beth walks over to the counter and eyes it strategically.

"Don't you dare try to jump up here," I say, sliding off so I can lift her up onto the counter. Then I hop back up beside her.

We sit side-by-side on the counter, swinging our legs in unison like a couple of little kids, as the washing machine whirs away behind us. She holds her palm out to me, and I snag a grape, tossing it into my mouth.

Cooper walks through the open doorway. "How are you getting along with the washing machine?"

I roll my eyes at him as Beth snickers. "I know how to operate a washing machine. It's not rocket science, you know."

Shane follows Cooper into the room, his eyes widening when he sees Beth perched up on the high counter. "What are you doing up there?" he says, coming to stand in front of her, wedging himself between her knees. He puts his hands on her waist, and for a second, I think he's going to set her down on the floor.

"Eating grapes with my BFF," she says, batting her sex-kitten eyelashes at him.

"She looks so innocent, doesn't she?" Shane says, shaking his head as if he knows something we don't. "Don't believe it for a second."

Beth plucks a grape off the stem and pops it into Shane's mouth. He chews it, then kisses her. "Please be careful, sweetheart. When you're ready to get down, let someone help you, okay?"

Now it's her turn to roll her eyes at me, and we both laugh.

Shane looks at Cooper. "Are you sure this is a good idea? Letting these two live under the same roof together?"

Cooper shakes his head. "Probably not. I think we're just asking for trouble. But it's too late now."

We hear the chime over the intercom system that announces the arrival of the elevator. A moment later, Lia's voice filters down the hallway toward us. "Where the hell is everyone?"

"We're in the laundry room," Shane calls back.

A moment later, Lia walks through the doorway. "Why is everyone congregating in the laundry room?"

Shane shakes his head at his youngest sister. "Don't ask." Then to Beth, he says, "I mean it. Don't jump down from there on your own." He looks at me. "Sam, you help her when she's ready to get down."

I salute the big boss. "Shane, I broke my leg, not my brain."

Shane and Cooper leave us to our own devices.

Lia gives me a curt nod. "Hey, red, how's it going?"

"Fine, shorty. Where's your better half?"

"He's at the bar, talking to Jamie and Molly. They rode up in the elevator with us."

"Oooh, cool," I say, hopping off the counter. "I want to meet this Molly. I saw her briefly at Beth's wedding, but I really didn't get a chance to talk to her. I didn't know they were serious."

I grasp Beth by the waist and set her down on the floor.

"They're definitely serious now," Beth says. "Molly's been living with Jamie since her crazy ex-husband broke into her apartment and attacked her. Now Jamie and Molly are inseparable."

"Wait—what?" I say. "What the hell did I miss? Who attacked Molly?"

"Oh, that's right," Lia says. "You weren't here when all that drama went down. You were on your" —and then she makes air quotes— "walkabout." Molly's asshat of an ex-husband broke into her apartment and assaulted her in her own bed, and my big brother took him out."

I'm shocked I'd never heard anything about this. "Are you kidding me? Was she okay?"

"Yeah, she was okay," Lia says. "Jamie got to her in time, before her idiot ex could do much damage. Jamie squashed him like a bug." Then Lia makes a slashing motion across her throat.

"Jamie killed him?" I say, surprised.

"Dead," Lia says. "Well, technically, Jamie didn't actually kill him. The guy fell on his own knife." She makes a scoffing sound. "Hey, my brothers don't mess around."

* * *

When we join everyone in the great room, Jake and Liam have arrived as well, and the party is underway. Everyone is congregating around the bar, where Cooper and Jake are acting as bartenders, and someone started up the sound system.

"Hey, what's with the extra security in the lobby?" Liam says, taking the beer bottle Cooper hands him.

"I don't suppose it has anything to do with our friends down in Sweetwater, does it?" Jake says, eyeing Cooper.

Cooper frowns at Jake. "You should go talk to Shane about that," he says, nodding in the direction of Shane's office.

Jake accepts a bottle from Cooper and heads toward Shane's office. I'm tempted to go with him to find out more about the additional security arrangements. I guess I'm not surprised. Shane's not going to take any chances with his pregnant wife living in the building.

I see Jamie and his new girlfriend sitting on barstools at the end of the bar, and I make my way down to them. "Hey, Jamie," I say, giving him a heads-up to my presence before I lay my hand on his shoulder in greeting. For a change, he's not wearing his dark glasses.

In fact, I don't think I've ever seen him without dark glasses on. His eyes... damn, they look so real. I'd never guess they were prosthetic.

"Sam!" he says, smiling as he turns to me. "Welcome back, man." He offers me his hand, and we shake. "This is Molly Ferguson, my girlfriend. Did you meet her at the wedding?"

"I did, sort of," I say, offering my hand to the attractive brunette. "I'm sorry I wasn't at my best at the wedding. I didn't really get a chance to say 'hi.'"

"That's quite all right," she says, hopping off her barstool as she meets me halfway to shake hands. "I'm glad to see you up on your feet again. How's your leg?"

"It's not bad. I'm not back to one hundred percent yet, but I hope to be able to return to work in a few weeks."

Jamie reaches for Molly, and she catches his hand. He pulls her close, and she leans into him, putting her arm across his shoulder and smiling contentedly as she drops a light kiss on his lips. His smile says it all.

I'm glad Jamie's met someone special. He's a great guy—I've always liked him. And they seem so comfortable together, as if they were made for each other.

Up close, I can see a faint starburst pattern of tiny scars around his eyes, but the damage isn't that noticeable. I know that he lost both eyes in an explosion in Afghanistan, and that he wears prosthetics. But honestly, even this close, I can't tell just by looking that his eyes aren't real. And the way he moves his head and blinks is so natural, someone who didn't know he was blind would never realize it just by looking at him. "I don't think I've ever seen you without your glasses before."

He grins bashfully. "Yeah, Molly likes to see my eyes, so I've stopped wearing them around family."

"You should listen to Molly. You look fantastic."

The elevator chimes, and a moment later Shane's eldest sister, Sophie, walks in. Damn! I'm not into women, but even I can admit she's a knock-out. A tall, curvy brunette, she reminds me of an old-fashioned Hollywood movie star. Dressed in a form-fitting, cobalt blue sheath dress with matching heels, a string of pearls around her neck, she's all glam. Her long, lustrous hair is pulled up into a complicated do, and she's wearing an impressive pair of diamond drop earrings.

Sophie smiles warmly at everyone, but she heads right for Beth, giving her an affectionate hug. "Hi, sweetie," she says to Beth, kissing her on both cheeks. "How are you feeling?"

"I'm feeling great," Beth says. "I'm so glad you could make it this evening."

With her arm still around Beth, Sophie turns her attention to me, giving me a gracious smile. "I wouldn't miss this party for the world. Hello, Sam. Welcome home."

* * *

The rest of the guests arrive—Gabrielle Hunter and the uniformed caterers from Rinaldo's, Erin and Mack from the bookstore, and Shane's parents, Calum and Bridget McIntyre. Beth's pretty mom, Ingrid, arrives, along with her intensely hot—and way too serious—brother, Tyler Jamison, who absolutely looks boss in his black suit, white shirt, and black tie.

"Sam!" Erin cries, running into my arms. "Oh, my God, it's so good to see you."

I hug the little pixie back, then shake hands with Mack, who never seems to wander far from Erin. At six-foot-six, Mack towers well over little Miss Erin O'Connor, and he shadows her like an avenging angel. I know she's got the biggest crush on the man, but he's way too old for her, and now they're sort of stuck in limbo.

"Hey, welcome back, Sam," Mack says as he releases my hand. "I could sure use you back on duty, man. I'm feeling a little out-numbered by all the females in the store." He says this peering down at Erin with a rueful smile.

Erin turns to Mack and smacks him on the arm, grinning. "Oh, stop. You are not."

"Don't worry, I hope to be back on duty in a few weeks," I say, bumping fists with the big guy.

I'd forgotten this party was being held in my honor until I noticed a meet-and-greet line forming behind Erin and Mack. When Erin and Mack move away to grab drinks from the bar, Beth's brother, Tyler, who looks every inch the uptight homicide detective that he is, approaches. It's hard for me to believe he's Beth's brother. He's dark and moody and so damn serious all the time, while she's all sunshine and light. They couldn't be more different. The only physical trait they share is their eyes, which are a gorgeous blue-green. On her, with her blonde hair, the eye color isn't unusual, but on him, with his dark hair and even darker demeanor, it's very unexpected. And he's technically old enough to be her father, so there's the age difference thing as well.

"Sam," Tyler says, shaking my hand. "Welcome home. I'm glad to see you're recovering well from your injuries."

"Hey, Tyler. How's it going?"

He tightens his hold on my hand. "I can't thank you enough for what you did for Beth. If you hadn't been there—"

"Hey, it's in my job description, right?" I say, laughing off his praise. I don't need to be thanked for protecting my best friend. I would do the same thing all over again, without hesitation.

Tyler doesn't even crack a smile. "I'm in your debt, Sam."

"It's okay, Tyler," Beth says, linking her arm with his and effectively pulling him away from me. "I'm okay. The baby's okay."

Tyler kisses the top of his sister's head. "Hello, kiddo."

"Here, Tyler," Cooper says, reaching over the bar counter to hand him a tumbler of what appears to be a double shot of whisky. "You look like you could use this."

Beth's mother pulls herself away from Bridget McIntyre to join us, giving me a heart-felt hug. "Hello, dear boy," she says, kissing my cheek. She pulls back and looks me over from head to toe. "You look wonderful. So much better than the last time I saw you, which was at Beth and Shane's wedding. How are you? How's your leg?"

"Almost as good as new, Mrs. J."

At that moment, Gabrielle Hunter walks into the great room in a pristine, white sous chef uniform, which contrasts dramatically with her thick braid of bright red hair. Behind her are two Rinaldo's catering staff members, also in uniform, pushing two industrial carts laden with stainless steel covered containers.

"I hope you guys are hungry," she says. "We brought a ton of food."

19

Cooper

While everyone's shooting the breeze in the great room, waiting for dinner to be announced, I wave Liam and Mack over to the bar. "Take over for me, will ya?" I say. "I need to talk to Shane."

I head for Shane's office, where I'm guessing he's in a pow-wow with Jake, making plans for how they're going to handle the fact that Roger Stevens skipped out on bail. I rap once on Shane's office door, then open it and walk in. Shane's leaning against his desk, and Jake's standing by the window looking out over the congested street traffic.

Roger Stevens is my fucking problem, and I'll be the one to solve it. I look Shane in the eye, expecting to see censure, but there's no blame or resentment in his steady gaze. Just the determination to do whatever it takes to keep this family safe. I take a breath. "I'm sorry—"

"Stop right there," he says, lifting a hand to cut me off. "None of this is your fault."

"Bullshit. If Stevens comes to Chicago, it's because of me, so hell yes, this is my fault."

Shane shakes his head, dismissing my attempt to shoulder the blame. "No. You did the right thing by going to Sweetwater to try to settle that mess. The fact that Stevens skipped bail is not your fault. What we need to focus on now is how we secure this building. If Stevens is headed this way, we need to stop him from getting inside."

Before he can hurt Sam, or indirectly Beth. He doesn't come out and say that, but that's exactly what we're all thinking.

Jake speaks up from across the room. "I'll set up perimeter security around the building twenty-four-seven. He won't even make it to the lobby doors, I guarantee it."

Shane nods to Jake. "Do it. I don't want this fucker stepping foot inside my building." Then, to me, he says, "If I get wind that he's here in Chicago, I'll have to move Beth to Kenilworth. I'd rather not do that if I can help it, because I don't want to upset her. But if Stevens makes it this far, I'm not taking any chances."

I nod. I can certainly understand why Shane wants Beth moved somewhere safe, and frankly, I want Sam to go with her. The difficulty will be in convincing him to go. He hates it when I coddle him—I get that—but he doesn't realize how irrational I can be when it comes to his safety. The thought of him getting hurt—especially because of *me*—makes me break out in a cold sweat.

Jake's on his phone, sending text messages as he heads out. "I'm on it."

Shane turns his attention to me. "I've doubled security in the downstairs lobby and added security outside the entrances. I've also posted extra security on the penthouse elevator, both in the lobby and in the parking garage. That's about as far as I can go without completely freaking Beth out."

I nod, regretting that any of this is necessary. Regardless of what Shane says, I can't help feeling responsible.

"I want Beth to work from home until this is resolved. And one of us—you or I—has to be here at all times. If Stevens does manage to get inside this building, you and I are the last lines of defense. If that fucker steps one foot on this floor, I'll blow his head off myself."

I laugh, but the sound is bitter. "Get in line, Shane."

* * *

After coming up with a work schedule and putting a plan in place to keep the penthouse secured, Shane and I return to the party and do our best to be sociable. Heaven help Roger Stevens if he bursts into this penthouse tonight. Easily, six of us are packing heat, and that includes Tyler Jamison, who wouldn't hesitate a second to put an end to any threat that could possibly reach his sister. But Tyler, and even Shane, would have to stand in line behind me. I'd give anything to drill a few slugs into Stevens's head and end him right now.

As usual, most everyone is congregating around the bar, talking and laughing, with plenty of good-natured ribbing. Ingrid and Bridget are chatting on the sofa in front of the fire...most likely obsessing over the arrival of what will be the first grandchild for each of them.

Shane heads straight for Beth, who's currently being entertained by Calum telling stories about his kids when they were little. Shane walks up behind her and slips his arms around her burgeoning waist, linking his fingers over her baby bump. He leans down and kisses the side of her head. "What lies is my dad telling you now? Don't be-lieve a word he says. I was a perfect child."

"Ha!" Calum scoffs. "Don't listen to him, lassie. He was a trouble-maker from day one, just like your little guy will be too, if he's any-thing like his old man."

I shake my head, smiling and so damn thankful for this family. "I think you might be right there, Calum," I say.

"Oh, you'd better believe I'm right!" Calum grins at Beth. "If you don't believe me, young lady, go ask his ma. You know she'd never lie to you."

"Dinner's ready! Come to the table," Gabrielle says as she walks out of the kitchen.

The long dining table is already set, and a few extra places have been added to accommodate this big crowd. I'm looking forward to the day when we have to add a highchair as well. The one thing this family needs more of is kids underfoot. I have a suspicion that we'll be adding some of those over the next few years with all these new couples forming. I fully expect that Jonah will eventually man-age to sweet-talk Lia into marrying him. And I wouldn't be sur-prised if Molly and Jamie tie the knot before too long—they are two halves of the same soul. Yeah, this family needs a new generation of troublemakers.

Shane sits at one end of the table, with Beth to his right, and Ga-brielle next to Beth. I sit at the other end with Sam. The table fills up quickly as the caterers begin carrying in platters of delicious Italian cuisine, courtesy of Rinaldo's five-star restaurant, including sever-al entrees to choose from, and a variety of side dishes, salads, and bread.

Sam smiles at me, looking relaxed and happy to be home and among friends and family again. I reach over the table for his hand, giving it a squeeze. The dazzling smile he gives me in return is like a one-two punch to my gut, making me dizzy with desire. I can't wait to christen our shared bed tonight. I will wring every drop of pleasure I can out of his body, until he's rendered boneless and satiated.

The caterers are courteous and efficient as they bring refills and pour glasses of expensive red wine, and bubbling grape juice for our expectant mother.

Once everyone is settled and has started eating, Shane stands, raising his glass of wine.

"I'd like to make a toast," he says, his gaze singling out Sam at the opposite end of the table. He looks at Sam for a long moment, long enough that everyone grows quiet. I can see the tension in Shane's body, his expression equally tight. He swallows hard. "I'd like to make a toast to Sam Harrison, in honor of the brave and selfless act that saved the life of not just my wife, but also our unborn son." Shane pauses a moment, taking a deep breath as his words sink in. "We're glad you're home with us, Sam. It just wasn't the same around here without you."

Beth smiles first at Shane, and then at Sam, not bothering to hide the tears forming in her eyes.

Shane starts to speak again, then stops to take a breath and clear his throat. He's obviously shaken. "I'm eternally indebted to you, Sam," he says. "There's no way I'll ever be able to repay you."

Shane glances at Beth, who nods at him, smiling tearfully. "As you all know, Beth and I are expecting a son this summer. We've decided to name him Lucas Samuel, in honor of his guardian angel, Samuel Harrison."

The sighs and gasps in the room are audible. Sam reaches blindly for my hand, squeezing it hard. Tension radiates through him, and his hand is shaking. He looks from Shane to Beth to me, his brown eyes glittering too. Hell, I don't think there's a dry eye in the room right now, including mine.

For once, Sam is speechless as he scans the eyes on him. Giving him my undivided attention, I swallow my anxiety and raise our clasped hands to my mouth and kiss the back of his hand. If I'm going to be his boyfriend, now's as good a time as any to show him I can do it. The look on his face is priceless.

Someone starts clapping, and soon everyone has joined in. I hear a few hoots and hollers, at least some of which I know are coming from Lia.

Sam blushes, but his eyes are locked on me. "Jesus, Cooper," he says, stunned by my actions.

"What?" I say, shrugging it off like it's no big deal that I just kissed my boyfriend's hand in front of a room full of people. That's what he wanted from me, right? To act like a boyfriend. And that's what I'm doing.

"Get a room, will ya?" Lia says, shaking her head.

* * *

Dinner proceeds with plenty of great food and lots of conversation. As usual, there's a lot of joking and ribbing at the table. Lia and Sam, in particular, can't help taunting each other—they're worse than children. I sit back and enjoy watching everyone.

It's nice to see Gabrielle Hunter again. She doesn't often get to visit us because of her busy schedule at Rinaldo's. As a sous chef, she works her butt off, hoping to be promoted one day to chef. Peter Capelli would be a fool not to promote her.

Jamie and Molly are for the most part wrapped up in each other, leaning close and talking. Jamie has his hand on the back of Molly's neck, gently massaging it. He says something to her and she smiles at him, then kisses him.

Erin is telling a story about something that happened at Clancy's, and I notice how Mack hangs on her every word. He tries to act aloof and unaffected by her, but he's not fooling anyone. I feel for him. Shane has warned him more than once to keep his distance from Erin. She's what—a sheltered, twenty-two-year-old virgin, and he's thirty-five years old, former military, who's been around the block more than a time or two. Shane's made it perfectly clear that Mack will have to deal with *him* if he hurts Erin.

Erin, on the other hand, is completely oblivious to Shane's threatening glances at Mack. She's hanging on Mack's every word and gazing at him with blatant puppy-dog longing. Poor Mack, he'd have to be a monk to remain indifferent to her.

Of course, I have no business judging Mack for the age difference between him and Erin. I have no room to talk—Sam's practically half my age. I'm the true letch, setting my sights on a much younger man. But hey, the heart wants what it wants, right? Age doesn't really factor into that. As long as everyone involved is a consenting adult....

Speaking of my much younger man, I'm keeping my eye on him as he smiles and chats with everyone at the table. He's clearly a social butterfly, at ease with everyone, while I'm more comfortable silently observing.

I notice that he's hardly touched any of his food tonight. He's had two glasses of red wine, not to mention the bottle of beer he drank before we were seated at the dining table, but not much food other than a few bites of his salad.

I lean toward him. "Aren't you hungry?"

He gives me a knowing glance, and I smile at him. I know exactly what's on his mind. He's anticipating the fact that I'm going to be fucking the daylights out of him in a few hours. "Got butterflies?"

Sam shrugs, but he can't manage to hide the flush creeping into his cheeks. He looks at me, pretending to be shocked. "Who are you, and what have you done with Cooper?"

Once everyone is done with their meals, the caterers come by with a dessert cart laden with every sugary concoction imaginable. Sam eyes a bowl of chocolate mousse topped with whipped cream and chocolate curls, but ends up passing on it. Damn, he is nervous. He's passing up chocolate?

As the evening wears on, he grows more and more quiet, and I start to get the feeling this is more than just bedtime jitters. I lean toward him, close enough to whisper, "What's wrong?"

He shakes his head, not even bothering to make eye contact with me. *Damn.* Something is bothering him.

* * *

Dinner is followed by more drinking and lots of laughter and conversation. Sam crashes on one of the sofas with the girls, but he still seems kind of quiet to me. The guys are mostly hanging out at the bar. A lot of these folks live in the building, and the others came by Uber rides and will leave the same way, so finding designated drivers really isn't an issue.

As the clock approaches midnight, folks begin to head home. It's a Friday night, so most of them can sleep in tomorrow. Beth certainly will. She's half asleep on the sofa right now, leaning against Shane, who has his arms around her and his hands clasped over her belly. Sam seems pretty subdued still, which doesn't reassure me.

When it's just the four of us left, Shane lifts Beth into his arms. "Time for bed, young lady." Then he looks at me. "You'll arm the security system?"

"Yes. Go to bed."

"Goodnight, guys," Beth says, making no protest when Shane carries her out of the room and down the hallway that leads to their suite.

I walk up to the back of the sofa and reach over to massage Sam's shoulders. "How about you? Shall I pick you up and carry you to bed, too?"

He laughs. "You wouldn't dare."

"Don't tempt me." I lean over the back of the sofa and kiss the side of Sam's neck, making him shiver. "Why don't you go get ready for bed while I lock up?"

"All right." Sam rises from the sofa and walks around to meet me. He slides his hands up my arms, squeezing my biceps. Then he leans closer and kisses me gently. "Thank you."

"For what?"

"For being my boyfriend tonight."

I smile at him, feeling a pang of guilt, as if he's giving me way too much credit. All I did was touch him a few times and hold his hand and kiss the back of it. "I didn't do all that much."

"You did plenty. It made a difference."

I pull him into my arms so he can feel my erection. I've been biding my time all evening, pacing myself, and now it's *our* time. Now I can have him all to myself.

I thread my fingers in his upswept hair, holding him fast. "I can't wait to get you into our bed." I plant another kiss on his lips and reach around to swat him on his ass. "Now, go get ready."

$\wp$ 20

Cooper

When the penthouse security is locked up tighter than Fort Knox, I head to our suite and rap lightly on the closed door before opening it. There's no answer, but I wasn't expecting one. He's likely in the shower. There's a single light on in the room—the lamp on the nightstand. The door to the bathroom is ajar, and I can hear the water running. I smile, imagining Sam getting ready for bed. I imagine his nerves getting the best of him. This is just our second time to have sex since reuniting, and the anticipation is likely killing the both of us.

The room is already tidy, so all I have to do is pull down the sheets. I'll leave the nightlight on so he can see when he comes out of the bathroom.

I head for the closet to ditch my boots and socks in the closet, along with my T-shirt. I leave on my jeans that hang low on my hips because he thinks they're hot.

While he's in the separate shower room, I take care of business and brush my teeth. I already showered before the folks arrived for dinner this evening, so I'm fresh as a daisy and ready for my guy. Then I head back into the bedroom to wait for him.

The water shuts off before long, signaling that his shower is over, and I wait for him to appear, perhaps with nothing more than a towel around his waist. I wait, and wait, but there's no sign of him, which is odd. I sit on the side of the bed, giving him a little more time, but still he doesn't show. After giving him another ten minutes, I know something's wrong.

I find him seated on the wooden sauna bench outside the walk-in shower, wearing nothing but a towel wrapped around his hips. He's just sitting there, leaning forward, his elbows on his thighs, staring numbly at the tile at his feet. "Sam?"

He glances up at me from beneath his dark lashes, but he says nothing.

At the haunted look in his eyes, my heart rate kicks into overdrive. "What's wrong?"

"This is all my fault."

I crouch down in front of him, laying my hands on his knees to balance myself. "What is?"

"All the extra security on the building. I know Shane's worried about Beth, and I don't blame him. God, if anything happened to her because of me—"

"Whoa, stop right there, kid," I say, looking up into his eyes. His gaze is anywhere but on me. "Sam, look at me. How is any of this your fault?"

"The only reason you went down there to confront those assholes was because I pushed you into it."

"That's not true."

"Yes, it is! I gave you an ultimatum. I told you if you couldn't open up, we were through. It's because of me that you went down there in the first place."

I sigh. "Sam, this was something I've been needing to do for years. I just kept sweeping it under the rug because I didn't want to face it. And honestly, I should have done it years ago. None of this is your fault."

He lowers his head into his hands and grips his tousled wet hair, tugging on the strands.

"I'll get your comb," I say, patting his knees as I rise. I grab his comb off the counter and begin combing through his mop of tangled hair, gathering the long top layers into a bun and securing it with a hair tie I find lying on his pile of discarded clothing. When I'm done, I run my fingers gently through his undercut, smoothing the strands. I hate that he's hurting because of me. "Honestly, baby, this is not your fault."

"Shane probably thinks it is."

I grasp his chin and force him to look up at me. "No, he doesn't."

His eyes fill with tears. "They're planning to name the baby after me. I don't deserve that. If anything happened to Beth, or to the baby—"

"Nothing's going to happen to Beth. Shane will move her to Kenilworth if it becomes necessary. Nothing can touch her there." I reach for his hands and pull him to his feet. "Come to bed. We don't have to have sex. Just let me hold you, okay? This is our first night together in our bed. It should be a happy time, and I'm not going to let you beat yourself up for something that's not your fault."

His towel falls to the floor, revealing a body that's nothing short of a work of art. As I look my fill at those long, muscled limbs dusted with auburn hair, his gorgeous dick starts to harden. My gaze sweeps upward, past abs and a chest that is cut with muscles that look like they could have been sculpted.

"Come on." I lead him to the bed and, after shucking off my jeans, I climb in after him. "Come here, baby," I say, pulling him into my arms. He lays his head on my chest, and I wrap my arms around him. Shane's not the only one with someone to protect. If the shit hits the fan, I'll hogtie Sam myself and send him to Kenilworth right along with Beth, whether he likes it or not.

Absently, I stroke Sam's back, running my blunt nails along his spine. He shivers and groans, pressing his face into my chest.

He teases my nipple with the tip of his tongue, making it tighten. And when he licks the tight little point, the sharp pleasure draws a cry out of me. He comes up onto his elbow and leans over me to tongue circles around the peak before drawing it into his warm, wet mouth.

"Jesus, Sam!" I gasp, my back arching off the mattress.

"I want you to fuck me," he says, shifting so he can kiss his way down the center of my torso. He skims his tongue down my abs, stopping to tease my belly button, then continues down to the thatch of hair at the base of my cock. He grips me firmly and licks his way up the shaft to the crown and over the tip.

I exhale a rough breath as heat and aching pleasure sweep through me. "Slow down, baby," I gasp as he works me into a frenzy. "I'm already so close, and you're nowhere near ready for me."

Sam lunges up and opens the nightstand drawer, pulling out the bottle of lube, which he hands to me. "Make me ready. I want you."

He rolls over onto his belly, wrapping his arms around his pillow and opening his legs.

"Are you sure?" I say. "We don't have to—"

"Yes. Make me ready."

I kneel between his open thighs and take my time lubing him up, stretching him slowly. I slide one slick finger into his body, relishing his groans as I make small teasing circles inside. When he's ready, I add a second finger, gently opening him up and stretching those tight muscles. When my finger glides repeatedly over his prostate, he groans, pressing his face into the pillow to muffle the sound.

Impatient, Sam suddenly rises up onto his knees and presses me down onto my back. He grabs the lube and slicks up my cock. Then he throws his leg over my hips and hovers with his ass poised right above my erection. His expression is breathtaking as he reaches behind himself to position my cock at his opening.

I skim my hands over his thighs, murmuring encouragement as he sinks down on me, slowly working the head of my cock inside. When he starts to move, I run my hands up and down his chest, stopping to tease his nipples and piercings. I love watching him work himself on me, rising and falling on my shaft, his teeth gritted with a mixture of pleasure, tension, and a tiny bite of discomfort as he waits for his body to fully accommodate me.

"You okay?" I say, gripping his taut thighs.

He nods, breathless, now moving faster as his body gradually opens for me. He grips his own cock, stroking himself firmly as he watches my face. We're both groaning now, both of us straining and close.

I sit up, wrapping one arm around him to hold him close to me. Then I turn us so that he's lying on his back beneath me. His thighs open, cradling me as we lie missionary style.

He relaxes beneath me, and I sink deep with a satisfied groan. He answers my groans with his own, and soon we're both breathing hard. I start to move, slowly at first. I withdraw and add more lube, just to be sure he's comfortable. Then I feed myself back into him, all the way, and he exhales, forcing himself to relax as his body adjusts to being penetrated.

He pulls me down for a kiss, and I drink in his moans. I cup my hands around his head and gaze into his beautiful brown eyes, gauging his arousal. He slips his hand between us and pulls on his cock, stroking himself in time with my short, quick thrusts. I know when I'm brushing against his prostate because his eyes widen and his breaths shallow until he's fairly panting.

With a loud cry, I rise up and arch my back, filling him with spurt after spurt of liquid heat. My thrusts turn slow and gentle as I lose myself in him. He tugs and strokes himself until he joins me, crying out as he comes in wild spurts on his stomach and chest. Once he's finished, I pull out and sink down beside him, and we hold each other.

After a quick clean-up, I tuck him into bed with me, spooning behind him. I trail kisses along his shoulder and up his throat, feeling his pulse pounding beneath my lips. I smile, breathing in his intoxicating scent. "I love you."

He cradles my arm tightly to his chest. "I love you, too," he says, yawning.

* * *

The next morning, I leave sleeping beauty to his well-deserved rest and grab a quick shower before pulling on a pair of jeans and a T-shirt. I head to the kitchen to start the coffee. The kids like using the Keurig machine and drinking their fussy caramel mocha lattes, but I'm old school. I like grinding my own beans and making coffee the old-fashioned way. It's just about six a.m., so Shane should be coming out of their room any second now for his morning caffeine fix on his way out the door. He usually grabs breakfast at the café in the McIntyre Security building.

A half-hour later, when he hasn't appeared, I glance down the hallway that leads to their suite and see the light on in his home office. I head down that way and quietly rap on the door.

"Come in," he says.

I push the door open to find him seated at his desk, working on his laptop. He's wearing a white dress shirt, unbuttoned at the neck, sans tie, and his suit jacket is hanging on a hook on the wall behind his chair. "What are you still doing here?"

He leans back in his chair and motions me inside. "Have a seat. I have a proposition for you."

I take one of the seats in front of his desk, leaning back and getting comfortable. "What did you have in mind?"

"I was thinking this morning that one of us should be here at all times, until Stevens is apprehended. I don't want to leave Beth here without protection. She'll be working here from home until further notice."

"Sam will be here too, you know."

"I know. But, technically, he's not back to work yet."

"He can still fire a gun."

Shane nods. "I'm sure he can, but he'll be concentrating on physical training. I'd feel better if one of us was here at all times. I imagine you have work to do this morning at the shooting range, so I'll work from home for half a day while you take care of business at the range. Then you could come home for the afternoon."

I nod. "That sounds good. I am a little backlogged at the range. I need to catch up on scheduling some assessments, and I can easily do that from home this afternoon."

"Good. Why don't we keep this schedule, working half days here at home, until this blows over."

"That works. Hey, while I've got you, I was wondering if you could help me with something."

He looks surprised. "Of course. What is it?"

I scrub my hand over my beard, not sure exactly how to start this conversation. It feels awkward at my age to be asking these questions. "As you know, Sam wants me to act more like a boyfriend. The truth is, I'm not sure how to do that. I've never seriously dated anyone before Sam. It's always been temporary hook-ups, you know, with no long-term expectations on either side. This is kinda new territory for me."

Shane grins as his brow furrows. "Are you asking me for dating advice?"

"Don't sound so shocked. Yes. I need some advice. I've never done this before."

"Just do things for him. Make him feel special."

"Such as?"

Shane laughs. "Really? Do I have to spell it out?"

"Yes, please, because I'm clueless."

He shakes his head. "Ask him out to dinner. Make reservations somewhere nice. Wear a jacket, dress up. Open doors for him. How about Tavern on Rush? Take him there for a nice steak dinner and some wine. Do it tonight. I'll get you a table, and I'll arrange for someone to drive you. Take the Mercedes. Go all out."

"That's it?"

He laughs at me again. "It's not that hard, Cooper. Just plan things for the two of you to do together. If the weather's decent, you could take him for a walk along the lake—that's romantic. Beth loves it when we do that. Or take him to the park. When I plan stuff like that for Beth, she looks at me like I'm some kind of god. Take him shopping at his favorite store. Take him to a pub to listen to music, or to a concert. They just want to know that we're thinking of them... thinking about what they might like to do. They want us to make them feel special. It's not that hard. And honestly, if you just make an effort, he'll be happy."

"Tonight's Saturday. I guess that would be as good a night as any to take him out to dinner."

"It would be perfect. Just let me arrange for a driver and security. Under the circumstances, I think it would be prudent if you had someone watching your back so you can relax and concentrate on Sam. I'll call Killian, see if he's available."

"Killian Deveraux? Hell, are you trying to make me look bad?"

Shane laughs. "Relax. Sam doesn't have eyes for anyone but you."

"Yeah, but Killian? He's too damn pretty. He would turn anyone's head."

"Trust me. You don't have to worry. Also, ask Beth for some ideas. She knows Sam well. She knows what he likes."

"I will. Thanks." I rise from my chair. "I'll go put in half a day at the shooting range, then I'll come back to spell you for the afternoon."

ꙮ 21

Sam

When I awake, the bedroom is lit with morning sunshine streaming through the sheer curtains. I stretch, moaning loudly. Cooper's already up, but that's no surprise. Looks like he let me sleep in today.

I just lie here for a few minutes, enjoying the residual echoes of pleasure coursing through me. When I tighten my ass, I feel a slight twinge—a pleasant reminder of the mind-blowing sex we had last night. He puts all my past lovers to shame. Compared to him, they were just a bunch of fumbling high school and college boys who didn't have a clue what they were doing, not with their own bodies or with mine. The first time Cooper and I had sex, he absolutely blew my mind, and I've never been the same since. Now, just the thought of bottoming for him makes me weak in the knees. He's such a force of nature, so strong, so overwhelming, and yet he always makes it good for me. When I'm with him, the rest of the world falls away and I'm in this special place only he can bring me. He brings out this sexually submissive side I never knew I had. And he makes me *like* it. Crave it, even.

After cleaning up and dressing, I go looking for my sexy top. But instead of finding him in the kitchen, I find Beth heating up a covered plate in the microwave. She's wearing a pair of light blue fleece pants and a matching maternity top, her hair up in a messy pony tail. I'm pretty sure she just rolled out of bed herself. "What's for breakfast, princess?"

"Cooper left for the shooting range early this morning, but he left breakfast plates for us to heat up." She shows me her plate. "There's one for you too."

"He's gone?" I feel a swift pang of disappointment that he didn't say good-bye before he left.

"Yeah." She sounds apologetic. "But he left a note for you." She picks up a hand-written note that's lying on the breakfast bar and hands it to me.

> Sam – You were sleeping so soundly I didn't want to wake you.
> Breakfast is in the fridge. Work on physical training & keep Beth
> company. Shane's working at home this morning. I'll be home @ 12:30.

"Shane's still here?" I'm surprised. He's usually at the office by the crack of dawn.

Beth nods as she takes a bite of scrambled eggs. "Apparently, we're being babysat. Shane has the morning shift while Cooper's at the shooting range, and then they'll switch after lunch. Cooper will be home all afternoon while Shane goes to the office." Beth laughs.

"What?" I say, laughing too, just because she's laughing.

"We're such a modern family, aren't we? It's like we have two dads."

"Yeah, I guess we are." I heat up my breakfast plate and join her at the breakfast counter. When I sit down on the wooden seat, I feel a tender echo of discomfort deep inside and make a small sound of protest, shifting in my seat.

Beth gives me a too-innocent smile. "Something the matter?"

"No." I try hard to keep a straight face, because I know what she's thinking. And she'd be right.

She grins. "I just thought maybe your bum is a little sore, that's all."

I wad up my napkin and throw it at her just as Shane comes in to the kitchen to grab a refill of coffee. "Why are you throwing things at my wife?" he says, giving me a level stare.

"Because your pretty little wife has an evil streak."

Shane laughs. "She does, eh?"

"You'd better believe she does."

"Good morning, sweetheart," he says, leaning over the counter to kiss Beth's forehead just as she bites into her buttered toast. "Did you sleep well?"

"Mmm-hmm," she says, chewing.

"Good morning, Sam," he says, not wanting to leave me out of the conversation. "I trust you slept well?"

Beth giggles, and it's my turn to glare at her.

Shane gives us both considering looks. He points at Beth. "You, behave yourself." Then he points at me. "You, strength training. I want you back to work ASAP."

I salute the big boss. "Yes, sir."

* * *

After breakfast, while Beth runs off to get dressed, I change into my workout gear and head to the fitness room. Of course Shane has a fully-outfitted fitness room in the penthouse—this place is not lacking any amenities of creature comforts. After a thorough warm up, I drop down onto the mat to crank out a ridiculous number of push-ups. My goal is eighty push-ups in two minutes. That's ten push-ups every fifteen seconds. Damn. I think Shane's trying to kill his employees. When I gripe about how grueling the physical requirements are, he reminds me that it's less than what the SEALs are expected to do. That just stirs my Army pride and makes me want to show the Navy dweebs what-for.

I'm on my third rep of push-ups when Beth comes breezing in, looking chic in a black tunic maternity dress, gray leggings, and black ankle boots. "Can I help?" she says.

I stop mid-push-up and roll to my back, drawing up my feet so I can work on sit-ups instead. "Sure. You can sit on my feet."

She stares at me as if I just said something obscene. "I said *feet*, Beth. Sit on my *feet*. Jeez, get your mind out of the gutter."

"I do not—oh, never mind!" She sits on my running shoes and wraps herself around my shins to hold on while I start.

"How's your leg?" she says.

"Better. Occasionally it aches, but not all the time. I'm definitely on the mend."

I hand her my phone. Give me two minutes on the stopwatch. When she signals for me to start, I crank out as many sit-ups as I can before the timer goes off. "Seventy-two! I'm getting closer."

After a few more tries, Beth scoots off my feet and I stand, shaking out my legs and stretching. "I need to try running." Unfortunately, there's not a running track in the penthouse.

"There's a running track downstairs in the fitness center. Shane runs down there all the time."

"You wanna come with me?"

"Sure," she says. "I can't really run, but I can walk. I could certain-ly use the exercise."

She's already dressed comfortably enough to walk on the track in the fitness center—she just needs to exchange her boots for sneak-ers. After she makes a quick stop in the ladies' room, we meet up outside Shane's office door, which is wide open. He stops what he's doing and looks at us quizzically.

Beth leans into the open doorway, smiling. "We're going down to the fitness center to use the track."

"To run?" Shane says, looking at her skeptically.

She points at me. "He's going to run. I'm going to walk. I need the exercise."

Shane hits a couple of keys on his laptop, then closes the lid. "Give me a minute to change, and I'll go with you. A run sounds good."

* * *

When Shane comes out of their suite dressed in a pair of black running shorts and a form-fitting black T-shirt that outlines every freaking muscle in his torso, Beth gives him the once-over and whis-tles. "My man looks good," she says, winking at me.

I laugh, as Shane rolls his eyes. "All right, let's go."

We take the private elevator down to the fitness center, which is rather crowded as it's a Saturday. We cross through the floor filled with weight machines, treadmills, and elliptical machines to the en-trance of the running track, which runs the perimeter of the large center, right along the windows, offering a great view of Lake Shore Drive and beyond that, Lake Michigan.

We all three sit on the carpeted floor just outside the track and stretch for a few minutes.

"Don't overdo it, sweetheart," Shane says to Beth as he stretches his calf muscles. "The last thing you need is a pulled muscle. Just take it easy, all right?"

"I know," she says, leaning into a stretch.

Shane stands when he's done, and he offers Beth his hand, helping her to her feet. I follow them out onto the track.

The track is four lanes wide, with the two inner lanes reserved for walkers, while the two outer lanes are designated for the runners. We all three walk the first two laps together, with Shane walking beside her and me behind them. Then, when it's time for us to break off, Shane plants a kiss on her cheek before he moves into the runners' lane and takes off at a nice clip. I watch his clean, easy gait as he quickly puts some distance between us.

"Don't overdo it, okay?" Beth says, when I move up beside her. "You have nothing to prove."

I give her a thumbs' up, then take off after Shane, hoping I don't make a complete fool of myself. This is the first time I've tried to do any serious running since breaking my leg.

I catch up to Shane easily enough, but I don't think he's putting much effort into it yet. We run one full lap around the track, side by side, passing Beth twice. She's got her ear buds in and is listening to music, completely oblivious to us or anyone else around her as she strolls leisurely along, apparently in no hurry.

"Doing okay?" Shane says, as I manage to keep pace with him.

"Yeah." I'm already a little breathless, which just underscores how out-of-shape I am after three months of decreased physical activity. "No problem."

The third time we pass Beth on the track, Shane reaches out and smacks her lightly on her ass. She jumps, squealing, then laughs when we pass her.

After half a dozen laps, my leg starts aching, and I have to slow down a bit. Shane slows down as well, keeping pace with me. "You don't have to babysit me, you know," I tell him.

He shrugs. "I don't mind."

The next time we pass by Beth, Shane checks on how she's doing, and she gives him a thumbs'-up.

"He's really trying, you know," Shane tells me two laps later.

"What? Who?"

"Cooper. He's really trying."

I feel myself blushing, remembering him reaching for my hand at dinner last night, and the sex we had last night after my little emotional melt down. "Yeah, he is."

"This is all pretty new for him, you know. He's never dated anyone before you."

I smile. "I know."

Shane gives me a satisfied nod. "Just give him a chance."

Now that I'm a little more warmed up, Shane and I pick up speed until we're running at a pretty good clip, buzzing right past Beth. Halfway around the track again, I glance over at Beth and see she has acquired some company. Some guy who looks to be in his forties is walking with her, talking her ear off. I glance at Shane, not surprised to see his gaze locked on Beth and her new friend. When the guy pats her on the back, she shrugs away from him and starts scanning the track, presumably looking for Shane. This guy encroaching in her personal space has got to be setting off her anxiety something awful.

Shane immediately kicks into overdrive, leaving me far behind.

I watch, more than a little amused, as Shane catches up with Beth and this fool who's blatantly hitting on her, effortlessly inserting himself between them. He puts his arm around Beth, clearly marking his territory. The guy has the balls to scowl at Shane. Beth leans into Shane, clearly looking relieved.

I cut across the center of the track to intersect the three of them, putting myself right in the guy's startled face. "Get the fuck away from our girl, asshole, or I'll break your god-damn arm."

It's all I can do not to laugh in the guy's face when he blanches, turning white as a ghost. Eyeing both me and Shane warily, he mumbles an apology and rushes ahead, trying to put as much space between us and himself as he can.

When I catch a glimpse of Shane's expression, I don't blame the guy one bit. Shane can be a scary son-of-a-bitch when he wants to.

22

Sam

That guy had some nerve," I say, as we head back upstairs in the elevator.

Beth's standing between me and Shane, and Shane's got his arm around her, holding her close.

She still looks a little shell-shocked. "He came out of nowhere. I was just walking, and then there he was."

"What did he say to you?" I say.

She frowns. "He asked me if come here often—what a lame pick-up line."

"Don't worry, sweetheart," Shane says, leaning over and kissing the top of her head. "Sam put the fear of God into him. I think he got the message loud and clear."

When we arrive upstairs, we find Cooper in the kitchen, grabbing a cold drink from the fridge. "Hey, there you are," he says to us. "I wondered where you'd all gone."

"Downstairs to the fitness center," Shane says.

"Until Beth got hit on by this older guy," I say.

Cooper grins at me. "Hey, watch it. Don't disparage the older guys." Then he sobers, looking at Beth as he meets her halfway, holding her at arm's length to get a good look at her. "Are you okay, honey?" he asked.

She nods, if a little bit reluctantly. "I'm okay. He just made me nervous."

"I've got to grab a shower before I head to the office," Shane says. He kisses Beth's temple and rubs her back. "Are you sure you're okay?"

She nods.

"All right then. You guys have fun."

"Wait, I'm coming with you," Beth says, following Shane to their suite.

Cooper walks into the kitchen and opens the fridge door to see what we have on hand. "You hungry?" he says.

"Yeah. I only ran a mile, but I worked up an appetite."

He pulls out a package of deli meat. "How about a turkey bacon melt?"

"Sounds great."

I take a seat at the counter as he pulls out a pan and gets busy cooking. Once he's got the bacon frying in the pan, he pulls two bottles of water out of the fridge and hands me one. "How's your leg after that run?"

"Not too bad." I reach down and rub my left thigh. "It aches a little."

"Want some pain killers?"

"Nah. I'll tough it out."

He nods, then looks away, seeming distracted all of a sudden.

"Something wrong?" I ask him.

He scratches the back of his neck, looking nervous.

When he doesn't answer me, I say, "What's wrong? Spit it out." His apparent nervousness is making me nervous.

He exhales a long, heavy breath. "Nothing's wrong. I was just wondering something."

"Yeah?"

He turns away to start making the sandwiches. For a moment, I think he's not going to say anything. Then, he suddenly turns to me and blurts it out. "Would you like it if I took you out for dinner tonight?"

My eyes widen, and my pulse starts racing. I'm not even sure I heard him correctly. "Are you asking me out on a date?"

He gives me a classic *duh* look. "Yes, I'm asking you out on a date."

"In public?"

He frowns. "Yes, of course in public. How about Tavern on Rush? Shane said—"

I set my water bottle down hard. "Oh, my God, yes! Of course, I want to go out on a date with you! Tonight? Really?"

He smiles, apparently satisfied with my reaction. "Yes, really. Don't sound so surprised."

I give him a look. "Cooper, we've been together for two years now, and you've *never* asked me out for dinner. Not on a date anyway, and certainly not in public."

He shrugs. "I guess we're overdue then. Shane got us reservations for six o'clock."

I shake my head in disbelief, my mind already jumping ahead to what I'll wear. I know this restaurant. It's pretty swanky, so my ripped jeans and snarky tees won't cut it. "I don't have anything to wear."

"I'm sure you can come up with something."

"What are you wearing?"

He shrugs. "Black dress slacks and a white shirt. Maybe a tie."

A tie? Holy shit. Other than when he officiated at Beth and Shane's wedding, I've never seen Cooper in anything other than jeans or sweats. "You're serious about this, aren't you?"

He nods, looking a little green around the gills. "As a heart attack."

* * *

I lurk outside Beth and Shane's suite until Shane comes out, dressed for work.

"See ya, Sam," he says, walking right past me.

"Is she decent? I need to talk to her. It's urgent."

Shane grins. "Yes, she's decent. You can go in."

I knock on their door, and Beth calls out, "Come in!"

After stepping inside and scanning their spacious suite, I spot her sitting on the sofa by the fireplace, dressed in her fluffy robe. Her hair is loose around her shoulders, the ends a bit damp. It looks like she might have assisted Shane in his shower.

Her bare feet are tucked up beneath her on the sofa, and she's reading something on her phone. "What's up?" she says. "You look like you're about to bust a seam."

"I need your help," I say, dropping down beside her. "It's urgent."

She lays her phone in her lap and gives me her full attention. "Okay, shoot."

"Cooper asked me out on a date—a real date, tonight."

She beams at me. "That's wonderful!"

I shake my head. "Well, yes, it is, but the problem is I don't have anything to wear. He's dressing up in slacks and a dress shirt, maybe even a tie. I don't own anything other than ripped jeans and snarky T-shirts."

She looks suitably concerned, which makes me feel better. "All right," she says, thinking aloud. "So, we need to go shopping, right? What time is your date?"

"Six."

She glances at her phone screen. "It's only one o'clock. We have plenty of time to find you something suitable to wear." She hops up and heads for her ginormous walk-in closet. "I'll get dressed and meet you in the great room. We'll go find you something nice at Water Tower Place."

I head out to the great room and find Cooper seated at the breakfast bar with a cup of coffee and a copy of the *Chicago Tribune*. "Beth and I are going out. Shopping."

He spares me a quick glance before returning his attention to the newspaper. "No, you're not."

At that moment, Beth comes scurrying into the great room, slipping on her sneakers. She's dressed in blue jeans and a pink maternity blouse and white sweater. "Ready," she says to me, a little breathless.

"You're not going anywhere," Cooper says, giving us both a stern look.

Beth glances at me, looking wary. Oh, no he doesn't. I am not going to let Cooper pull this I'm-the-boss-of-you shit right now. This is too important. It's our first real date, and I need to go shopping.

"We're just going to Water Tower Place," I say, keeping my voice level. "We won't be gone long."

"I said no. Shane and I don't want you two running around the city until Stevens is apprehended."

"Who knows when that will be?" Beth says, sounding frustrated. "We can't just put our lives on hold forever."

Cooper eyes us both, then shakes his head. "It's not worth it."

I start to say something, but Beth shakes her head, cutting me off. Then she walks up beside Cooper and lays her arm across his shoulders. She leans into him. "It's just a quick trip," she says. "Just to Water Tower Place and back, I promise. Please, Cooper. Sam seriously needs to go shopping for your date tonight. This is a big deal for him. Please don't spoil it."

Cooper sets the paper down on the counter with an exasperated sigh. "All right, fine. But you're taking security with you."

"But I have Sam," she says.

Cooper shakes his head. "Technically he's not back on duty yet, so you will take someone who is."

"Okay, fine. Who?"

Cooper picks up his phone and makes a call. "Hi," he says into the phone. "Can you spare someone for a couple of hours to escort Sam and Beth to Water Tower Place?" He pauses as he listens. "Yes." Another pause. "I know, but they really want to go. It's just for a couple of hours." Another pause. "Okay. Thanks. Send him up."

Cooper ends the call and sets his phone down. "You have two hours," he says. "I mean it. Two hours, and then I want both your butts back here."

"Thank you!" Beth says, hugging Cooper as she kisses his cheek.

"Who's sending someone up?" I ask.

"Jake has a perimeter security team downstairs. He'll lend us someone for a couple of hours."

A moment later, the elevator pings, and the doors slide open. Killian Deveraux walks through the foyer door, his tall, lean gait as seductive as a panther on the prowl. His dark hair is tousled on top, and he's got a short dark beard. And those eyes—damn! His irises are so dark they look black.

When Beth turns to see who's arrived, her eyes widen in appreciation and she gives me a quick glance. Apparently, no one is immune to this guy's looks.

"Eye candy," she whispers to me. "You can look, but don't touch."

I jab her with my elbow as Killian reaches us. I've met this guy a few times at the McIntyre Security office building, but I don't know him well. I've heard rumors about the Cajun—that he used to wrestle alligators bare-handed as a kid back in the bayou. Looking at him, I can easily believe it. He's whipcord lean and muscular, a deadly combination. There's something wild about him—he almost seems feral.

"Killian," Cooper says, standing to shake the man's hand. "Thanks for stepping in this afternoon. I appreciate it."

He gives Cooper a curt nod, then he eyes me and Beth, a hint of a smirk on his too-handsome face. "I heard we have a shopping emergency," he says in his low Cajun drawl.

"Hey, don't make fun," Beth says, laughing. "It's important. Sam has a *date*."

Killian raises an eyebrow, his gaze going first to me, then to Cooper. "Why didn't you say so in the first place? Let's get a move on."

"Two hours, max," Cooper says, using his stern drill sergeant voice. Then he looks at Killian. "Don't let them talk you into anything more."

"Aye, sir," Killian says, winking at Beth as he salutes Cooper.

Killian had already called for an Uber, so within minutes, there's a black SUV waiting for us outside the front lobby doors. As we step outside, I immediately scan the property and three vehicles parked strategically along the outer perimeter of the parking lot. I see Jake's black Tahoe, although it's currently empty. I see Cameron Stewart in another SUV. The third vehicle is a beat-up pick-up truck, but it's empty as well. Presumably, that's Killian's pick-up truck.

"Hi, guys," Jake says, joining us beside our Uber ride. He claps me on the back. "Stay close to Killian."

I roll my eyes. "Yes, dad."

Jake narrows his gaze at me. "Don't get smart with me, or we'll call this little expedition off."

I shake my head at Jake as Beth smiles brightly. "We'll be on our best behavior," she says. "Promise."

Killian opens the rear passenger door for Beth, and she scoots inside the vehicle. I slide in beside her, and Killian sits in the front passenger seat. Our driver is Middle Eastern, with a thick head of black hair and a heavy accent. He's got a sizeable collection of tiny Minion figurines hanging from his rear-view mirror.

Once Beth has her seat belt latched, we're off.

* * *

As soon as we set foot inside the impressive entrance to this shopping heaven and ride up two sets of escalators to the main floor, Killian does an amazing job of blending into the scenery and becoming essentially invisible. I know he can't be far away—he knows better than that—but he's not easy to spot. He leaves us alone to do our thing, and I appreciate that. It's bad enough being babysat, without being smothered too. Damn, I really need to get recertified at work. If I were back on the job, Beth and I could have done this alone, just the two of us.

"Where shall we start?" Beth says, as we reach the first floor of shops. She tilts her head back and gazes up through the center open space. It's an impressive sight, seven levels of glass, gold trim, and sparkling lights. "And no, we're not stopping at the Lego store," she says, as she catches me eyeing an impressive Lego display sitting inside a Plexiglass case.

They have all the cool clothing shops here, but I'm not looking for jeans or tees. I have plenty of those. Beth takes my hand and drags me to the glass elevator, which we ride up to the fifth floor. There, she leads me to Armani Exchange. "Here," she says, pushing me through the entrance. "Very chic, classic style. It's perfect for impressing your date."

"This is Cooper we're talking about," I remind her. "I don't think he'll be impressed by what I'm wearing."

"True. But you still need to look amazing."

We peruse the store, and I end up trying on half a dozen pairs of trousers in varying shades of black and gray as she waits for me to model them.

"Those!" she says, when I step out of the changing room wearing a pair of slim profile black trousers. "Hot damn!"

I laugh at her enthusiasm as I check out the fit in the mirror. They're comfortable, but they're a little dressier than I'm used to.

"Now a shirt," she says, pulling me to some racks of long-sleeved patterned shirts. She rifles through their selection and settles on a long sleeved button-down shirt with a subtle, black-and-white design. "This!" she says. "With a black jacket and black boots. That would look awesome."

I try on the shirt, and it's a perfect fit. And I like it. Then she drags me to the jackets, and I pick out a light-weight, slim black bomber jacket.

When I come out of the dressing room wearing the entire ensemble, her eyes widen appreciatively. "Very metrosexual," she says, nodding her head.

I grin. "I'm homosexual, not metrosexual."

She swats my arm. "They're not mutually exclusive, you know. In fact, aren't most gay guys good dressers too?" She gives me a dismissive wave of her hand. "You notwithstanding."

"You are stereotyping, princess," I tell her, dragging her toward the shoe department. "I want some new boots that will go well with these pants."

I end up selecting a pair of low-profile, black leather Chelsea boots that work great with the slacks, and to finish off the outfit, a pair of dark aviator sunglasses. "I look sick!" I say, staring at my reflection in the mirror.

Beth laughs. "Yes, you definitely look sick."

Then she talks me into getting a second pair of these trousers in a dark gray, and a few more shirts. "You're twenty-eight, Sam, soon to be twenty-nine. It's time for you to move beyond ripped jeans and snarky T-shirts. Besides, Cooper might ask you on a second date, and you'd have nothing else to wear."

"It took him two years to ask me out on our first official date. I'm not holding my breath that there will be another one any time soon."

Beth fiddles with my jacket, admiring my new threads. "I wouldn't be so sure about that," she says. "I think he's really trying hard. Don't underestimate him. Besides, when he sees you dressed up like this, he's gonna be like, 'Damn, I need to take Sam out more,' right?"

I shake my head as she says this last bit in her best Cooper impersonation. "Are you okay?" I say, as I feel her forehead.

She ducks her head, swatting my hand away as she laughs. "I'm fine!"

As we head to the check-out so I can pay for my new threads, I catch sight of Killian standing just outside the store's entrance, monitoring our progress. He's dressed in all black—the bodyguard's dress code—and I know he's packing heat beneath his jacket. It's strange being on the receiving end of protection. I'm used to being the one doing the protecting, not the other way around.

I've accomplished all my shopping in less than an hour. "We still have some time to kill, you know," I tell Beth. "Is there anything you want to do?"

She grins. "Can we go look at maternity clothes? And maybe baby clothes?"

On another floor of the shopping center, we come across a mom-and-baby shop. Beth tries on several casual maternity dresses and picks out a mint green floral chiffon dress that looks amazing with her blonde hair.

"How about a lingerie set?" I suggest, when we come across a display of sexy little two-piece outfits. "Pick out something sexy and slinky to surprise Shane with tonight."

"I can't."

I laugh. "Why not?"

Her hand automatically goes to her baby bump. "I'm showing."

"Oh, for God's sake, don't be ridiculous. You realize your husband is smitten with you, right? You could wear a brown paper sack and he'd be all over you. Honestly, sweetie, he'd love to see you in new sexy lingerie, baby bump or not. Besides, in case you've forgotten, he's the one who put that baby in you in the first place."

She grins, turning a pretty shade of pink when I point at a mannequin wearing a cream-colored babydoll lingerie set, with a sheer gauzy and lace top and matching barely-there string panties with a tiny little swath of fabric barely big enough to cover her pussy.

"That's really pretty," she says.

"Hell, yes, it's really pretty. It's fucking awesome. You definitely need to wear this tonight, for Shane's sake. I guarantee you, he'll love it."

But the best part of the trip is when we come across the baby clothes section. I've never seen so many cute little outfits in my life. "No wonder people have babies," I say. "They want an excuse to buy all these darling clothes."

Beth picks out a few cute little newborn sleepers. I pick out a onesie that says *Daddy's Mini Me*, cause I figure this little guy is going to be a chip off the old block.

Once our purchases are made, we still have twenty minutes to spare before we turn into pumpkins, so we stop for ice cream cones and sit down at a little bistro table to eat them. Killian lurks just on the edge of my peripheral vision.

I tip my head in Killian's direction. "Don't you think it's kind of ridiculous, how good looking he is?"

Beth nods as she licks her ice cream. "Mm-hmm. He's really nice, though, and I love that Cajun accent. I wonder if he has a girlfriend."

I shrug. "I have no idea, but seriously, all that hotness is going to waste if he doesn't."

Beth leans back in her chair and groans as she stretches her legs. "My feet hurt." She licks her ice cream cone. "Are you excited about tonight?"

"Yeah. And nervous, too."

"Why are you nervous?"

"He's never done this before. What if someone makes some dumb-ass comment? I don't know how well he'll handle it. I guess I'm afraid something will happen to mess up tonight and make him regret taking me out in public."

"I don't think you need to worry about that." Beth lays her hand on my arm and gives me a reassuring pat. "He really wants to make you happy, Sam."

When some random guy approaches our table, asking for money for bus fare, Killian pushes away from the wall and heads right for us. I hand the guy a five-dollar bill, and he thanks me and walks off.

"What was that all about?" Killian says, when he reaches us.

"Nothing. Just a guy asking for money. No problem."

Killian nods and then checks the time. "Are you two ready to head home?"

I stand. "We are." I hold out my hand to Beth, and she lets me help her to her feet. "I think our expectant mother is worn out."

~ 23

Sam

Once we're back at the penthouse, Beth disappears into her suite to do some schoolwork. She's halfway done with a business degree from University of Chicago, where she takes classes online. Personally, I think it's just an excuse to take a quick nap—she seemed pretty tired after our outing.

Cooper is in his home office, catching up on rescheduling the monthly weapons assessments that had to be postponed when we went out of town. We have a few hours to kill before our big date, so I head back into the fitness room in the penthouse and work on lifting free weights and doing some pull-ups. I'm tired of being treated like an invalid—I want to get recertified to work as quickly as possible.

I keep watching the clock and pacing myself, not wanting to overdo it. And to make sure I have plenty of time to shower and get into my new clothes.

Shane arranged for us to have a driver tonight. Our reservation is at six, and as the restaurant is practically just around the corner, we don't have to leave until a quarter 'til six. At five, I jump in the shower, letting the hot water soothe my aching leg. So much for not overdoing it.

I hear someone putzing around in the bathroom, so I assume Cooper's getting dressed as well. But when I get out of the shower, he's gone already, so I don't get a sneak peek at what he's wearing. Darn it.

After drying off and putting up my hair, I dress in my new clothes and boots and head to the great room about five-thirty. Cooper's in the kitchen, putting two covered plates in the warming bin, presumably dinner for Beth and Shane.

When he turns to me, I whistle at the sight of him. He didn't shave—I'm glad of that because I like him with this short beard—but he is dressed up in black slacks and a white dress shirt with a black tie. He's also wearing a black blazer, which looks really sharp on him. The dark clothing really makes his silver hair stand out.

"Damn," I say, looking him over. I wink at him. "You look hot. For an older guy, I mean."

He smirks at me. "Funny." Then he walks right up to me and pulls me into his arms for a kiss. "You look incredible, as always. I mean, I love seeing you in ripped jeans and a tee, but this—you look edible. And I'm going to enjoy eating you up tonight."

Before I can respond, the elevator pings and the doors open. We both turn just as Killian steps out of the elevator. "Are you studs ready for a night out on the town?"

"You're our driver?" I say, surprised to see him twice in one day.

Killian shrugs. "Only the best for you, son. The boss reassigned me to this building until that Stevens motherfucker is caught, so I might as well escort yawl to dinner. Besides, Tavern on Rush has some mighty fine Jambalaya on the menu—good enough to make my mama proud. At least I won't starve babysitting the two of you."

Shane and Beth surface from their suite just in time to see us off. Shane shakes hands with Killian and gets a status report on the building's perimeter security. There's been no sign of Roger Stevens anywhere near the property. But the authorities in Sweetwater have had no luck locating him either, so his current location is anyone's guess. Until he's located and apprehended, Shane and Cooper both are going to be on high alert, so we might as well all get used to it.

* * *

We head down to the underground parking garage with Killian taking the lead. He's got one of Shane's shiny black Mercedes sedans ready to go. Acting the chauffeur, Killian opens the rear passenger door for us, and both Cooper and I slide into the back seat. Killian drives us ten minutes to the restaurant and parks in a spot marked VIP.

"Shane's got connections," Cooper says, when I raise my eyebrows.

I follow Cooper up to the front entrance to the restaurant, Killian following a few yards behind. I guess it's time for his disappearing act to begin. When we check in with the hostess, she gives us a big smile and says our table is ready. As she escorts us to our table, I turn back and see that Killian has disappeared already. Presumably he's lurking somewhere out of sight. I hope someone takes pity on the guy and feeds him.

The hostess leads us to a corner table for two, in a semi-private setting. The dinnerware is fancy, and there are wine glasses on the table and an antique silver candleholder. She lays our menus on the table and lights the candle before walking away, after promising that our server will be at our table shortly to take our drink orders.

Cooper's hand brushes lightly against my hip, just a gentle caress, as he reaches around me and pulls out my chair. I sit, and he helps me push my chair in. Glancing around us, I feel a little self-conscious on his behalf, but no one is paying us any mind. So I relax into my seat and watch him take his seat across the table from me.

Honestly, I am blown away. I would have been happy if he'd taken me to a crowded, dark sports bar, and we'd had hot wings and beer. But this—this is over the top. I never expected anything like this.

Feeling a little out of my element, I pick up my menu and scan the list of entrees. They're famous for their steak and seafood, so I figure I'll get a small ribeye steak and a salad.

I watch Cooper as he pulls a pair of reading glasses out of his jacket pocket and slips them on so he can read the menu. He looks damn hot in glasses.

A cute blond guy arrives at our table to take our orders. We both end up ordering steaks, and Cooper orders a bottle of very expensive red wine. It's a good thing we have a designated driver tonight.

"What are you looking at?" Cooper says when he catches me watching him.

"Just admiring the view."

He smirks. "Don't be a smart ass."

"I'm serious. You look handsome as hell dressed up like that. Why don't you do it more often?"

He shrugs. "I don't have any use for monkey suits. That's more

Shane's style. Besides, a suit would be impractical at the shooting range. Speaking of, you need to come in and complete your shooting recertification. You could come with me to the range just to practice, too. Spend a few hours there with me, and then I'll send you home."

Just the mention of the shooting range makes me smile—it brings back fond memories of how we first met. I laugh, blushing at the memory, and he smiles too. I'm pretty sure we're thinking about the same thing.

I'd applied for a job at McIntyre Security shortly after recuperating from the parachuting accident that ended my military career. It was just a training jump, nothing strenuous, but my chute didn't open. I fell into a Maple tree—thank God, it cushioned my fall—and I managed to break only fourteen bones. It was enough to end my career in the Army.

A former Army colleague—Miles Bennett—told me about this great company he worked for in Chicago, McIntyre Security, Inc. He told me the company specialized in personal protection, and that it was run mostly by former special-ops military guys. That sounded good to me, so I came to Chicago to check it out. Shane interviewed me, then sent me to the company's shooting range for a weapons evaluation. And that's where I met my guy.

Just out of the blue, this hot older guy walks up to me, a Glock tucked into his chest holster, looking all bad ass and so damn fuckable. I was practically drooling over him. He watched me shoot off a couple magazines at some paper targets. When I was done, I took off my ear protection, and then there he was, standing right behind me. He leaned close and whispered in my ear.

"Have you ever kissed a man?"

I swear, that was the hottest thing anyone had ever said to me.

"Yes," I'd answered, nearly choking on the sudden knot in my throat.

"Did you like it?"

"Yes."

Damn! Just thinking about that day puts a smile on my face.

Cooper grins. "What are you thinking about?"

"The first time we met. When you asked me if I'd ever kissed a man."

He grins. "Well, it worked, didn't it?"

"You took a hell of a chance, you know. What if I hadn't been gay?"

He smiles. "I knew you were."

"How could you have been sure? We'd barely spoken a word to each other before that."

"Because you were just too pretty not to be, sweetheart. Life couldn't be so cruel as to drop you in my lap, so to speak, and not give me a chance to make you mine. Hell, I knew you played on my team. And when I asked you if you'd ever kissed a man, you looked me straight in the eye, all balls and brawn, and said 'yes' without batting an eye. At that moment, I knew I wanted you—bad. I didn't give a damn that you were too young for me. I just wanted you in my bed. Shane read me the riot act for even thinking of pursuing you, but I wanted you more than I wanted my next breath...and now here we are."

My throat tightens painfully at his declaration, and I swallow hard as I try to hold it together. "And now, here we are. On a date."

He frowns as he reaches across the table for my hand—holding my God-damned hand in a dining room filled with over a hundred people. "I'm sorry I disappointed you at Beth's wedding. I think about that day a lot, and I regret it so much." He shakes his head. "If I could go back and do things differently, I would. When I discovered the next morning that you'd left town—you'd left *me*—I panicked. I really thought I'd lost you."

A sharp pang of guilt stabs me in the chest. "I'm sorry. I shouldn't have—"

"No," he says, squeezing my hand, shaking his head. "Don't apologize. I needed to be shaken out of my paralysis. You have nothing to be sorry for."

Our meals arrive, along with the bottle of wine, and we dig in to our food. The steaks are amazing, flavorful and tender, and the wine is the best I've ever tasted. Several times during the meal, Cooper reaches for my hand and gives it a squeeze, holding it for a few minutes before letting go. I don't know if it's the food, the wine, or the company, but I feel really warm and mellow. But as much as I'm enjoying our meal—and our first real date—my mind is on what's going to happen when we get home.

I hear thunder just as rain begins to pelt the windows. An early spring rainstorm. It makes me want to go home and curl up in bed with Cooper and forget the rest of the world. There's something so romantic about a thunderstorm, especially when you're holed up inside, all cozy with the man of your dreams.

I suspect Cooper's thinking along the same lines because his gaze is hot on me, his expression darkening with hunger—and not for food. We've pretty much satisfied that already. All I can think about now is getting home and putting my mouth on him. I want to kiss and lick and suck—.

"Are you ready to go home?" Cooper says, laying his napkin on the table.

I feel my face heat up as I grin at him. Yeah, we're thinking along the same lines. The way he says *home* gives me butterflies. I nod.

Our server brings the check, and Cooper pays the bill in cash, leaving a generous tip. As we head for the exit, Killian appears out of nowhere, falling in at the front, leading us out to the car. Damn, that guy's quiet.

"Did you get something to eat?" I ask him.

"Sure did," he replies, a telling grin on his face. "That hostess is a very accommodating woman."

* * *

It's just eight o'clock when we arrive back at the penthouse. Killian drops us off in front of the private elevator in the garage, and once we're safely inside the elevator car, he leaves to check in with Jake.

We take the elevator upstairs, and when we step into the great room, we find Shane and Beth curled up on the sofa. There's a fire in the hearth and a basketball game playing on the big flat-screen TV, the volume set on low. Even though it's only eight o'clock, Beth's in her PJs already, with her feet tucked up on the sofa, cuddling with Shane beneath a fleece blanket. It's all very cozy.

Shane turns to glance at us over the back of the sofa. "Hey guys, how was dinner?"

I come around to sit beside Beth, putting her feet in my lap. "It was fantastic. The food was great, and my date was very gallant."

Cooper sits in one of the arm chairs near the fireplace and smiles at me. "Very nice." Then he sets our wine bottle, which is still about half full, on the coffee table. "Can I interest anyone in a glass of wine? It's good stuff."

"Sure," Shane says, shifting as if to get up. "I'll take some."

Cooper rises to his feet. "Stay where you are. I'll get you a glass."

Cooper heads for the bar and grabs three wine glasses, bringing them back to the seating area by the fire. He sets them on the coffee table and splits what's left of the wine among the glasses. He hands Shane a glass, then hands one to me, keeping the last one for himself. "Sorry, none for you, kiddo," he says to Beth.

Beth snuggles closer to Shane. "That's okay. I've had so much water today my bladder is in danger of exploding."

We finish off the wine while watching a bit of the game on TV, Chicago Bulls versus Dallas Mavericks.

After he finishes his glass of wine, Cooper returns to the kitchen and tosses the empty bottle into the recycling bin. I hear him turn on the faucet in the kitchen sink.

"Anyone want coffee?" he says, filling a pot with water.

I abandon Beth to her husband and her iPad and join Cooper in the kitchen.

Walking up behind him, I slip my arms around his waist and rest my chin on his shoulder. "Thank you for a wonderful dinner tonight. That was the best date I've ever had."

He chuckles. "It was just dinner. It was hardly that big a deal."

"Yeah, but you took me *out*, and that makes it a big deal."

I kiss the side of his neck and smile when he shivers. He's warm, radiating heat, and smells so damn good. I run my nose along his neck, breathing in his masculine scent. "How about a movie?" I say. "We could watch a movie in bed." I pull his hips back against mine, and I know he can feel my erection straining against the front of my slacks.

He makes a low sound deep in his throat.

"You can even pick the movie," I say, sweetening the deal.

Cooper shuts off the faucet and sets the pot of water in the sink before turning in my arms and putting his own around me. He glances past me at our housemates, as if checking to see if we have an audience, but when he relaxes in my arms, I know no one's paying us any attention.

"I accept," he says. His hands slide down to cup my ass.

"Perfect."

Since no one else wanted coffee, Cooper abandons the pot of water, leaving it for morning. I take his hand and lead him across the great room, stopping briefly behind the sofa. "We're calling it a night," I tell Shane and Beth. "See you in the morning."

Beth pops up to look at us over the back of the sofa, blinking drowsily. "You're going to bed already?" Then she notices that I'm holding Cooper's hand. "Oh. Well, good night then." She grins at me. "I'll see you in the morning."

"Night, guys," Shane says, his eyes glued to the basketball game.

When we step into our room and shut the door behind us, I grab the remote and turn on the TV. "What do you want to watch?"

Cooper deliberates for a minute. "How about a western?"

"Okay." Not my first choice, but I did offer to let him choose. "Which one?"

"Magnificent Seven."

"The old one or the new one?"

"The new one. I like the cast, especially Chris Pratt and Denzel Washington."

While I cue up the movie, Cooper heads for the closet to undress. By the time I join him there, his jacket is off and hung up, and his tie is off. He's still wearing the white dress shirt, which his broad shoulders fill out quite nicely.

I walk to him and brush his hands aside as he begins to unbutton his shirt. "Allow me."

He raises an eyebrow and smiles as he lowers his arms to his side. "Be my guest."

I think back to the guys I dated in high school and shortly after. They were pretty fit, but they were boys. Their bodies pale in comparison to Cooper's. His is a man's body, with well-delineated musculature, rough-hewn muscles that make me want to stroke and touch. The hair on his chest is a total turn-on for me... just enough to make me think about sex and hot, sweaty bodies.

As I unbutton his shirt, I let the backs of my fingers brush along his torso. His expression darkens as he makes eye contact with me, and his nostrils flare as his rate of breathing picks up. His shirt falls open, and I skim my gaze down his torso, from his throat and clavicles, down to his sternum, past his ridged abdomen, to his belly button. His dark chest hair converges into a line that disappears beneath his waistband, and I'm itching to follow it to its destination.

I push the sides of his shirt off his shoulders—exposing well-defined, firm muscles—then let the fabric fall away, leaving his chest fully exposed. His nipples are tight little points peeking out of the hair on his pectorals, and I'm tempted to lick one just to hear his reaction.

I love bottoming for Cooper, but sometimes, like tonight, I just want to devour him. I don't know if it's the date, or the excellent wine...but I feel aggressively aroused. I've topped him before, and I know he would be open to letting me do it again if I wanted to. Sometimes I think I want to, but then I'd miss out on how amazing it feels when he takes me.

I maintain eye contact with him as I reach down and unbuckle his leather belt, pulling it from the belt loops of his trousers. I toss his belt to the floor, then reach for the fastener of his slacks, slowly undoing them and unzipping them, exposing his underwear. My eyes widen at the sight of his sexy black silk boxers, which are a far cry from his usual and very utilitarian cotton boxer briefs.

I run the back of one hand along his cock, brushing it through the cool, silky material, feeling it harden further. He makes a noise and closes his eyes for a moment, reveling in my touch. When he opens them again, they're burning. He moves to unbutton my shirt, but I shake my head and take a step back. No, this is for him. This is his reward for being such a good boyfriend tonight. This is his reward for *trying*.

I tug his slacks and boxers down his legs, dropping them to the floor, and motion for him to step out of them. Then I relieve him of his socks, leaving him naked.

"Thank you for this evening," I tell him once more, wanting him to know how much our date meant to me. There was a time when I was sure he'd never do something like that for me. But tonight, he did. I guess miracles do happen.

I lean closer and kiss the curve of his neck, tasting his warm, slightly salty skin, licking his pulse point. When he groans loudly, I smile, happy that I can pleasure him. I kiss my way down his chest, taking time to flick my tongue against the hard peaks of his nipples, first one, then the other. Then I follow the path of his chest hair, lower, past his abs and his belly button, to his thick cock, which is at full mast, defying gravity as it strains upward. I drop to my knees and grasp his impressive erection, directing the tip of it into my mouth, where my tongue flits against the crown before licking over the tip.

"Jesus, Sam," Cooper says in a wonderfully gruff voice that sends a shiver down my spine, directly to my balls. He grasps the sides of my head, but refrains from directing me or thrusting. I draw him into my mouth, as far back as I can take him, wetting him with my saliva. Then I pull back and work him with my hands and mouth, teasing him and driving his arousal higher and higher, until he can't help himself any longer. He grasps my head tightly and holds me in place as he begins to thrust in earnest. "Oh, God," he groans, thrusting long and deep. He threads his fingers through my hair, gripping my topknot and using it to direct my movements.

I relax my throat muscles and breathe slowly through my nose, loving how he lets himself use me like this. I want to please him, I want to blow his mind. He thrusts faster and faster, rocking me on my knees as I brace myself. His moans and grunts are erratic now, almost desperate, and I know he's close.

"I'm coming!" he says, making a move to pull out.

I grab his ass and hold him tightly to me, his cock buried deep in my throat. When he does blow, he arches his back and cries out loud enough to shake the rafters. I swallow every drop, my hands and mouth gentling as he slows his movements and gradually comes to a stop. His cock is hyper-sensitive, and he gasps when he eventually pulls out.

Cooper reaches down and hauls me to my feet, pulling me in close for a hot kiss. He devours my mouth, his tongue thrusting against mine.

"I thought we were going to watch a movie," he says, a little breathlessly, but obviously sounding pleased.

"We are. But first I needed to do that. Once I got the idea in my head at dinner, I couldn't let it go."

Cooper makes short work of my clothing, stripping me down to my birthday suit. We both head for the bathroom to take care of business and get ready for bed because neither one of us will want to move a muscle once we're wrapped up in each other's arms.

Once we're in bed, propped up on pillows and lying in each other's arms, we start the film and lie back to watch. The room is dark, but there's enough light coming from the television screen that I can make out what Cooper's doing as he casually reaches over to open the nightstand drawer and pull out a bottle of lotion. He tosses the bedding aside, then squirts some lotion into his hand.

I don't say a word, but instead just lie there and try to watch the movie as he grips my cock, his big hand leisurely stroking me from base to tip. As his grip tightens, I moan, turning to press my hot face into his shoulder. He's going to torture me like this—I just know he is—keeping me on the edge of arousal as long as he can, before he eventually lets me come. Before long, I'm breathing hard, like I've just run a marathon, and groaning shamelessly against his shoulder. He continues jerking me off, squeezing and stroking and tugging on me until I'm squirming, desperate to come. My body tenses and my ballsac draws up tight. Fire races down my spine and into my balls, and I muffle my cry against him as I erupt in thick, scalding ribbons of come that shoot onto my belly and chest. He continues to milk me, alternately murmuring to me and kissing me as I gradually come down from the high.

After a quick clean-up with a hand towel, we both settle into each other's arms and watch the last of the film. When the credits roll, I turn off the TV and turn toward Cooper. He pulls me into his arms, my head tucked into the crook of his shoulder, my body warm and sated.

I've never felt so contented in my life. "I love you." Three short words, and yet they carry so much meaning.

He clears his throat, swallowing hard. "I love you too, baby."

24

Sam

When I awake the next morning, Cooper's gone, presumably to get an early start at the shooting range. He and Shane still have this ridiculous babysitting arrangement going between them. I'm so fucking tired of being treated like an invalid. Beth was right—we do have two dads. I don't mind Cooper bossing me around in bed, but out of bed—hell no. And Shane—he might be my boss, but he's not my daddy. I've really got to get my ass in gear and get back to work.

I lie here for a few minutes, thinking about last night. An actual dinner date, then a bit of mind-blowing sexy fun, followed by a shoot-'em-up, high-body-count movie. I could definitely get used to this.

After stretching and groaning like a bear coming out of hibernation, I hit the john, then throw on my workout clothes. I'll grab a little bit to eat, some coffee, and hit the gym.

As I walk into the kitchen, Beth waves from her spot at the breakfast counter. She's got a bowl of oatmeal in front of her, as well as her laptop.

I glance at the screen. "Doing schoolwork?"

"Yeah. I've got a management paper due today."

I grab a bottle of orange juice from the fridge and pour myself a glass.

"Cooper left you a plate in the warmer," she says, pointing.

I grab my juice and plate and sit beside her, and we eat in silence, as I don't want to interrupt her school work.

I don't know about her, but I'm really feeling the strain of being cooped up in the penthouse. I imagine she's itching to get back to work, too. "Shane's in his office?" I say.

She nods. "I overheard him telling Diane to reschedule all of his morning appointments this week because he'll be working from home. Ugh. I've got cabin fever. I just want to get back to our old routine, you know? I want to be able to go out."

"Yeah. This is getting old."

She takes a sip of milk and looks at me pensively. "How much longer do you think it'll be until you can get recertified for work? If you can come back to work, I'm sure Shane will let me leave the penthouse and go to Clancy's. I miss Erin. And Mack. I miss my store."

I lean over and kiss her cheek. "I miss them, too."

After I finish my food, I rinse off my dishes and put them in the dishwasher. "I'm going to go work out. My leg feels good, and I think maybe I can really push myself to hit my targets today. At least I'll give it my best shot."

"Don't overdo it!" she calls to me as I jog down the hallway toward the fitness room.

* * *

After a 20-minute warm up, I hit the treadmill. I take it easy the first mile, just letting my leg get reaccustomed to carrying my weight at a steady pace. The second mile, I jack up the speed a bit, and by the third mile, I increase the incline. I'm going for endurance right now. I need to rebuild my stamina to get back to peak performance.

I feel energized after yesterday. Cooper taking me out to dinner was pretty momentous for me. I know it was just a dinner, not a marriage proposal, but it signified something.

Beth joins me in the fitness center, listening to an audiobook as she walks on the treadmill beside mine, while I put myself through my paces. When I'm done, I wipe the sweat from my face with a hand towel. Then I drop down onto the mat and churn through an ungodly number of push-ups. I push myself, and then I push myself some more. I realize I've gotten lazy and far too complacent since the accident, almost seeing myself as an invalid. It's way past time to get over that.

"Hey, will you come sit on my feet?" I ask Beth, after catching her attention. She shuts off the treadmill and obliges me by sitting crosslegged on my feet, clinging to my shins. This time, I actually hit my target spot on.

The next morning, I go to the shooting range with Cooper to do some serious target practice. After I squeeze off my third magazine into the paper targets suspended at the end of my shooting lane—having clearly decimated the head and chest regions of my imaginary foes—I remove my ear protection just in time to hear a low chuckle coming from behind me. I look back to see Cooper grinning at me.

He lays a warm hand on my shoulder and gives it a squeeze. "Looks like you haven't lost your edge, kid. Consider yourself recertified on weapons."

Yes! One assessment down. Now I just have to pass the physical tests.

I grab an Uber ride back to the apartment building and head upstairs to the penthouse to put some more miles on the treadmill. When I walk through the foyer into the apartment, I see Beth seated at the breakfast bar doing her school work.

"Hey, princess," I say, tugging on her ponytail. "Study hard. I'll be on the treadmill."

She laughs. "You're certainly in a good mood this morning."

"I am. Cooper signed off on my weapons certification."

"That quickly?"

I shrug. "What can I say? I have good aim. It's like riding a bike—you never forget how."

Shane walks into the kitchen carrying a coffee mug. "You never forget how to do what?"

"Sam got recertified on weapons this morning," Beth says. "Now he just has to pass the physical assessment."

Shane pours himself a fresh cup of coffee.

"That's all?" Shane says, smirking at me.

"Hey, give me until the end of this week, and I'll be there. I guarantee it."

"Thank God," Beth says. "I'm so bored staying home all the time. I want to go back to work."

I bump Beth lightly with my hip. "Don't worry, girlfriend, I got this."

For the rest of the week, I train my ass off, sometimes with Beth's helpful company, and sometimes without. I work hard all morning, and then I usually hang with Beth in the afternoon, watching movies or playing video games.

By Wednesday, I've got the upper body and core strength exercises mastered—the sit-ups, the push-ups, and the pull-ups. I'm still working on that run. Once I have that down, I can schedule with Liam for a physical assessment at the office.

On Thursday, Beth and I head downstairs to the building's fitness room so I can do some serious running. With her cheering me on, I nail the run—a mile and a half in under ten minutes. My leg is finally on board again.

"Call Liam," Beth says, handing me my phone. "If you can pass the physical assessment tomorrow, then I can go back to work on Monday."

"You got it." I call Liam and make the appointment to see him Friday morning. Then, the rest of Thursday morning and into the early afternoon, I run through the drills twice more, just to be sure I have the endurance to keep it up.

That evening at dinner, with the four of us seated at one end of the dining room table, I tell Cooper, "I have an appointment with Liam in the morning. I'm ready to pass my physical assessment."

Cooper raises an eyebrow. "Really? You think you're ready for that?"

"Yes."

"Yes, he is," Beth says.

Cooper's phone chimes with an incoming call, and when he sees who's on the line, he picks up immediately. "Jenny? What's the news?"

"Jenny Murphy," I whisper to Beth. "She's the editor of *The Sweet-water Gazette*."

At first, Cooper looks pensive as he listens to Jenny talk. Then his expression goes from skeptical to wary to relieved. "Really? He's sure?" Pause. "He obtained a reliable visual sighting?" Pause. "And it's the right vehicle?" Pause. "All right. Thank you. Please keep me posted."

Cooper ends the call and lays his phone on the table. "I'm sure you picked up on the fact that was Jenny Murphy, from Sweetwater. She said the local authorities found Roger Stevens' vehicle abandoned at the edge of a state forest. A local guy, an avid hunter who knows Stevens well, said he saw Roger Stevens in the woods yesterday. After a search, the feds found the remains of a campsite. They found physical evidence that Roger has been camping out in the woods for a few days."

"If he's still down near Sweetwater, then he can't be in Chicago!" Beth says, grinning at me. "That means we're no longer under house arrest."

Shane looks far from happy when he frowns at Cooper. "But they don't have him in custody?"

Cooper shakes his head, looking just as unhappy as Shane. "No."

Beth looks from Cooper to Shane, and she frowns. "But someone spotted him down there, someone who knows him. Surely that's enough evidence—"

Shane reaches for Beth's hand and squeezes it. "Sweetheart, jumping to conclusions is a great way to get someone killed." Then he picks up his phone and keys in a text message. "I asked Jake to meet us here."

After we finish our meal, Cooper and Shane hole up with Jake in Shane's office for a pow-wow. Beth and I clean up the dinner dishes. I'm feeling pretty damn good. I'm about to get the OK to go back to work, which means Beth and I can get out of the apartment. It looks like Roger Stevens' escape from justice might have been a false alarm—maybe the guy just went on a walkabout in his own backyard, managing to avoid the authorities for the better part of a week. And I'm finally shacking up with my true love. "Hey, smile," I say, bumping hips with Beth. "Life's pretty damn good."

She laughs. "Yes, it is. I can't wait to call Erin and tell her the good news. She'll be ecstatic."

✑ 25

Cooper

I relayed Jenny's account to Jake as he and I sat in the chairs across from Shane's seat. When I finished, Jake looked just about as unimpressed with the news as Shane and I felt.

"What do you think?" Jake asked Shane.

Shane's mouth flattened. "I don't think this report changes anything. We have nothing definitive. No one's apprehended Stevens, which means he could be anywhere."

"But they do have his vehicle," Jake points out. "And physical evidence that he's been camping out in the woods. Is he an outdoorsman? Does he have survival skills?"

I nod. "Jenny said he does. She said he's a member of a local hunting club. She also mentioned he's a member of a survivalist group down there. They do monthly exercises in the woods, camp rough, that sort of thing."

Jake still doesn't look convinced. "And there's no report of any stolen vehicles in the area? No evidence that he might have rented a car, or perhaps a buddy of his rented a car for him? Or loaned him a car?"

"According to Jenny, none," I say.

"Well, we have no evidence he left the state," Jake says. "And we have no evidence he's here in Chicago." He looks at Shane. "So, what's the plan?"

Shane blows out a heavy breath as he runs his fingers through his hair. "We've got a bunch of hearsay, that's all. I'm not willing to bet anyone's safety on hearsay." Shane looks to me for my opinion.

"Sam's going in to see Liam tomorrow morning, to get recertified for work," I say.

"Do you think he'll pass?" Shane says.

I nod. "He'll pass, or he'll kill himself trying. He's tired of being cooped up. He and Beth both need some freedom back."

Shane shakes his head. "I don't like this one bit. There's nothing more than anecdotal evidence that Stevens is still in Sweetwater, and none that he's here, and yet I can't shake the bad feeling I've got."

"How about this," Jake says. "Until Stevens is captured, we keep the extra security inside the building lobby, and I'll reassign Cameron and Killian to the bookstore. And Beth is limited to just going to Clancy's for now, nowhere else."

Shane looks pensive, and still not happy, but eventually he nods. "I can't keep her locked up here forever, or she'll mutiny. And if Sam's going to be back to work tomorrow, then it'll be impossible to keep the two of them cooped up in the penthouse." He blows out another heavy breath. "All right. We'll let them go to Clancy's, and we'll increase the security in the store. That sounds reasonable."

Then Shane looks at me. "Keep checking in with the authorities in Sweetwater for any updates on the search for Stevens. I want to know the instant that fucker is apprehended."

* * *

About eight o'clock that evening, the four of us are seated on the sofa by the fire, just relaxing, watching a movie on the flatscreen.

Shane's phone rings and he looks at the screen and frowns. As he accepts the call, I mute the audio on the movie.

"It's the front lobby security," Shane says, putting the call on the speaker phone.

A disembodied voice comes over the speaker. "Sir, there's a man in the lobby asking to see Mr. Harrison. What should I tell him? It's not Roger Stevens, sir. This is a younger man. Says his name is Craig Morrow, sir. He says he's a friend of Mr. Harrison's."

I look at Sam, who looks as surprised as I feel to hear that Craig is here in Chicago. "Are you expecting him? Did you know he was coming here?"

Sam shakes his head. "No. I haven't spoken to him since I left Dayton."

Shane looks at me first, then at Sam. "What should I tell him? Do you want to see him?"

Sam looks absolutely baffled by Craig's sudden appearance. He opens his mouth to answer, but nothing comes out.

"Send him up," I say, suddenly overwhelmed with the need to meet the asshole who tried to steal my guy. "I want to meet this guy."

"All right," Shane says. Then to the guard on the phone, he says, "Have someone escort Mr. Morrow up to the penthouse."

I jump up from the sofa and stand at the foyer doors, arms crossed over my chest, eager to meet this Craig. I hope he really is an asshole so I can kick him out. If he says one inappropriate thing to Sam, he's out of here.

Shane remains seated on the sofa, next to Beth, who's half-turned in her seat to watch the foyer door over the back of the sofa.

Sam joins me at the foyer door. "Tone it down, babe," he says, nudging me with his elbow. "You look like you're ready to kill someone."

I scoff at him. "Maybe I am."

Sam rolls his eyes at me. "Relax. He probably just came here to check on me. Stop worrying."

"Who says I'm worried?"

Sam gives me a flat look. "Give me a break." He runs his hand down my arm, squeezing my muscles. "You're too tense. Relax. Craig's harmless."

My heart rate is indeed pounding, and my teeth are clenched so tightly I'm afraid I might crack my jawbone. "Why is he here, Sam?"

He shrugs. "Honestly? I don't know. I'm as surprised that he's here as you are. I made it clear to him that I was taken."

"Did you guys talk about seeing each other again? Did you make plans with him?"

He cracks a smile. "Oh, my God, are you jealous?"

"This isn't funny, pal. Just answer my question."

"No, we didn't make plans to see each other again. When I left Dayton, I said goodbye to him. I never expected to see him again."

I hate how cavalier Sam is acting about Craig's arrival. I'm practically having a panic attack here, and he's grinning at me like a fool, telling me to relax. "Don't tell me to relax."

The elevator pings as the doors open. Craig steps out of the elevator, accompanied by a uniformed, armed security guard.

The guard stops at the foyer door, eyeing me directly. Smart guy. "Mr. Cooper. Sorry to bother you, sir, but Mr. Harrison has a guest."

Craig looks a little shell-shocked as he glances around the spacious great room, his blue eyes widening. When his gaze finally lights on Sam, he smiles and visibly relaxes. "Sam, hi!"

Sam steps closer to Craig and offers his hand for a shake. "Hi, Craig. Welcome."

Instead of shaking hands, Craig pulls Sam into his arms, catching him by surprise with a bear hug. "Surprised to see me?" Craig says.

Sam pulls back from the hug. "Yeah, you could say that. I wasn't expecting you."

Tired of being left out of this little welcoming party, I step forward and lay my arm across Sam's shoulders. Subtlety is not my strong suit. "Aren't you going to introduce me to your friend, baby?"

Sam rolls his eyes at me. "Cooper, this is Craig, the guy from Dayton I told you about. Craig, this is my boyfriend, Daniel Cooper."

Disappointment flickers across Craig's face when Sam refers to me as his boyfriend, but I have to admit it gives me a hell of a lot of satisfaction.

"Hi, Dan," Craig says, hesitating a moment before he smiles and offers me his hand. "It's great to finally meet you. You're all Sam talked about in Dayton."

Reluctantly, I shake Craig's hand, squeezing a little harder than necessary. When Craig makes a face and pulls his hand free, I smile. Hopefully like a shark. "It's Cooper." I cross my arms over my chest again, wishing like hell I was wearing my gun holster. I have no plans to shoot the prick, but it wouldn't hurt to let him know I mean business. "So, what are you doing here, Craig?" I ask him, point blank.

Craig laughs, obviously nervous, as his gaze darts from me to

Sam. I'm sure he's looking for Sam to help him out here. "I just wanted to check on Sam, you know. See how he's doing? We got to know each other pretty well in Dayton, and I just thought—"

"You thought what?" I say, glaring at Craig.

Sam jabs me with his elbow, but I don't let up on the glaring.

Craig shifts his attention back to Sam, looking for support. "I just wanted to make sure you were doing all right. You know." Even as he's talking to Sam, his gaze keeps jumping back to me.

"I'm fine, Craig, really," Sam says.

"Oh?" Craig says. He stands there for a long, awkward moment, as if waiting for Sam to elaborate. Craig leans closer to Sam. "Can I talk to you? In private?"

I bristle at the suggestion, but Sam puts his hand on my shoulder, giving it a firm squeeze. I get the message. *Calm down.*

"Yeah, sure," Sam says, looking at me to judge my reaction. "Come on, Craig. I'll give you a tour of the fitness room."

Then Sam looks right at me. "Wait here. We won't be long." Then he motions for Craig to proceed him down the hallway to the right. "It's this way."

* * *

I pace the floor outside the foyer, glaring down the hallway where Sam and Craig disappeared into the fitness room.

Shane levels his gaze at me from over the back of the sofa. "Cooper, for God's sake, sit the hell down."

"Not helping, Shane."

He and Beth both are watching me, Beth looking worried, Shane looking partly amused and partly exasperated.

"I could go—" Beth starts to say.

"No," Shane says, pulling her into his arms. "You stay out of this pissing match."

"They're just talking, Cooper," Beth says, smiling at me. "Don't worry."

I check my watch. "I'm giving them five minutes. Then I'm going in there."

Shane shakes his head at me. "You don't honestly think Sam would—"

I glare at Shane. "I'd like to see you remain calm if it was Beth and some admirer of hers shut up alone, out of your sight."

"That's different," Shane says, looking affronted.

"No, it's not."

"Are you saying you don't trust Sam?"

"Of course, I trust Sam!"

"Then relax, man. He's a big boy. He can take care of himself."

* * *

I waited a full five minutes, just as I promised—five fucking long minutes—and then I took off down the hallway to the fitness center. I could hear Shane getting to his feet to follow me, instructing Beth to stay put on the sofa.

When I get to the fitness room, I don't bother knocking, but instead shove the door wide open and walk into the room, interrupting a rather heated conversation. Craig is practically in Sam's face, gripping Sam's biceps hard.

"Get your fucking hands off him," I say. It comes out more like a growl, but I can't help that. All I can think about is that this asshole is trying to make a move on my guy.

Sam looks surprised by my entrance, but also relieved, as he gives me a rueful smile. I expect he's going to chew my ass off, but instead, he surprises me. "I'm actually surprised you waited this long."

"But he doesn't deserve you!" Craig says to Sam, completely ignoring my entrance and shaking Sam as if he's trying to talk some sense into him. The guy really has no sense of self-preservation.

Sam looks Craig in the eye. "My relationship with Cooper is my business, and no one else's. I'll decide who deserves me. I don't need anyone's help."

"But you said it yourself! Cooper can't meet your needs. You need someone who—"

"Things have changed—he's changed. But I don't need to explain anything—"

"Oh, come on, Sam," Craig says. "No one changes that quickly. He's doing a snow job on you."

Sam sighs, showing far more patience than I ever could. "Craig, I think it's really...um, considerate...of you to come all this way to check on me, but a text or an e-mail would have sufficed. If you came here to talk me into leaving again, well, I'm afraid you've wasted your time. You should have just called."

"But—" Craig huffs with frustration, glancing back nervously at me. Then he turns back to Sam, lowering his voice. "Look, is there somewhere we can go, just the two of us? Somewhere private? Let's go out for a drink."

I'm so fed up with this guy, I'm ready to kick him out of our apartment. But I can't do that to Sam. Sam has to make his own decisions.

"I'm sorry, Craig," Sam says. "There's no point in us going anywhere. My answer's not going to change. You're welcome to stay here and visit for a while, but I'm not leaving with you to go out for drinks, not unless Cooper comes with us, which I really don't recommend. You should have called me first."

"But I drove all this way to see you, man," he says.

This asshole walks into my home, trying to sweet-talk my lover... not cool. "Well, now you've seen him," I say. "You can go."

Sam glares at me over Craig's head. "Not helping, babe."

Craig's gaze scans the room, going from Sam to me to Shane and Beth, who are standing out in the hall. I guess he can tell he's waging a losing battle, because his shoulders slump in defeat. "It was worth a try, Sam," Craig said. "You were worth a try."

* * *

Craig leaves as quickly as he arrived, with little fanfare and his tail tucked between his legs.

"Huh," Shane says, after the elevator doors have closed on Craig and the security guard who'd escorted him up. Then he looks at Sam, a quizzical gleam in his eye. "Do you have any more secret admirers we should know about?"

"No," Sam says, looking almost bashful. "Can I help it that I have a certain effect on people?"

Sam seems oddly subdued, and I wonder if he's feeling bad for Craig, having come all this way just to be rejected.

"Can we talk?" I say, nodding toward our suite.

Sam nods, then heads toward our room. He doesn't say anything as we step into our room and I close the door quietly.

"Sam? Are you okay?"

He nods. "I'm sorry about that. I had no idea he'd come here. We were friends, buddies, and that's it—I swear. I never gave him any indication that there was anything romantic in our future."

I walk right up to him, eye to eye, and lay my hands on his shoulders. "I know you didn't."

"I never gave up on us, Cooper. Even while I was away, I always had it in the back of my mind that we'd somehow work things out."

I nod, realizing just how close I might have come to losing Sam. I have to admit, Craig's a good-looking guy, and he's close to Sam's age. Sam could have easily decided I wasn't worth the effort and just given up on me.

I cup the back of his head with one hand and meet him halfway for a kiss, teasing his lips apart, while my other arm snakes around him so I can draw him even closer.

We stand there for a few moments, just kissing.

Damn, I came so close to losing him. "Hey, what do you say we go away for the weekend? We could leave tomorrow, after you pass your physical assessment test."

Sam pulls back, his eyes widening. "Really?"

"Yeah. A romantic getaway, just the two of us."

I can tell by the smile on his face that it's the right move.

"What did you have in mind?" he says.

"Somewhere private, some place secluded, where we can relax and do whatever the hell we want. We can spend the whole weekend naked in bed if you want to. I'll ask Jake if we can borrow his cabin up in Harbor Springs."

Sam pulls me into a bear hug, nestling his hips against mine. "Yes!" he murmurs against my lips. "I would love that."

26

Sam

I get up early Friday morning and join Cooper for breakfast. Since Shane's been sleeping in with Beth lately, it's just the two of us up at this quiet hour. While Cooper cracks some eggs and starts the coffee, I make toast. He's already dressed for work, but I'm still wearing my fleece pajama bottoms and nothing else.

While he's standing at the stove, cooking the eggs, I come up behind him and slip my hands around his waist, linking my fingers over his washboard abs. "Don't forget to pack your hiking boots for the weekend," I say. "I feel like getting back to nature."

He laughs. "Will do."

We finish preparing breakfast together, then sit at the counter to eat. I love being with him like this, quiet and domestic. It makes me think about crazy things, like one day the two of us getting married. It's so easy to picture him as my husband. Last night he made love to me with such a sense of urgency, which I attributed to him still being worked up over Craig's unexpected appearance.

I reach over and brush my thumb across the back of his hand, tracing the path of a sexy tendon. "Craig was never more to me than just a friend, you know that, right? I was always planning to come back. I just needed some space."

His throat works as he nods. He takes in a deep breath, then blows it out. His eyes are pained when he looks at me. "I know I drove you away. I don't blame you—it was my fault. I deserved it."

"No, I—"

"No, don't. Don't let me off the hook by giving me an excuse. I was a coward, and I let you down. I'm sorry."

I slide off my barstool and turn Cooper's seat so that he's facing me. I step between his knees and bring my hands up to cup his face. "I understand better now where you were coming from, and I don't blame you for your fears. I know now that they were valid ones. We get a do-over now, all right? We get to start over."

I kiss him then, and he squeezes his eyes shut.

* * *

After we finish eating, I clean up the kitchen while Cooper finishes getting ready for work. When he's done, he returns to the kitchen to give me a mint-flavored good-bye kiss. I walk him to the foyer.

"Good luck with your assessment test today," he says. "Don't be too disappointed if you don't pass this first time."

"Oh, I'm going to pass. You can bank on it."

He smiles at me. "Good. Then we'll have something extra to celebrate this weekend."

I give him one last kiss before he steps inside the elevator. We're so domestic—I could get used to this. And I really like the idea of going away with him for the weekend—we can play house out in the woods together and get into all kinds of trouble.

"I'll make arrangements with Jake to borrow his cabin," he says, just as the doors begin to close. "We'll leave this afternoon."

"Perfect."

Once he's gone, I head to the fitness room to do some stretching and warm up to get in a couple of good practice sessions. I can crank out the push-ups, sit-ups, and pull-ups now...exactly as prescribed. And I can do the run, so I'm all set.

A bleary-eyed Beth, still in her PJs, comes to find me in the middle of doing another set of pull-ups on the chin bar.

"Today's the day," she says, grinning at me. "Do you think you can do it?"

"I know I can do it. Consider yourself on parole starting around noon today."

"Can I come with you? We could stop at Clancy's afterwards. I need to see Erin and check on my books."

"They're your books, huh? All seventy thousand of them?"

"Yes, they're mine." She frowns. "Besides, I miss my store, and I miss my friends."

"All right, you can come with me—you'll be my good luck charm—and afterwards we'll go Clancy's."

Once we're ready to leave, we stop at Shane's open office door.

"I'm going with Sam to the office for his assessment. And then afterwards—when he passes—we're going to Clancy's for a while."

Shane looks up from his desk, his brow furrowing as he considers her statement. I don't think he missed that fact that she was *telling* him, not *asking* him. My girl is developing a backbone!

Shane leans back in his chair, looking pensive. "Sounds like a great idea," he says, and I think he managed to surprise us both.

"Really?" she says.

"Yes, absolutely. Have fun." He hits a few keys on his laptop and closes the lid. "In fact, I might as well go back to the office. I'll ride along with you."

I have to give the guy credit—that was slick. He let her have her way without exposing her to any potential risk in the process. He drives us in the Escalade and parks in the garage beneath the McIntyre Security, Inc. building. Once we're in the elevator, he presses the buttons for the third and twentieth floors.

"Good luck, Sam," Shane says, when the elevator doors open on the third floor, and Beth and I step out. "I would say 'break a leg,' but under the circumstances, I don't think it would be wise."

Shane leaves us as he heads up to the floor where his office is located. Beth follows me into the martial arts studio, and we find Liam on the mats with a small group of female employees. He's barefoot, dressed in a pair of black cross-trainer shorts and a gray McIntyre Security T-shirt. The women, all ages and levels of fitness, are going through some repetitive motions.

I'm a few minutes early for my appointment, so I steer Beth to sit in the row of chairs at the side of the room while we watch Liam conclude what appears to be a self-defense class.

"You should take a self-defense class," I whisper to Beth.

"I tried that once. Shane freaked out every time someone threw me down onto the mat."

I laugh. "Why does that not surprise me? Maybe he'd be okay if Lia taught you some moves."

"She did teach me a few things."

Liam's class finishes up then, and the women head for the locker rooms to change.

Liam joins us. "Hi, sis," he says, kissing Beth's cheek. "Hi, Sam. You ready?"

I rise from my chair, leaving Beth to sit and watch. "Yes. Let's do this."

"What do you want to do first? Run or the mat work?"

"The mat work."

"Okay." He motions me toward the mats. "Go for it."

I shuck off my sweatpants, leaving me dressed in workout shorts and a T-shirt. I take a seat on the mat, and Liam crouches at my feet.

"I'll hold your feet," he says, gripping my ankles. He's got a stop watch suspended from a chain around his neck. "Ready?"

"As I'll ever be."

"Go, Sam!" Beth yells, offering some inspiration. "You can do it!"

Liam glances at Beth, grinning. "You brought your own cheerleader?"

"Yeah."

I crank through the sit-ups and push-ups with a few seconds to spare each time. Then I move to the bar anchored to the wall and power through the required number of pull-ups.

"Great job," Liam says when I drop to the ground. "Ready to run?"

"As ready as I'll ever be." I head for the oval running track that hugs the perimeter of the room. I have ten minutes to run a mile-and-a-half, which is 18 laps around the room. Liam gives me the go-ahead, and as I start running, he goes to sit with Beth, the two of them chatting as I run my ass off.

I'm tired from the mat work, but also energized that I'm close to being able to get back to work. I power through the run, digging hard for the speed and stamina I need to beat the clock. Beth follows my progress with her gaze, waving at me every time I run past her position. There's a large digital timer on the wall I can use to measure my progress. Finally, with thirty seconds to spare, I hit my target and jog over to Beth and Liam.

Liam stands and offers me his hand. "Good job. Welcome back to work, dude."

Beth jumps to her feet and gives me a hug, despite the fact that I'm a hot mess. I leave them to their conversation as I head for the men's locker room for a quick shower and to change back into my street clothes.

After I'm changed, I say my good-byes to Liam, and Beth and I take the elevator up to the twentieth floor.

I pull out my phone and send Cooper a quick text.

I passed.

Cooper sends me a prompt reply.

I knew you would. We'll celebrate tonight at the cabin. Your ass is mine. Be ready.

She watches me out of the corner of her eye. "What are you grinning about?" she says.

"Nothing."

She pokes me with her elbow. "Liar. Did you get a text from your *boyfriend*?"

I try to hold back my smile, but I fail miserably. "Yes."

"Is he proud of you?"

I nudge her with my hip. "Yes. He's taking me away for a romantic weekend. We're going to spend the weekend up at Jake's cabin."

"Oooh, I love Jake's cabin. You're going to have so much fun, just the two of you rolling around in the leaves."

When the elevator stops, we step out into the corridor in front of the administration suites. A glass wall has the McIntyre Security, Inc. logo etched into it. I hold the door for Beth, and we head to the desk belonging to Shane's executive assistant—a sweet little lady with short, curly white hair and softly wrinkled skin.

"Hello, dear," Diane says, beaming at Beth. "How are you feeling?"

"Fine, thanks," she says.

"And Sam, it's so good to see you back again. How's your leg?"

"Right as rain," I say. "I'm officially recuperated and back to work."

"Do you know if Shane's busy right now?" Beth says.

Diane's face lights up, her blue eyes crinkling at the corners as she smiles. "Beth, honey, he's never too busy for you." She picks up her landline. "Hold on, sweetie. Let me tell him you're here."

Barely a moment later, Shane's door opens, and he walks out of his office looking all GQ in his gray suit, white dress shirt, and black tie. *Damn.* I'm certainly not coveting my best friend's husband, but even I have to admit the man is smoking hot.

"Hi, sweetheart," Shane says, pulling her into his arms for a quick kiss. Then he extends his hand to me for a handshake. "Liam just called. He told me you passed with flying colors. Congratulations, Sam, and welcome back."

"Thanks. It's good to be back."

"And now that my bodyguard is back, we're free to roam the city," Beth says.

Shane raises an eyebrow as he shakes his head. "Roam the city? I don't think so. You can go to Clancy's and that's it. Until further notice, all right?"

"All right, fine," she says, tugging on my arm. "Come on, let's go. I need to see my store."

Shane gives Beth a light kiss on the lips. "Have fun."

* * *

Beth and I catch a taxi to the bookstore, which is little more than a mile from the McIntyre Security, Inc. building on N. Michigan Avenue, right in the middle of shopping heaven, just blocks from Water Tower Place and other iconic Chicago shopping destinations.

Her enthusiasm for getting back to a sense of normalcy is contagious. It's been over three months since I've been able to escort her to Clancy's. I guess we're both ready to get back to our familiar routine.

When we walk through the front doors, we're greeted by a cheering crowd.

Erin is right in front of said crowd, and she practically launches herself into my arms. "Sam! You're back!"

Mack shakes my hand, as does the dozen Clancy's employees gathered around. I recognize some of them from the business offices upstairs, and some from the customer check-out lanes. I'm surprised to see Cameron Stewart here, too—I guess he's part of the temporary increase in security. It's quite a festive environment with clusters of colorful helium balloons perched on almost every table top.

"Thank God you're back," Mack says. "I've been so outnumbered."

"Oh, I'm sure you can hold your own against the ladies," I tell him, glancing pointedly at Erin, who's currently deep in conversation with Beth. I nod toward Cameron. "And it looks like you have some extra help."

Mack nods. "Cameron and Killian are both helping out here for the time being, until your fugitive-from-the-law friend from down south is captured."

Erin and Beth start walking away, arm in arm, heading deeper into the store. "If you'll excuse me," I tell Mack, pointing at the girls, "duty calls."

I'm still high from passing my physical assessment—thank God I passed the first time. Cooper would never have let me live it down if I'd failed. Everything just seems to be coming together. Cooper is opening up to me, I'm back to work. My sexy guy is stealing me away to a remote cabin in the woods for the weekend. I can see it now— long, romantic hikes in the woods followed by wild make-out sessions in front of the fire. God, I hope there's a fireplace.

I follow the girls at a respectful distance, giving them a little privacy to catch up on all the girl time they've been missing. They seem deep in conversation, although Erin's doing most of the talking. She's probably catching Beth up on what's been going on here at the store, and maybe throwing in a little bit of gossip about what Mack's been up to.

Poor Mack. I sympathize with the guy. Erin is one adorable little female—yeah, adorable. That's the best way to describe her, *adorable* like a favorite little sister. Petite, dark hair, blue eyes and freckles. She's twenty-two, but she looks younger, which just adds to both her frustration and his. And while Erin looks like a little woodland fairy, Mack is built like a tank, six-six with muscles to spare. My God he'd crush her in bed. Which is partly why Shane put the fear of God into Mack, threatening him with bodily harm if he ever did anything to hurt little Miss Erin O'Connor.

Of course, I guess you could say Shane's being a bit hypocritical, as he's the same age as Mack, and Beth's just two years older than Erin. So, it's definitely a case of the pot calling the kettle black, if you ask me. And Mack, well he's a good guy. Very chivalrous. And that's why little Miss Erin makes him so nervous. When she bats those baby blues at him, fluttering those long dark eyelashes, he gets hives.

As I follow the girls through the magazine section, I grab the closest thing that looks interesting—*Modern Gun*—so I have something to read while they're catching up on whatever important things they need to catch up on. With these two, there's no telling. It could be work, or it could be the latest viral video of a cute baby or a cat.

After they make a complete circuit of the first floor of the bookstore, they head up the curved staircase to the second floor. I follow a dozen yards behind them, close enough to step in should I need to, but not close enough to eavesdrop on their private talk. They turn right and disappear down the hallway that leads to the administrative offices, and I join them in Beth's office.

"I knew you would do great," Beth says to Erin. "Didn't I tell you? The store's running perfectly, like a well-oiled machine. You're a natural leader."

Erin's pacing like a nervous sparrow.

"Just like old times, eh?" I say. My comfy sofa is right where I left it, in front of a large picture window that overlooks N. Michigan Avenue. Ah, yes, it's good to be back.

Beth gives me a pleading look. "You tell her."

"Tell her what?"

"Erin doesn't think she can manage the store when I go on maternity leave this summer."

I put my arm across Erin's shoulders and pull her close. "Of course, you can do it, Erin. You're a natural, and everyone here loves you." *Including the head of security.*

"You're doing great," Beth tells her. "And you have three more months to get used to the idea. I'll help you."

Erin doesn't seem convinced, but at least she stops fidgeting.

Now that the drama seems to have died down somewhat, I plop down on my favorite sofa and put my feet up on the coffee table. "Who's hungry? I just busted my ass at McIntyre Security, and I'm starving. Let's order something in. Who feels like Chinese?"

Beth drops down onto the sofa beside me and pats my leg. "I'm so glad you're back."

"Me, too, princess. Now, let's call in some food."

I phone in an order for delivery from our favorite Chinese restaurant, while Beth and Erin go over the new book orders for the next couple of weeks. While the girls are talking numbers and new releases and book clubs, and all that shop talk, I entertain myself catching up on my favorite YouTubers. Half an hour later, Mack knocks on Beth's door, then walks in carrying our lunch order.

"Somebody ordered Chinese?"

"Yes!" Beth says. "Thank goodness, because we're starving."

There's plenty of food here, so we talk Mack into joining us for an impromptu lunch. We grab our beverages of choice from the refrigerator in Beth's office, then sit down to enjoy our food.

Beth sits at her desk to eat, while the rest of us sit on the sofa. Erin sits between me and Mack, and I watch her nibbling on her Veggie Delight—barely eating enough to keep a bird alive. Mack makes up for her slack by eating a mountain of food, but I guess it takes that much food to power his big body.

I watch Mack out of the corner of my eye and can't help noticing that he spends most of his time watching Erin, offering her a veggie spring roll or a napkin or more rice. I'm sure she has absolutely no idea of the power she has over him.

When we're done eating, Mack heads back downstairs to work, and Erin goes off to place the book orders that she and Beth pored over. Beth comes to sit beside me on the sofa.

She leans her head against my shoulder and sighs. "We should get going. You need to go home and pack for your getaway weekend. Do you know what you're going to bring with you?"

"Beth, we'll probably spend the entire weekend hiking, so all I need are jeans, sweatshirts, and hiking boots."

She gives me a lewd grin. "I don't think hiking is the only thing you'll be doing. Besides, you might want to go into town to eat. There's a nice diner there, and Lucky's Tavern serves great food. The owner, Hal, is really nice, and he's friends with Shane."

"Isn't that the bar where Lia and Jonah nearly got their asses kicked?"

"Hardly," Beth scoffs. "Nobody kicks Lia's ass. It was the other way around. Now, come on, back to what you're going to pack."

"Hey, as long as we have plenty of lube, I'm good to go."

27

Sam

I'm just about finished packing for our trip when Cooper strolls into our bedroom, a bit breathless. He whips off his jacket and tosses it on the bed. "Sorry I'm late. I had a steady stream of folks at the shooting range all day."

Cooper smiles at Beth, who's sitting on our bed watching me fold my T-shirts before I put them in my duffle bag. "Hey, kiddo," he says, barely sparing her a glance. And then, to my utter shock and delight, Cooper leans in and kisses me right on the lips, in front of Beth. "Hey, baby." When he pulls back, he winks at Beth, and she laughs, her cheeks turning pink.

"I need to grab a quick shower," Cooper says, pulling off his sweat-shirt as he heads for the bathroom.

"Well," Beth says, grinning at me. "It looks like Cooper's really coming out of his shell. I can't believe he actually kissed you in front of me."

"I know, right?" Ever since our trip to Sweetwater, Cooper's been much more relaxed when we're around others. Of course, Beth hardly counts as others—she's family. But still, he's much more comfortable in public, and I love it. I never dreamed this would happen. I don't expect him to hold my hand in public and declare his undying love in front of an audience, but if he can keep doing what he's been doing these past few days, I'll be one happy camper.

I grab my hiking boots from the closet and socks and briefs from the dresser. "That's about it for my clothes." Then I head into the closet and bring out my portable handgun backpack and check its contents. I have three handguns in there, with plenty of magazines for a short, weekend trip—not that we'll be doing any shooting, they're along for the ride as a precaution—as well as a first-aid kit.

Beth frowns at the guns. "You're bringing guns? Why?"

I give her a *duh* look. "Two gay men alone in the woods? Really? I'd rather be safe than sorry."

Her eyes widen, and I feel like a heel for saying what I did. The last thing I want is for her to worry about us. I set down the gun pack and take her hands in mine. "Hey, relax. I just want to be prepared, that's all. There's nothing for you to worry about."

I can tell that her mind is working over what I said. "The cabin is pretty isolated," she says. "And there's no reliable cell signal out there—not in the woods anyway. In town, yes, but not at the cabin. Jake does keep a satellite phone in the cabin for emergencies."

Ah, shit. Now I've scared the daylights out of her. "Hey, come here." I pull her off the bed and into my arms for a bear hug. "I'm sorry. I shouldn't have said anything. Don't worry."

"Don't worry about what?"

We both jump at the sound of Shane's voice coming from the open doorway. When we look his way, we see him leaning against the door jamb.

"You do that a lot, you know," I say.

"Do what?"

"Sneak up on people and join their conversations. You scare the shit out of me sometimes."

He shrugs. "So, what's my wife not supposed to worry about? Why are you scaring her?"

Beth glances at the gun case. "They'll be okay out at the cabin, right? It's pretty isolated, and there's no cell signal out there."

Shane pushes away from the door and walks into the room. "They'll be fine, honey. You don't need to worry."

Shane glares at me over the top of Beth's head, and I receive his message loud and clear. *Quit scaring my wife.* "I'll give Mitch a call to let him know they'll be staying at the cabin. He can keep an eye on things."

"Who's Mitch?" I say.

"Sheriff James Mitchell," Shane says. "He's a good friend. You can count on him."

Cooper comes out of the bathroom with only a towel wrapped around his waist, water droplets clinging to his chest. He pauses for a moment, eyeing us all warily. "I didn't know we were having a party."

Shane laughs as he leads Beth toward the door. "Sorry. We'll get out of your hair."

Shane closes the door as they leave, and I take advantage of the opportunity to lay my hands on Cooper's bare chest. No man has a right to look this good, I think, as I run my hands across his well-defined pecs, up and over his broad shoulders, then down his arms, squeezing his rock-hard biceps.

I feel heat and desire pool low in my belly, and all I can think about is sex. I dip down to flick one of his nipples with the tip of my tongue, teasing it. He arches his back and makes a low, rough sound. His chest expands with a deep breath as his hands come around me to grasp my ass.

"We're supposed to be packing," he says, groaning again when I switch to his other nipple, licking it before I trail kisses up to his neck.

I laugh. "I am packing."

He swats my ass, chuckling. "I mean packing clothes, for our trip."

I groan when I feel his dick stir beneath his towel. My hand drops down to palm him through the damp material, and I rub him from root to tip, feeling him thicken beneath my palm

I kiss my way up to his ear and whisper, "Are you going to make me wait until we get to the cabin tonight?"

He laughs, the sound a little ragged. "Hell, yes, I'm going to make you wait. I'm going to keep you hard all evening until we settle in. Then I'll take you in front of a blazing fire."

I sigh, knowing it's useless to try to change his mind. He loves having the upper hand where my dick is concerned.

"Did you pack *everything*?" he asks, pressing his erection into my hand.

I moan into the curve of his neck, taking in the scent of his warm, wet skin and a residual hint of soap. "Yes."

"Good. Now let's finish packing and get on the road. We have a two-hour drive ahead of us, and it'll be a while before I can get you naked."

* * *

We commandeer an Army green four-wheel drive, reinforced Jeep from Shane's fleet for our trip...just in case we want to do some off-roading. With our bags in the back, my handgun case, a sack of groceries, and cooler full of beer and ice, we set off for the great wilderness.

"Two hours, huh?" I say, turning on the radio to the local pop station.

"Yep. Straight north, follow the lake. Harbor Springs is a small, out-of-the-way fishing village. Jake's cabin is about a mile out of town, deep in the woods. He owns about ten acres of dense forest. Very secluded. We'll stop in at the little grocery store on the way into town to pick up some steaks and other perishables."

Cooper is driving, so I settle back in my seat and get comfortable. "We should get some marshmallows for the bonfire." I give him a sideways glance. "In case you were wondering, there will be a bonfire."

He smiles. "Not a problem. Jake's probably got two years' worth of seasoned wood stacked in the shed."

"Good. What else is there to do, besides build fires and hike?"

"It's mostly woods. There is a stream nearby that ends at a waterfall. That's a nice hike. There's a small downtown with a diner, a bar, and a wharf. We could fish, if you want to, or rent a boat. Other than that, prepare to be ravished. I'd be fine with never leaving the cabin. Hell—I'd be totally fine with never leaving the bed."

I grin. "I'm on board with that."

It's dark when we arrive at Harbor Springs, so I can't see much. Cooper stops at a little mom-and-pop grocery store on the outskirts of town to pick up enough groceries to get us through the weekend.

It's another mile before Cooper turns onto a nondescript lane that leads deeper into the woods. It's a narrow lane, just wide enough for one vehicle to pass along the rutted dirt path. It's spring, so there's been a lot of rain, and the ground is soft. It's a good thing we brought a four-wheel drive vehicle.

The lane eventually opens up into a spacious clearing, in the center of which stands a quaint, one-story wood cabin with a covered front porch.

Cooper parks the Jeep near the front door, and we unload our gear and carry it up to the door. In contrast to the rustic nature of the cabin, there's a sophisticated electronic panel beside the door. Cooper enters a numeric code, and then the system beeps as the door unlocks. Inside, there's another panel embedded in the wall, just inside the door, providing a schematic of the cabin's floorplan.

"Jake didn't mess around," I say. "This place is wired."

It takes two trips for us to carry in our duffle bags, my gun case, and the groceries.

Standing in the center of the living room, Cooper gives me a quick rundown of the place. "There are two bedrooms, with a shared bathroom. The kitchen's there, and behind the kitchen is a small workout room. There's a back porch, too, with a grill and a hammock. Out back there's a shed with firewood and kindling."

The living room offers the basic comforts: a long, comfortable-looking sofa, a coffee table, two rocking chairs, and stone hearth. There's a large, flat-panel TV hanging above the fireplace and a bookcase holding a small library of DVDs and books. The wood floors are old, but well maintained.

Cooper carries our duffle bags into the back bedroom and sets them on the bed. As I stand in the doorway, watching him unzip his bag, a sudden wave of emotion comes over me. I know this isn't a honeymoon, but God, it sure feels like it could be.

I walk up behind him and slip my arms around his waist. Leaning forward, I drop a kiss on his shoulder, and am gratified to feel him shiver. Then I kiss the side of his throat, slowly, letting my lips linger over his pulse point. The feel of his skin beneath my lips, his heat and scent, make me hard. God, I want to christen this bed right now.

He turns in my hold and wraps his arms around my waist, and we stand perfectly eye-to-eye. My throat tightens when I think of how close I might have come to ending us. I was so angry after Beth's wedding—when he refused to dance with me at the reception. Angry, and so bitter. I could have ruined everything with my impulsive reaction.

"Thank you for bringing us here," I tell him. There are so many other things I should say.

Thank you for not giving up on me.

Thank you for trying to meet me halfway.

His eyes turn pained suddenly, as if he can read my mind. "Thank you for coming back," he says. He swallows hard, and his fingers grip my shirt tightly as if he's hanging onto me physically, afraid to let go.

My eyes burn as tears form, blurring my vision. "I love you." I've said it before to him, and he's said it to me, but somehow it means more this time, in this quiet space, with just the two of us.

He reaches up to brush the lone tear tracking down my cheek, catching it just before it disappears into my beard. "Sam." He runs the pad of his thumb along the top edge of my beard, stroking my face. "I—the words 'I love you' don't even begin to do justice to what I feel for you. I don't deserve you. I don't deserve *this*."

I grab his hands, which are cupping my face now, and latch onto him. "Why do you say that?"

"I've spent my whole living either running or hiding from who

I am. I look at you, and I'm ashamed of myself. You've never hidden who you are. You face life head-on, with so much courage and determination."

"We were raised differently. You can't expect yourself—"

"No, don't make excuses for me. I should have manned up a long time ago. But for some lucky reason, you're still here, and I get another chance to win you."

I laugh. "You don't have to win me. You already have me, babe."

At that moment, my stomach betrays me by letting loose a loud growl. I grimace. "That was so not sexy."

Cooper laughs as he pats my stomach. "How about I make us some dinner while you bring in the firewood. We'll eat in front of the fire, and then see where things go from there."

"Deal. I can tell you right now where things are going to go." I slip my hands down to his waist and pull his hips forward to meet mine. We're both hard. "We are so going to fuck tonight."

Chapter 28

Sam

While Cooper cooks chicken breasts on the back porch grill, I head out to the shed to gather some dry kindling and logs for the fireplace. It's pitch black outside now, but there's a solar-powered light inside the shed that provides adequate light. I certainly wouldn't want to come face-to-face with an irate raccoon out here in the dark.

I step up onto the back porch with an armload of firewood, pausing to look my fill at the hot guy manning the grill. "That's a good look for you," I tell him.

He grins at me, and I could swear he's blushing. He gives me the once-over in return. "That's a good look for you," he says. "Very lumberjack. I could get used to this."

I glance down at my red plaid flannel shirt. "Beth picked it out. Pretty cool, huh?"

I carry the wood inside and deposit in the rack beside the fireplace. Then I grab two cold beers from the cooler we brought and carry one out to the back porch for Cooper.

"Thanks," he says, bringing the bottle to his lips for a long pull. "That sure hits the spot."

We sit outside in the chilly night air, in our jackets, until the food's ready. Then we head inside and eat our grilled chicken and salads seated on the sofa in the living room. The TV reception out here is nonexistent, but there's an ancient DVD player hooked up to the TV.

I scan the collection of DVDs on the bookcase. "The selections are decent, if a bit outdated," I say. "What do you feel like?" I ask Cooper. "Sci-fi? Action? Western?"

He waves his fork at me. "It's your turn. You choose."

I pull out a copy of *Fast and Furious 7*. It's a few years old, but it's a classic. I pop it in and sit back on the couch beside Cooper.

"What's this?" he says, when the opening titles roll.

"*Fast and Furious 7.*"

"What's it about?"

"Fast cars, hot guys, and crazy-ass stunts."

He shrugs. "Okay. Sounds good."

We settle back and watch the movie while we eat. I grab us a couple more beers and sit back to watch Cooper watching the movie.

"Oh, come on!" he yells at the screen when six vehicles roll out of an airplane with parachutes strapped on. "That's not realistic!"

I pat this back. "Babe, it's a movie. Of course it's not realistic. When was the last time you saw a movie that was realistic?"

He continues to groan and grumble with each new impossible stunt, and I find him even more entertaining than the movie.

After we're done eating, we wash the few dishes, then stretch out together on the spacious sofa to finish the movie. It's pretty cozy in the cabin with the lights off and the fire blazing brightly. The pop and sizzle of the burning wood, combined with the smell of wood-smoke, is downright romantic, and now I'm far more interested in Cooper than in any movie.

Cooper's lying behind me, spooning. His arm is slung around my waist, and his fingers are fiddling with the hem of my shirt, every once in a while slipping beneath the fabric to stroke my lower abs. Every time he runs his fingers up and down my torso, electricity zips along my spine, right down to my balls, making it hard for me to breathe.

His teasing becomes more and more insistent when his hand drops down to the front of my jeans, and he presses his palm against my growing erection. I groan loudly, but he pretends not to notice. But when his fingers trace the outline of my cock through my jeans, I throw my head back with a moan. "Cooper."

"Shh. Watch the movie. Don't pay me any mind."

I nearly choke on my laughter, as it's absolutely impossible to ig-nore the fact that he's unsnapping my jeans and lowering my zipper, giving himself easy access to what's inside my briefs. He slips his hand inside my underwear and wraps his fingers around my cock.

"Oh, God," I groan, closing my eyes as I arch my neck. I love it when he teases me like this, but it also drives me insane, to the point I'm reduced to begging.

He kisses his way along my throat to just beneath my ear. My heart is pounding, and I'm practically panting. The movie is com-pletely forgotten now, just so much background noise, because all I can think about is the firm grip he has on my dick.

I lie my head down and close my eyes, thrusting shamelessly into his hand. He makes a rough noise deep in his chest, and the sound goes straight to my cock, making me even harder. When he presses his hips firmly against my ass, I push back, creating delicious friction, and then it's his turn to groan.

"Are you taking me to bed, or what?" I ground out.

He laughs. "What about the movie?"

"Forget the movie. Just take me to bed, damn it, now."

He begins stroking me slowly from base to tip, his fingers catching my pre-come and using it to lube my shaft.

I'm not above begging. "Shit, Cooper, please."

More soft laughter. When he play-bites my shoulder, I growl in frustration.

"All right," he says, finally showing me some mercy. He releases my cock and smacks my hip lightly. "Go get ready for me. I'll lock up the cabin and check in with Shane. I want to see if there's any news on Roger Stevens."

* * *

The shower stall in the bathroom is barely big enough for one, let alone two, so co-showering this weekend is out of the question. I shower quickly. Cooper's teasing has gotten me so hot and bothered, all I can think about is getting him inside me. At this rate, I'll die of blue balls.

When I leave the bathroom after toweling myself dry, wearing nothing more than my birthday suit, I find Cooper pacing the living room, the satellite phone in his hand. When he catches sight of me bare-ass naked, his eyes widen, and he grins.

"All right," he says into the phone, never once taking his eyes off me. "Thanks. Yeah, I'll check in with you in the morning to see if there are any updates. Give our love to Beth."

Cooper ends the call and sets the sat phone down in its charging base.

"Any news?" I say.

"No." He pulls me into his arms. "The feds found a second campsite just a half-mile from the first one, with evidence that Stevens had been there. A couple of hunters said they thought they spotted him earlier today."

"You don't seem very happy about the news."

Cooper frowns. "I'm not. It doesn't make sense. We're supposed to believe he's just out there, camping in the woods, and neither the feds nor the local authorities have caught him? So far all the evidence is circumstantial and hearsay. There's nothing concrete. I don't like it. He can't hide in the backwoods of Sweetwater forever. You'd think he'd move on, otherwise he's a sitting duck."

"They'll apprehend him soon," I say, tugging his hand. "Now, you come with me. We have business to attend to."

"Business, huh?" Cooper says, laughing as he follows me to the bedroom.

"Yes. Your job is to make me come my brains out. So, get over here and get busy."

"Then get your ass in the bedroom." Cooper turns me to face the bedroom, then he walks me to the bed and pushes me down onto my back. He motions for me to scoot up, so that my head is on a pillow, and he crouches over me, reminding me of a big, prowling cat.

"You're still dressed," I point out.

He grins. "All in good time, pal."

He rises up onto his knees and whips off his shirt, tossing it to the side. Then he unbuckles his belt, pulling it from the belt loops. My gaze skims his torso, from his broad shoulders down to his ridged abs, and I'm absolutely mesmerized by the sight of him. When I make eye contact with him again, his gaze is hot.

I watch his hands as he unfastens his jeans and lowers the zipper. He shoves his jeans and briefs down past his thighs in one fluid motion, freeing his thick erection to bob in the air before me, thick and bold.

I sit up, wrapping my fingers around his cock and licking the tip, my tongue tracing the underside of the crown, making him groan. I wet my lips, then draw him into my mouth, using my tongue and lips to caress him, while I stroke his shaft with my fist.

"Fuck, Sam," he grates, shoving himself deeper into my mouth as he grips my head.

I suck in air before taking him as deeply as I can, sucking and licking and stroking him, letting my throat muscles tighten on him. I can feel him thickening still with each thrust.

"Oh, shit, baby," he groans, thrusting long and slow into my mouth.

I cradle his balls and gently caress them. When I feel this ballsac begin to tighten, he pulls back, his steely erection slipping from my mouth with a wet sound.

I gasp for air, looking up at him, waiting for his cue.

He pulls back to stand at the foot of the bed and shucks off his boots, socks, and the rest of his clothes. Naked, he crawls back onto the bed and pushes me onto my back so he can loom over me. He lowers his mouth to mine, his lips hot and hungry as he practically devours me. "You make me so damn crazy," he says against my lips, his voice little more than a growl.

I smile, gripping his thighs. "That goes both ways, babe."

Cooper open my legs and bends them at my knees so he can kneel between them. He reaches for my cock, taking me in a firm grip. The air whooshes out of my body when he strokes me from root to tip, catching my pre-come. I'm already hard as a rock and aching for release, but I know I'll have to wait.

He leans across me and grabs the bottle of lube off the top of the nightstand, where I'd left it for him. He pops the cap and dribbles some of the liquid between my legs, letting it run down my crack. Then he squirts some onto his finger and reaches between my legs.

I grasp the sheet as he lubes me up, stretching me, stroking me deep inside and driving me crazy. A second finger joins the first one, and I groan as he stretches me.

"You want me inside you?" he says.

"Yes," I gasp.

He curls his finger inside me and strokes my prostate with diabolical precision, and before long, I'm about to lose my mind. My balls are tightening, and the base of my spine is tingling. Just as I feel an orgasm looming, he withdraws his fingers and reaches for more lube.

"You are so cruel," I say, watching him slick up his cock.

"You can wait."

He moves in closer and begins teasing my hole with the tip of his cock, brushing against me, teasing my nerve endings and heightening my anticipation. He's always a lot to take, but God damn, it feels so good.

He looms over me, missionary style, holding my gaze firmly as he slowly presses the broad crown inside. I take a deep breath, then blow it out slowly, forcing my body to relax for him.

As he begins to rock in and out of me, pressing deeper each time, I clutch his thighs, holding onto him. I feel so connected to him as I watch those steely blue eyes bore into me, so expressive. Reading his obvious desire drives mine even higher.

Cooper sinks all the way inside me and leans forward to kiss me, his breath coming rapidly. He's as jacked up as I am. His lips are hungry on mine, almost desperate. I reach between our bodies to tug and stroke myself as his mouth devours mine. We're both moaning shamelessly, grunting from a combination of pleasure and physical exertion.

He leans back and angles his thrusts so that he's hitting my prostate, and oh, my God, I see stars. He's relentless in his determination to push me over the edge. But he's just as lost in the pleasure as I am, and it's not long before Cooper stiffens above me, gritting his teeth as he sinks deep inside me and comes, filling me with a throbbing heat. He arches his neck, his neck muscles standing out in stark relief, and he looks magnificent. He shouts to the rafters, his voice deep and raw, and continues to fuck me through his orgasm, my passage so much slicker now.

As his movements slow and his cock begins to soften, I allow myself to finish, my own cries joining his as I blow my load on my abs and chest.

Breathing hard, Cooper pulls out and falls to my side, his chest heaving. When I turn to face him, he kisses me gently.

"You are going to be the death of me one day," he says, smiling against my lips.

"I'll be right there with you, babe."

"Give me a minute," he says, still trying to catch his breath, "and I'll fetch a towel."

My bones have turned to liquid, and I couldn't move a muscle if I had to. "No problem. I'm not going anywhere."

* * *

After a quick clean-up, Cooper slips beneath the covers with me, spooning behind me. He wraps his arm around my waist and slips one leg between mine. I shiver when he skims his lips down my neck and along my shoulder.

"Thank you for coming back," he says. "For giving me a second chance."

I look back at him. "Of course I came back. I never intended to stay away permanently."

He levels me with a look. "Don't you dare tell me you were never once tempted to take Craig up on his offer."

I grin guiltily. "I never would have—"

"But you were tempted, weren't you?" He glares at me, daring me to contradict him.

Cooper is baring his soul to me, so the least I can do is be honest. "I was tempted, sure. Craig represented everything I thought I wanted. And let's face it, he's pretty freaking hot. But he's not *you*, and that's what made the difference. I didn't just want any boyfriend—I wanted *you*."

"I'll give you freaking hot," he says, pushing me to my back and rolling on top of me.

He grabs my wrists and holds them pressed to the pillow above my head. Then he dips his head down to tongue one of my nipple piercings. "Oh, fuck," I moan, arching my back. "You don't play fair."

He raises his head to look me in the eye. "Where you're concerned, I'll never play fair."

And when he kisses me, it's with a mixture of reverence and demand that makes my head spin.

29

Cooper

Sunlight streaming through the uncovered window wakes me, and I snuggle closer to Sam. I don't ever want to sleep without him in my arms again. Those three months that he spent in Dayton nearly killed me. Now that he's back, I won't ever give him a reason to leave again.

I carefully extricate from the tangle of our arms and legs and head to the john to empty my bladder. I wash up and brush my teeth, then head back into the bedroom to dress quietly.

He looks so damn young when he's sleeping, it kills me. I'll never understand what he sees in a grizzled old bear like me. But at least he looks well rested, and I know he's well fucked. I must be doing something right.

Once I've got my socks and boots on, I leave sleeping beauty to his well-deserved rest and head to the kitchen to make coffee. Then I'll think about fixing us a hearty breakfast to tide us over through the long morning trek ahead.

On today's agenda is a ten-mile hike through pretty rough terrain. The first couple of miles are easy, but after that, it's an uphill hike for about eight miles to the ranger station in the adjacent state forest. I'll pack some sandwiches for lunch, bottles of water, and nuts for some much-needed protein and fat. It'll do us both good to sweat a little and remember what it's like to work hard.

I make a quick call to Shane on the sat phone to get an update on Roger Stevens.

"There's nothing new to report," he says, sounding less than thrilled.

"Something's off," I say. "Stevens isn't skilled enough to evade both the feds and the local police department for this long. Not if he's still living rough in the woods outside Sweetwater."

"Check in with me after your hike. I'll let you know if I've heard anything new."

"Will do."

The sausage is done, and I'm frying up some eggs and potatoes when my baby staggers out of the bedroom dressed only in a pair of black boxer briefs, looking like he's still half-asleep.

"Good morning, sunshine," I say, reaching for my coffee mug.

He runs his fingers through the long strands of his hair, which came loose in the night, and gazes at me with bleary eyes.

"How many beers did I drink last night?" he says, groaning.

"A few. Sorry. Suck it up, buttercup."

He laughs. "Hey, that's my line."

I nod toward the stool at the breakfast counter. "Have a seat, and I'll pour you some coffee."

Sam drinks his first cup of coffee black, while I finish preparing breakfast. Then I fill two plates with food, grab my second cup of coffee for the morning, and join him at the counter. With him sitting there half naked, I have a hard time concentrating on my food.

We both eat our fill, because we know we have a long day ahead of us. Sam nurses his second cup of coffee as I wash the dishes.

"I'll dry," he says, indicating the dishes sitting in the dish drainer.

"No, you go get dressed. I'll finish up here."

* * *

Twenty minutes later, Sam comes waltzing out of the bedroom, dressed in jeans, his red plaid flannel shirt, and a black leather jacket. His hair is freshly washed and pulled up into a top knot, and he looks raring to go. I'll carry a pack filled with our food and drink for the day. He'll carry his gun pack.

"Looks like we're good to go," I say. After a quick trip to the bathroom to freshen up, we're out the door.

It's still early, not even nine o'clock yet, and we set off with a map, compass, and a GPS device. Besides the handguns, just for precaution, we have our cell phones, even though we probably won't get a signal in the woods.

We hike the easy first two miles to the falls, which border on the state forest, and stop to admire the view. From there, we pick up the trail that leads into the state forest and hike due west, deeper into the woods.

The weather is perfect for a hike—sunny, but cool enough that we're not going to burn up the entire day. I take the lead, and Sam follows behind me, both of us happy to stretch our legs and give our muscles a good work-out. The farther west we go, the rougher the terrain becomes, and we face a steady incline in elevation. It should take us about five hours to reach the ranger station and visitor center, which is our destination. Then it'll be about a four-hour hike back as we'll be going downhill most of the way back.

While we're hiking, I mull over the fact that Sam has a birthday coming up. He'll be twenty-nine in a couple of weeks, and I want to do something special for him. I keep thinking back to when Beth organized a surprise birthday party for Shane at Rowdy's. Shane was really touched by that, and I think Sam would like it too. And he'd like it even more if I arranged everything myself and surprised him. I've never planned a birthday party for anyone before, so I mull over my to-do list in my head. I'll invite the whole McIntyre family, of course, as well as the McIntyre Security employees based in Chicago. I think that pretty much covers all of Sam's friends in the Chicago area. I should also invite his mother and sister.

About halfway to the ranger's station, we stop to drink water and each eat a trail bar for some quick energy. Sam takes off the gun pack and inspects its content.

I take a peek. He brought three Berettas and enough ammo for a small army. "Expecting trouble?" I say, laughing.

He shrugs. "No. But out here, it never hurts to be prepared."

We are pretty isolated out here. We haven't seen another soul all day. Lia and Jonah did have some trouble in Harbor Springs last year when they were staying at the cabin, but that was a separate incident. It has nothing to do with us.

Glancing deeper into the dense woods, I feel a frisson of unease crawl up my spine, and I shake it off. "Let's get going."

We collect our trash and continue on our hike, more than halfway to our destination. Twice on the trail, we hear rustling out in the deep undergrowth. The second time, we're rewarded by the sight of a beautiful doe and her two adolescent fawns from the previous season.

We make it to the ranger station, which is currently closed—probably due to budget cuts—and climb to the top of the look-out tower to gaze out over thousands of acres of pristine forest. We eat our sandwiches up there and munch on more dried fruit and nuts.

Sam finishes his food first, and after disposing of the trash, he steps between my legs and puts his hands on my hips. "Have I thanked you for bringing us up here?"

"Yes, you did. Last night. You're welcome."

"Remind me to thank you again, tonight, naked in front of a roaring fire."

I laugh. "That I will be happy to do."

Having rested and caught our breath, we climb down from the look-out tower and start on our journey back to the cabin. The return trip should be a bit quicker as we'll be going downhill, letting gravity work in our favor. The afternoon is wearing on and this deep in the woods, it's already starting to look like dusk.

Sam takes the lead this time, and we're a little more than halfway back to the cabin when fire tears through my right calf. My leg collapses, and I drop to the ground like a stone, gritting my teeth at what feels like a hot steel blade running through my leg. As I struggle to deal with the burning pain radiating through my leg, I hear the report of gunfire.

"Shooter!" I yell, rather unnecessarily, as I roll to my left side and shake off my backpack.

Sam's at my side a moment later, grabbing me under my arms and dragging me and my pack deep into the dense underbrush, about a dozen yards from the trail. Dropping down beside me in the waning light, he whips off his pack, opens it and pulls out a first-aid kit. He holds a penlight between his teeth and shines it on my leg as he uses a retractable knife to cut away my jeans so he can inspect the wound.

"Through and through," he says, sounding almost relieved. But the relief is short-lived when I start to feel blood streaming down my calf. "Shit. He nicked your fibular artery."

He pulls a roll of gauze dressing out of the first aid kit and wraps it tightly around the source of the fire in my calf. Then he applies a pressure bandage over top, holding the gauze in place. "The bleeding is manageable. This should keep you stabilized until we can get you to the hospital."

Reaching into his pack, Sam pulls out one of the Berettas, shoves in a magazine, then hands the gun to me, along with a spare magazine. Then he helps himself to the other two guns, loading them both quickly. One of them he tucks into the back of his waistband. The other one he lays at his feet. Then he shoves two spare magazines into his jacket pocket.

"Stay here and stay down," he says in a clipped, low voice. "If you hear anyone sneaking up on you, shoot to kill. Do you hear me? Do not engage. Do not hesitate. You shoot." Then he grabs armfuls of leaves and small branches and drags them toward me, using the foliage to cover me, providing camouflage. He reaches down and squeezes my shoulder. "Hang in there, babe," he says. "I'll take care of this asshole, and then I'll get you back to the cabin. Just lie still for now. Try not to move."

And just like that, he's gone.

Jesus, Sam.

My heart is in my throat, my pulse pounding. My leg is on fire, and the pain is searing. Shock must be setting in, because I feel cold all over, even as I'm starting to sweat and shake.

Feeling increasingly dizzy, I lay my head back on the ground and stare up at the late-afternoon sky, which is barely visible through the dense branches. It'll be dark in the woods in another hour, and I have no idea where Sam is, or what he's facing out there. Was this a hunting accident? Or was it something more nefarious? Sam's going into this blind, with no idea who's out there. And I have no way to help him.

My worst fears are realized when I hear the crack of a rifle shot split the air, followed by several pops from a Beretta in rapid succession. This was no accident. Sam's involved in a live gun fight, and I can't help him. I've never felt so fucking helpless in my life. He's out there, fighting my fight, risking his life for me.

My vision starts to darken around the edges, and I shake myself mentally, trying to stay conscious. I don't know how much blood I've lost, or how bad the injury is. And it's going to be dark soon, making it so much more dangerous for Sam to be out there with an active shooter.

As the sun drops, so does the temperature. The ground below me feels cold and damp, and I'm not sure how much of that wetness is my blood. If I bleed out here, I won't make it back to the cabin. Thank God he didn't hit my femoral artery, or I'd probably already be dead. At least with the fibular artery, I have a chance. And while I don't care about myself so much, I can't bear the thought of what Sam would go through if I bit it out here. I just can't do that to him.

I hear another crack of the rifle, way off in the distance, followed by the report of the Beretta. It sounds like Sam is running him to ground. "Jesus, baby, be careful."

♁ 30

Sam

As I work my way back toward the path and in the direction of the shooter, I'm reminded of my days in the Rangers when I trained endlessly for this kind of guerilla combat. And here I am, right back in the thick of it. Only this time, Cooper's life is on the line. I don't have much time. I need to neutralize this shooter quickly so I can get Cooper the help he needs. I have no illusions that he can survive for long out here in the cold, damp forest. Even with the pressure bandage, he's still bleeding pretty badly, and he's likely already in shock.

Keeping low to the ground, using the natural ground cover for camouflage, I make my way back to the path. I wait patiently for an indication of where the shooter is located, but I hear nothing. And as I don't have time to wait for him to make a move, I have to force the issue.

It's hard to believe he made it this far north, but my gut tells me we've located Roger Stevens. He must have seen us leave the apartment building and followed us to Harbor Springs.

"Show yourself, Stevens! Come out in the open and face me like a man, instead of hiding like a coward!"

The sound of a rifle shot coming from my right helps me pinpoint his general direction. I want to move the fight to him, to push him farther from Cooper's location.

Leaving my cover behind, I dart across the open path, risking exposure, and am met with two more rifle shots in rapid succession. He's not far from me, and he must have decent visibility. The shots sounded like they were coming from ahead and to my right. Using the undergrowth as cover, I make my way in his direction, hoping I can push him back a bit and eventually pin him down. Whatever I do, I have to do it quickly, as time is working against me. Cooper needs help fast.

"Is he dead?" Stevens calls out. "I know I hit him. I saw him go down."

I refuse to answer, instead using the sound of his voice to narrow down his general location. I keep moving in his direction, keeping low to the ground and moving as silently as possible. When I pause to get my bearings, I peer out from behind a tree trunk, and a rifle shot hits the trunk, splintering the bark off the tree several feet above my head.

"You're a fucking coward, Roger!" I yell. "Ambushing us in the woods, instead of facing us head on. That's what a coward would do. You're a coward now, just like you were forty years ago when you threw two teenage boys off a bridge to their deaths!"

"Shut up, you pervert! You're no better than Cooper! After I take you out, I'll find Cooper and finish him off, if he isn't dead already!"

I'm running out of time, so I step out into the open again, taking a chance as I attempt to draw him out. I'm close enough now to Roger that I can hit him at this distance with my nine millimeter if I can get a clear line of sight on him.

Just as he steps out from behind a tree, lifting his rifle in my direction, I shoot him square in the chest, sending him flying back onto the ground. Cautiously, I make my way forward, pretty sure he's dead, but not taking any chances. If I screw up there, Cooper's a dead man.

I quickly locate Roger Stevens' body, and sure enough, with a slug right to his heart, he's dead. I check his pulse, just to be certain, then quickly cover his body with branches and leaves. After cutting off a strip of my red plaid shirt, I tie it around the trunk of a sapling just a couple feet from the body so that the authorities will be able to locate it later.

* * *

"It's all right, babe—it's me," I say loudly as I stomp through the undergrowth on my way back to Cooper, making plenty of noise to alert him to my presence. It wouldn't do for him to shoot me now by mistake. "He's dead, Cooper. Roger Stevens is dead."

"Sam."

I drop down beside Cooper and retrieve the penlight so I can shine it in his face. "Yeah, it's me, babe. Damn, you're pale." I press two fingers to his carotid artery to check his pulse, which is slow and thready. He's in shock. Not a surprise. "Come on. Let's get you out of here."

Cooper grabs weakly at my arm. "Sam, just go. Get back to the cabin. Radio the sheriff. I'll be okay." He's shaking so hard, his words are barely legible.

"Fuck no, I'm not leaving you here! Are you insane?"

I brush the leaves and twigs covering Cooper aside so I can examine his wound with my light. "That fucker followed us here from Chicago. So much for the reports of him roughing it back in Sweetwater."

"He's dead?"

"Extremely."

I can sense the tension leaving Cooper's body at my declaration.

"Sam, you've got to leave me here," he says. "Go back to the cabin—"

"Shut up, Cooper." I relieve him of the Beretta I'd left with him and put it and one of my two guns back into the pack. I still have the one tucked into the back of my waistband...just in case Stevens wasn't out here alone. "All right. Let's go. We'll have to leave your pack here."

I rise to my feet and lift Cooper up and over my shoulder into a fireman's carry.

"You can't carry me all the way back to the cabin," he says, gritting his teeth against the jarring agony.

I scoff. "Hell, I carried guys bigger than you much farther distances back in my Army days."

Cooper bites back a cry with each agonizing step, and I feel awful for causing him more pain. But we have at least two miles of rough, downhill terrain to go. The fact that it's getting dark now just makes the job that much more difficult.

Whenever I stumble, coming into contact with a half-buried root or a stone, I quickly right myself, but not before causing Cooper more pain. "Shit, I'm sorry, babe," I say.

Every step I take pains him, and it kills me to add to his suffering. The trail is littered with fallen branches and roots and stones, making it difficult for me not to jostle him.

I'm grateful when I realize he's finally passed out.

I trudge ahead at a steady pace, using the penlight stuck between my teeth to light the way. I'm glad when we reach the falls, because that means we're just a couple miles from the cabin now, and the path is easier. I carry him over the bridge, then pick up the trail once more, heading for the cabin.

When we arrive back at the cabin, it's dark. I carry him inside and lay him down on the bed in the back room. Then I grab the sat phone and call 911 to request emergency medical evacuation. The dispatcher calls for paramedics and Sheriff Mitchell. Then I hang up so I can call Shane.

"Hi, Sam. How's it going?" he says.

"Not good. Cooper's been shot. Roger Stevens ambushed us in the woods."

"How bad is it?" Shane says, his voice now sharp and clipped.

"He's lost a lot of blood, and he's in shock. Medical evac is on the way. They'll transport him to the hospital in Stowe."

"What about Stevens?"

"Dead."

"I'll be there as quickly as I can, via helicopter. I'll meet you at the hospital."

Next, I hear the ping of the penthouse elevator doors, followed by the sound of muffled crying. I feel like an eavesdropper when I hear him say, "Sweetheart, no," in a gentle voice. "Stay here. Lia's on her way up. She'll stay with you until I get back."

Then I hear more crying.

"I know, honey," Shane says. "But you can't come with me. Cooper's going to be okay, I promise. Sam knows what he's doing. Please don't worry."

Shane returns to the line with me. "The helicopter's being prepped now. I'll be in the air within a half hour. I'll meet you at the hospital."

"All right. I'll see you there."

As I hang up with Shane, I hear a siren in the distance, alerting me to the arrival of Sheriff Mitchell. I leave Cooper just long enough to unlock the door and let him in.

"James Mitchell, sheriff," the man says as he comes inside. "Where is he?"

"Back bedroom."

The sheriff follows me to the bedroom and heads right for the bed. "How long has he been out?" he says.

"A little over two hours."

Mitchell turns to me. "What happened. Who shot him?"

"It's a long story, but I can tell you that the shooter is dead. I shot him myself."

"Do you know where the body is?"

I nod. "I can direct you to it—I marked the location—but he'll be impossible to find in the dark. You'll have to wait until morning. He's deep in the forest, and I covered his body with brush. But I left a clear marker."

Mitchell removes his hat and scratches his short blond hair. "I'll give it to you McIntyre Security folks. There's never a shortage of excitement when you guys come to town."

The emergency squad arrives just minutes later, and the paramedics perform a quick assessment of Cooper's condition, checking his wounds and his blood pressure, which is dangerously low.

"He lost a lot of blood immediately after he was shot," I say. "I managed to get a pressure bandage on him pretty quickly, though."

After getting his vitals and calling them in to the hospital's ER, the paramedics set up an IV, then transfer Cooper to a stretcher to take him out to the ambulance. I follow, locking up the cabin as I leave, taking only our wallets and phones.

"Where are you taking him?" I say, sticking close to the stretcher as they load him into the ambulance. Wherever they're going, I'm going too.

Sheriff Mitchell pats me on the back. "The nearest hospital is twenty minutes away, in Stowe. You can ride with him in the ambulance, and I'll follow in my squad car."

When we arrive at the hospital, Cooper is wheeled directly to the emergency room and immediately taken back for assessment. I stop at the registration desk just long enough to give the receptionist some basic information. I fill out his intake form and give them information about our health insurance.

"Who's his next-of-kin?" the woman asks.

I feel a moment of sheer panic, realizing they might keep me away from him as I have no legal claim on him. Technically—legally—I'm nothing to him. I don't even give it a second thought. "I am."

"What's your name?"

"Sam Harrison."

"And what's your relationship to Mr. Cooper?"

"I'm his husband." And even though it's a blatant lie, I didn't hesitate for a second. My throat tightens, and I feel tears forming. It shocks me how much I want it to be true.

The woman's eyes widen just a tad, and she gives me a sympathetic smile as she makes a notation on a paper attached to a clipboard and hands it to me. "Can you sign this, authorizing us to treat him?"

When I hand the signed authorization form back to her, she says, "Don't worry, Mr. Harrison. We'll take good care of your husband."

* * *

I head into the ER treatment area, desperate to find Cooper. When I finally locate him, he's lying in a hospital bed, deathly pale and still unconscious. They've already cut away his jeans and removed my make-shift field dressing.

An African-American woman is examining the entry and exit wounds. When she sees me, she glances up and smiles. "I'm Dr. Steadman. I'll be treating Mr. Cooper."

A nurse—*Amanda* according to her name tag—is taking Cooper's vitals, while someone else changes out his IV bag.

As I stand there watching them work, my heart pounds, and I feel light-headed. The doctor peppers me with questions about Cooper's general health history as she inspects the holes in his leg.

"The artery has stopped bleeding," she says to the nurse. "Let's get these wounds cleaned, and then we'll suture them."

Dr. Steadman removes her gloves, then offers me her hand to shake. "And you are?"

"Sam Harrison," I say. "I'm his husband."

She nods at me. "We'll take good care of him Mr. Harrison. No worries."

"Thank you."

Dr. Stedman leaves, and Amanda, the nurse, directs me to sit down in one of the two guest chairs in the room. Stress and crashing adrenalin are catching up to me, fast, and I feel like I could keel over at any minute. I drag a chair to the side of his bed and take a seat.

"When was the last time you ate something?" the nurse says, smiling sympathetically.

I shrug. "I had a trail bar this morning and a sandwich."

She shakes her head. "I think you should eat something before you pass out, too."

At that moment, Shane walks into the small, curtained-off room, his gaze quickly assessing Cooper, then me. Dressed in a suit and wearing a scowl, he looks intimidating as hell. I give him a quick run-down on Cooper's status.

"You don't look so hot yourself," Shane says, eyeing me. "When was the last time you ate something?"

"Why does everyone keep asking me that?"

Shane levels a glare at me. "Because you look nearly as bad as he does," he says, nodding toward Cooper. "Sam, go get something to eat. I'll stay with Cooper."

I shake my head. "I'm fine. I'm not—"

"I'm not *asking* you, Sam," he says, slipping into what Beth calls his bossy CEO mode tone. "I'm telling you. You can't help Cooper if you end up hospitalized for exhaustion. Go eat something. Now. That's an order. I'll stay with him."

I know Shane's right, but I hate leaving Cooper. I want to be there when he wakes up. I take the elevator down to the cafeteria and grab a sandwich and a cup of coffee, inhaling both and burning my tongue in the process. Then I'm back upstairs, all in under twenty minutes. Shane gives me a look when I rush back into the room.

"Is he still out?" I say.

"Yes." Shane rises from the chair beside the bed. "Here, sit down, before you fall down."

I take the chair Shane vacated and reach for Cooper's free hand. His right arm is immobilized now by an IV drip and secured to the bed. "What are they giving him?" I say, eyeing the bag of clear fluid hanging from an IV stand.

"It's saline," Shane says. "He's dehydrated. Plus, they're giving him an antibiotic and some pain medication. The wounds were pretty dirty. They're mostly worried about infection."

I watch the nurse as she continues cleaning the wound. I guess it's a good thing Cooper's still out cold, as I'm sure it would hurt like hell to have someone cleaning the entry and exit holes.

Just as the nurse finishes applying a fresh dressing, Cooper groans. I shoot to my feet and lean over him. When he does open his eyes, his gaze is unfocused, and he starts to struggle.

"Whoa, babe," I say, holding him down. "You're okay. You're in the hospital. Just relax."

"Sam?" His voice is as scratchy and dry as sandpaper.

"Yeah, it's me. Shane's here too."

Shane moves to the foot of the bed so he has a clear line of sight to Cooper. "Hey, buddy. Welcome back. You took a pretty long nap. I was getting worried."

Cooper looks at me, then at Shane, his brow furrowed. "What happened?" he says.

"Do you remember being shot while we were hiking? Roger Stevens ambushed us on the trail."

Cooper's color is rapidly coming back. He's no longer sickly pale, but rather looking a bit flushed now. I lay my hand on his forehead and glance back at Shane. "He feels hot."

Cooper shifts his position in bed and groans. "Damn, my leg hurts."

"You've been shot, babe. What did you expect?"

"I'll get a nurse," Shane says, walking out of the room.

31

Cooper

My lower right leg hurts like a bitch, and my head is pounding so hard it's hard to concentrate on anything else. The room spins, making me nauseous, as everything comes rushing back. *Hiking with Sam. My leg collapsing. Searing pain. The crack of a rifle shot. Sam dragging me into the trees.*

I glance up at Sam, who's hovering over me, worry etched all over his beautiful face. "What's wrong, Sam?" I say, reaching up to touch his face. "Oh, man, you're so beautiful."

He grins at me. "That morphine is some pretty good stuff, isn't it?"

I try to hug him, wanting to assure myself he's all right, but wince in pain when my right arm doesn't move as it should.

Sam presses my arm to the bed. "Whoa, careful. Watch the IV."

I frown as I try to think clearly. "That asshole shot me? Really?"

He laughs. "Yeah, really."

I look Sam over as best I can for any injuries. I have vague memories of him holding a gun in the darkness. "Are you hurt?"

"No, I'm fine. Don't worry about me."

A nurse appears suddenly beside my bed. "Hello, Mr. Cooper. Glad you could join us." She pulls some wand thing out of her pocket and swipes it across my forehead. Then she checks my pupils. "How are you feeling?" she says.

"I've been better."

She glances at Sam. "A slight fever, but that's not surprising. We'll keep an eye on it." Then she looks at me. "Mr. Cooper, can you tell me what day it is?"

I have to think for a minute. "We went hiking on Saturday. Is it still Saturday? I'm not sure."

She seems satisfied with my answer. "And can you tell me what year it is?" she says.

"Twenty-eighteen. You know, it's my leg that's injured, not my brain."

She chuckles. "I'm glad to hear it."

The nurse steps back to fiddle with the IV stand, and I notice Shane standing at the foot of my bed, frowning.

"When did you get here?" I ask him.

"About an hour ago."

"Where's Beth?"

"At home."

"You left her alone?"

"No, of course not. Lia's with her."

I shake my head. "She's probably worried sick." Her father was shot and killed on the job when she was just an infant. Now I'm the closest thing she has to a father. We practically adopted each other.

"Yes, she is," Shane says. "So get well quickly and come home."

The nurse checks the dressing on my leg. "Looking good," she says. Then she addresses Sam as if I'm not even here. "Dr. Steadman will be in shortly to suture the wounds. Then he'll be good as new."

"Hey, what about me?" I say. "I'm the patient."

The nurse pats my arm. "Don't worry, Mr. Cooper. Your husband is making sure we take good care of you."

My husband?

I glance at Sam, who gives me a wicked grin.

"Is there something I should know?" I ask him, after the nurse leaves.

He leans over to kiss me. "Yeah, we're married."

At the confused look on my face, he laughs. "I was afraid they wouldn't let me come back with you, so I told them I was your next-of-kin. Your husband, actually."

"Works for me," I say, trying to play it off as a joke. In reality, I'm desperately trying to ignore the rush it gives me. I would marry Sam in a heartbeat if I thought he was ready for a commitment like that. But he's so young—just twenty-eight. Actually, soon to be twenty-nine, as he has a birthday coming up in less than a week. I'm a lot older; I know exactly what I want, and that's to have Sam in my life. Forever.

* * *

Dr. Steadman returns a little later to suture my leg. After sticking some needles in my leg to numb it—ouch!—she gets busy with her needle and thread, patching up the holes in my body. Even with the local anesthetic, I can still feel the tug and pull of the needle and thread going through my flesh. Sam sits beside me, holding my left hand, wincing right along with me.

Shane walks back into the room. "Jake has collected all of your personal belongings from the cabin," he says, eyeing the doctor's sewing technique. "After we leave on the chopper, he'll drive the Jeep back to Chicago."

I nod, gritting my teeth. "Sounds good."

32

Sam

The next afternoon, Cooper is prescribed some oral antibiotics and pain killers, and is finally discharged from the hospital with instructions to follow up with his own physician. An orderly wheels him to the main entrance, and I help him walk to the waiting Jeep.

Sheriff Mitchell is there to see us off. "It's good to see you," he says, shaking hands with Shane. "Maybe not under these circumstances, though. How's your wife?"

Shane grins. "She's fine. We're expecting this summer."

Mitchell's eyes widen. "Wow, you're going to be a father. Congratulations, man." Then the sheriff shifts his attention to me and

Cooper. "Stevens' body has been recovered and will be transferred to Sweetwater."

The sheriff shakes my hand and then Cooper's. "I'm glad you two are all right." Then he looks at me. "You did well out there, Sam."

I laugh off his praise, patting Cooper's back. "Someone's gotta have this guy's back."

Cooper and I sit in the back of the Jeep, with Shane up front. Jake drives us to the small regional airport where the company helicopter and pilot are on stand-by.

It's a quick flight back to the helipad on the roof of the McIntyre Security building downtown. Cooper refuses crutches or a wheel-chair, so it's slow going to the elevator that will take us down to the underground parking garage, where Shane has a car and driver waiting to take us home.

When we arrive at the penthouse, Beth, Lia, and Jonah are waiting for us in the foyer. Beth is in tears when she sees Cooper limp out of the elevator, grimacing with each step. After being on his feet, even for a few minutes, he's white as a sheet, his expression pinched and drawn.

Beth walks into Cooper's arms and loosely wraps her arms around his waist. "Don't scare me like that," she says.

Cooper rubs her back. "I'm sorry, kiddo. I'll try not to get shot again."

She laughs around her tears. "It's not funny." Then her expression falls. "My dad was shot," she says, in an agonized voice. *And killed.* That part she doesn't say aloud. Her father, a Chicago police officer, was killed in the line of duty when she was just an infant. Cooper is, more or less, her adopted father. "I love you," she says, her voice little more than a whisper. "I can't lose you."

"I'm sorry, darlin'. Please don't worry about me. I'm far too ornery to die."

"You can say that again," I add, trying to lighten the mood. "Now let's get you to bed. You need to rest before you fall on your face."

* * *

It's a long, slow shuffle from the foyer to our suite. Cooper moves painfully slowly, gritting his teeth with every step. Shane offers to get him crutches or a wheelchair, but he insists on walking on his own power. The least he'll do is throw his arm across my shoulder and let me help support his weight.

"I could carry you, ya know," I say. "I've done it before."

"Don't you dare," he says, half laughing and half groaning. "I'll never live it down."

I can't help thinking back to November when I spent the better part of a week in the hospital, healing from a head injury and a broken leg. Cooper stayed by my side at the hospital, never leaving me. He was there all through my disorientation, through the seizures, through all the God-awful pain. He even brought me back here to the penthouse so he could nurse me back to health. "I guess the tables have turned, haven't they? Now it's my turn to take care of you."

"Yeah, but don't get any funny ideas, pal. I can still kick your ass."

I grin as I lean over to kiss him. "Hey, I'm the one who carried your heavy ass nearly four miles through rough terrain. I think I can take you."

We finally hobble our way down the hallway to our suite, and I push the door open. Inside, there's a huge vase of fresh-cut flowers with a single helium balloon attached. The balloon says *Get Well*.

I walk Cooper over to the bed and sit him down. Then I retrieve the card tucked inside the vase of flowers and hand it to him.

"Let me guess," I say. "Beth?"

He nods. "She says, 'Please don't get shot ever again. Love, Beth.' And there's a smiley face and a little heart with curlicues, too."

I sit carefully on the bed beside him. "I should check your bandages. Make sure all that walking didn't start you bleeding again."

He grunts noncommittally. "I was hoping you'd forget."

"Ha, no chance." I like playing nurse for him. I like the idea of taking care of him, seeing to his needs, helping him hobble to the bathroom so he can take care of business.

"Here, lie back," I tell him, pressing on his shoulders. His jeans were cut off right above the bullet wound, so I have easy access to the area. I remove his bandages and examine the sutures, looking for fresh bleeding or signs of inflammation. "Everything looks good. There's a little bit of seepage, but it's not blood, and your skin around the sutures is a bit pink, but I guess that's to be expected. I think you're okay."

"What I really need is a shower," he grumbles, after I apply a fresh dressing.

"No, you don't," I say, laughing. "Besides, you can't shower with the dressing on your leg. You're not supposed to get it wet. How about I give you a sponge bath in bed? That would be fun."

He scowls at me. "Oh, hell no. I'm not a feeble old man, you know."

I wink at him. "Come on. It'll be fun. I'll pay extra attention to your dick—make sure it's feeling the love."

He gives me a genuine smile, the first one I've seen from him all day. "You ass."

In the end, we compromise, deciding on a sponge bath in the bathtub. I help Cooper walk to the bathroom, and he climbs into the tub and sits on the built-in seat with his bandaged leg propped up on the side of the tub, out of the water. I soap him up while he rinses himself off with a hand-held sprayer. We can't quite manage to keep his dressing completely dry, but all in all, we do a pretty decent job of it.

By the time I get him back to bed, with his leg propped up on a pillow, there's a quiet knock on the door.

"Come in," Cooper calls, sounding resigned to receiving more attention than he's comfortable with.

Beth opens the door and sticks her head through the opening. "Peter Capelli is sending over dinner tonight. It should be here in about an hour. He sends his regards and says he's glad you're okay."

"Good," Cooper says. "I'm starved."

She steps halfway into the room, eyeing both of us warily, as if she's checking to make sure we're both fully dressed. "Do you guys mind if I come in?"

"Of course not, honey," Cooper says, holding out his hand to her.

She comes to him, and he pulls her onto the bed beside him.

She sits gingerly on the side of the bed, taking care not to jostle him. "I don't want to intrude."

"You're not intruding," I tell her. "Cooper just had a sponge bath, and now he's going to lie here and rest. You can keep him company."

Cooper gives me a dirty look, as Beth smothers a laugh.

Lia and Jonah walk into the room. "Who had a sponge bath?" Lia says.

"Cooper did," Beth says.

Lia comes to stand at the foot of the bed. "How ya doing, pops? I heard you had some drama up at the cabin."

Jonah offers his hand to Cooper for a shake. "I'm glad to see you're all right."

"Thanks, Jonah," he says, pointedly ignoring Lia's taunt. "Yeah, we had a little drama, but Sam took care of it."

"Way to go, red!" Lia says, offering me a fist bump.

I lean against the dresser, enjoying the family banter. Thinking back to Cooper's upbringing and the lack of support he received from his parents, I'm grateful that he has this family, who support him and love him unconditionally. And I'm grateful to be included now as well.

Shane walks into the room. "Molly and Jamie are on their way, and the food will be here soon. Why don't we take this party into the great room? I think we can make Cooper comfortable on the sofa. If you feel up to it?"

"Sure," Cooper says, sitting up in bed. "It beats lying in bed like an invalid."

I lend Cooper my shoulder again and help bear some of his weight as he shuffles toward the great room. Beth brings pillows and a blanket and makes a cozy bed for him on the sofa.

The elevator pings, and a moment later Molly and Jamie, along with Jake, walk through the foyer doors. Molly holds Jamie's hand, effortlessly guiding him to the sofa.

"Oh, my God, I'm so glad you're all right," Molly says, hugging Cooper.

Jamie sits on the coffee table in front of Cooper and shakes Cooper's hand. "Jake said this guy followed you from Sweetwater to Chicago to Harbor Springs? He was one of the guys you went to Sweetwater to confront?"

"He was. He's dead now. All three of them are dead. I'm not going to lose any sleep over that since they killed an innocent young boy."

Jake offers Cooper a bottle of beer. "Can you drink?"

"Hell, yes, I can," Cooper says, reaching for the bottle. "They gave me some prescription painkillers, but I'll pass on those. I'll make do with over-the-counter stuff."

The food arrives shortly, accompanied by two uniformed caterers and Beth's friend, Gabrielle, to supervise. The food—Italian Wedding Soup, salad, beef Bolognese, garlic bread, and a Lemon Mascarpone cake for dessert—is served at the big dining room table, but I make up plates for Cooper and myself, and I sit on the coffee table across from him while he eats in his makeshift bed.

"You holding up okay?" I ask him, when I notice him fidgeting and wincing occasionally.

"I'm hanging in there. The leg's a little sore."

"A *little* sore?" I laugh. "Dude, you were shot. I know—from personal experience—that hurts like hell. Do you want to go back to bed?"

"No. I'm all right out here for a while. It's nice being with everyone."

A burst of laughter from the dining room table catches our attention, and we glance over at the rest of the crowd. Jake is regaling everyone with the story of how I jumped off the Sweetwater River Bridge in practically my birthday suit.

"Oh, my God!" Lia says. "Please tell me you got that on video! It needs to go on Instagram."

"No, it does not!" Cooper yells across the room, eliciting more laughter.

"No, sorry," Jake says, laughing. "We didn't get any video. But maybe you can sweet talk Sam into recreating the event. He can always jump naked into the Chicago River."

"Oh, hell no!" Cooper says. "He's not jumping naked off any more bridges. My poor heart can't take it."

"Don't worry, babe," I say, patting his good leg. "I won't put you through that again."

Jake continues entertaining his rapt audience. "So, Sam finally climbs out of the water and up to the bridge, his balls frozen solid, and—just to add insult to injury—the deputy gives him a hundred dollar fine. And that's when we notice this sign posted on the bridge: NO JUMPING."

More laughter, all at my expense, of course.

When Cooper's finished with his meal, I take his plate and mine to the kitchen, then return to the sofa. He looks flushed, so I feel his forehead to make sure he's not got a fever. He feels cool to the touch. I just think he's exhausted. He's due for his medication, so I bring him his pills along with a glass of water.

He's starting to look a bit wan again. "Do you need anything?" I ask him.

"Just you."

He sounds tired. I stand and hold out my hand. "I think you should go back to bed now. Enough socializing for today, all right?"

He nods, almost reluctantly. "That's probably a good idea."

"Hey, guys, carry on without us," I say. "It's been a long day, and Cooper's tired. We're going to call it a night."

The girls come over to hug him and say goodnight. Beth, Molly, and Lia. Shane comes over to lay his hand on Cooper's shoulder. The two men eye each other solemnly.

"Yeah, don't make a fuss," Cooper finally says, blushing. "It's just a flesh wound."

It's obvious by Shane's expression that he's not amused. "Fuss? If that bullet had struck a foot higher, you would have bled out then and there. So, yeah, pardon me if I fuss a bit."

With teary eyes, Beth slips her arm around Shane's waist, and he puts his arm around her, drawing her close.

"Yeah, all right, I'm sorry," Cooper says. "I shouldn't make light of it."

The last thing I want to think about right now is what might have happened. What could have gone so horribly wrong out there in the woods. "Okay, that's enough what-iffing. The fact is, Cooper's alive and well, as ornery as usual, and we're going to make sure he stays that way. For now, I'm going to put his ass in bed."

Everyone laughs, as was my intention, as I walk Cooper out of the room and down the hallway to our suite. Once we're inside our room, I help him walk to the bathroom.

"I can take it from here," he says, limping into the room.

He's obviously in a lot of pain, and he's practically swaying on his feet from exhaustion. When he stumbles and nearly falls, just barely managing to catch himself on the bathroom counter, I step in, putting my arm around his waist. "Here, let me help you."

"I can handle it myself," he growls at me, giving me a glare that matches his mood.

I'm not surprised, or offended, by his belligerent tone. I get it. He's a tough guy—he doesn't take well to playing the invalid. But right now, whether he likes it or not, he is an invalid, and I'm the one who's going to take care of his grouchy ass—whether he likes it or not.

"No, you can't," I say, trying to tamp down my own frustration. "You need help—you need *my* help—unless you want me to call Shane or Jake in here."

His eyes narrow. "You wouldn't dare."

It's all I can do to keep a straight face, and I'm pretty sure laughing right now wouldn't help the situation. "Then shut up and let me help you."

He grits his teeth and hisses at me. "I don't need any help, damn it!"

I give him my best *oh, yeah* face. "Are we gonna fight about this?"

He scowls, his pale brow furrowing.

Oh, yeah, we're gonna fight. I sweep him up into my arms and carry him to the john, setting him down outside the door to the private toilet room. There's a hand rail in there, so I'm pretty sure he can manage by himself from here. "Don't be such a drama queen. I'm not going to let you fall on your ass just because you're stubborn."

He exhales heavily, his shoulder hunching. "I'm not good at this."

I think that's as close to an apology as I'm going to get. "It's okay. I am."

He chuffs. "Smart ass."

I help him by unsnapping his jeans, lowering the zipper and tugging the denim and his briefs down to his thighs.

"Okay, I got it," he says, hobbling toward the toilet.

I close the door partway to give him some privacy and brush my teeth at the sink while he takes a piss. Then I tidy up my top knot and strip down to my black boxer briefs and lean against the bathroom counter, waiting.

I hear a noise, then a thump, then a moan from the toilet area. Then, finally, a voice. "Sam?"

He sounds... defeated. When I pop my head through the open doorway, I see him leaning against the wall, holding himself upright using the hand rail. His briefs are halfway up his ass, his jeans down around his knees. He's a hot mess. "Yes?"

He peers up at me with pained eyes. "I need your help."

I refrain from saying I told you so, and instead I pull up his briefs and help him step out of his jeans. Then I pull his arm across my shoulder and wrap an arm around his waist and help him to the sink to wash up and brush his teeth. He looks like he's ready to keel over any second.

Once he's done, I lift him in my arms and carry him to bed.

"Thanks," he mumbles as I arrange the bedding over him.

"No need to thank me, babe."

After turning off the lights, I crawl in bed beside him, facing him, and lay my arm across his abdomen. "I'm glad we're home. In our own bed."

He lays his arm over mine and threads our fingers together. "Yeah. Me too. Thank you—" he starts to say.

"No. There's no need to thank me."

"But you risked your life for me, going after Stevens like that."

"Nobody messes with my guy."

"You probably saved my life."

"Oh, bullshit. Don't be so melodramatic." I lay my head on his shoulder and tighten my hold on him.

Shane was right, though, when he said that bullet came close—within a foot—of killing him. I shudder at the thought.

"Hey," he says, rubbing the back of my hand. "I'm not that easy to kill, you know. I faced a lot worse in the Marines."

I lift myself up and kiss a line along his jaw, then over to his mouth. It's just a gentle kiss, nothing sexual.

When I settle back down beside him, he puts him arm around me.

"Somebody has a birthday coming up in a couple of weeks," he says. "What do you want for your birthday?"

"Yeah, St. Patrick's Day. How about some green beer?"

He laughs. "What else?"

I lean closer and place a kiss over his heart. "You. I just want you."

He turns toward me and kisses me, giving me a long, lingering kiss that offers a bit more heat than I expected this soon. "I'm already yours, Sam. I've been yours for a long time."

When he continues kissing me, a shiver runs down my spinal

cord, lighting up my nerve endings and giving me the beginnings of an inconvenient and ill-timed erection. "Now you're not playing fair," I say against his lips. "You can't get me all hot and bothered when you're out of commission for the time being."

He laughs. "Who said love is fair?"

Two Weeks Later

Sam

E rin walks into Beth's office dressed in a Kelly-green skirt, white blouse, and big shamrock earrings. "Happy St. Patrick's Day!" she says.

I shake my head, grinning. "You look absolutely adorable."

She looks defensive. "Hey, I don't want anyone pinching me today."

Of course, I guess I shouldn't talk. I have my *Luck of the Irish* T-shirt on, also Kelly green. After all, it's St. Patrick's Day—also my twenty-ninth birthday. Beth and Erin took me out for lunch today to celebrate my birthday, and we're all still reeling from a few too many calories. Beth's office looks like a halfway house for birthday balloons—they're floating all through the room, attached to every flat surface available.

Erin hands Beth a sheet of paper. "Here are the May orders for the book clubs."

Beth skims the sheet. "Ooh, a new Kresley Cole is coming out? Order an extra copy for me, please." Beth hands the sheet back to Erin, who makes a notation on it. "Looks good to me."

"And accounting has completed the February profit-and-loss statement. Our profits were up twelve percent in February over the same month last year."

"Wow," Beth says, genuinely impressed. "Looks like your Valentine's Day specials really paid off. Good job."

Erin shrugs. "Oh, it was nothing."

Beth leans back in her desk chair, one hand absently stroking her growing baby bump. "I told you, you're a natural at this. You'll do fine—"

"No, don't say it!" Erin covers her ears. "You'll jinx me."

I laugh. "Erin, you'll be a great interim manager when Beth goes on maternity leave. Now, stop worrying, or I'll tell Mack to spank you."

"Oh, my God, you wouldn't!" she says, her face turning several shades of pink. Her blue eyes widen. "I mean—oh, my God, he wouldn't, would he? I mean, that's a joke, right?" Then she looks pleadingly at Beth. "He's joking, right?"

"Shall we try it and find out?" I say.

Erin looks utterly appalled.

Beth tries not to laugh as she sends me a mock glare. "Stop teasing her, Sam."

I shrug and prop my boots up on the coffee table in front of my sofa. "Who knows, she might like it. There's only way one to find out."

Beth wads up a piece of paper and lobs it at my head. "Samuel Harrison, you stop right this minute before you give Erin a heart attack."

Beth looks at the clock. "Oh, I forgot to mention I have to leave a little early today." She smiles. "I have a date tonight with my hubby. We're going out for St. Patrick's Day."

"I have to leave early, too," Erin says. "I'm going out tonight with my roommates."

"That works out well for me too," I say. "I have a date tonight. Cooper's taking me out to dinner for my birthday."

"The big twenty-nine," Beth says. "Enjoy it while you can. Next year, you'll join the ranks of the thirty-year-olds."

Mack pokes his head through the open door. "We need a manager downstairs to deal with a customer complaint."

Erin sighs. "Oh, I'll take care of it." As she walks past Mack, she gives him a wide berth, eyeing him warily.

"What was that all about?" Mack says, watching Erin as she walks away.

Beth points a finger at me. "Sam threatened Erin that you'd spank her. Never mind, it's a long story. But she was a little worried about it."

Mack levels me with his gaze. "Really, Sam?"

"You should have seen how she blushed. Honestly, I think she was intrigued by the idea."

"Do not antagonize her," Mack says. "I mean it."

I grin. "Oooh, Mack to the rescue."

"We're leaving early tonight," Beth says to Mack. "All of us—Sam, Erin, and I—we all have plans tonight."

"Good, because I have plans tonight, too." Mack points to his T-shirt. "Luck o' the Irish, green beer, and all that. I'm meeting some guys at the pub tonight. I'll take off right after you guys do."

* * *

Beth and I head out at four-thirty, catching a taxi home.

"What time is your date tonight?" she asks me as we ride up in the elevator.

I'm trying not to grin like a fool, but it's hard. This is the second time Cooper has taken me out on an official date, and I'm excited. "Six o'clock."

Beth nudges me with her elbow. "I'm sure you'll have a lot of fun."

Shane's waiting for Beth as we step out of the elevator. "Let's go, sweetheart," he says to her, checking his Rolex. "We don't want to be late for our reservation."

"Just give me five minutes to freshen up," she says, rushing down the hall to their suite.

Then he looks at me. "So, Cooper tells me you guys have plans tonight, too."

"Yeah. He's taking me out for my birthday."

Shane gives me an approving nod. "Things seem to be going well for you two."

I smile. "I think he's starting to get used to this boyfriend-slash-dating thing."

Beth comes rushing back, breathless, as she slips on her sandals. She changed her outfit and brushed out her hair, leaving it loose around her shoulders, and added a touch of lip gloss. She kisses me on the cheek.

As Shane pulls her into the elevator, she waves at me. "Have fun on your date tonight!"

It's not quite five o'clock yet, and our reservation isn't until six, so we have a little bit of time to kill. I head to our suite and find Cooper in the shower. That is just way too much temptation for me to resist.

Besides, it's my birthday.

Cooper laughs as I strip down in record time and climb into the shower with him, wrapping my arms around his wet, sexy body. He's in the process of soaping himself, so I add my two hands to the mix and spread soap suds across his broad chest, over his shoulders, and down his arms. Then I lean in and kiss him, smacking my lips playfully against his.

He smiles at me. "You're in a good mood this evening."

"Damn right I am. It's my birthday, and I'm going out with my favorite guy this evening. What's there not to like?"

Cooper pulls me into his arms, and we're standing chest to chest, the soap suds making our bodies slide against each other. Every time his nipples brush mine—or more specifically brush my nipple piercings—my knees go weak. When he flutters his tongue against one of the barbells, I sag against him. "So not fair," I moan.

He laughs, then gives me a deep, luscious kiss. "Let's finish getting ready. Our dinner awaits."

Half an hour later, we're both dressed and ready to go. Cooper surprises me by dressing up in black slacks, a white dress shirt, and a black leather jacket.

"Is this a dressy place?" I ask him.

"No. It's casual. You can wear whatever you want. I just felt like wearing this."

I'm wearing my favorite ripped jeans and a T-shirt that says *I'm With Him*, with a finger pointing to my right. Cooper raises an eyebrow at my clothing selection, but says nothing.

"Do I look okay?" I say, holding my hands out to my sides.

He nods. "Yes, you look fantastic."

* * *

We grab a taxi outside our building, and Cooper and I slide into the back seat. Cooper rattles off an address to our driver.

It seems like everyone is out this evening. The sidewalks are filled with pedestrians, many of whom are dressed in green for the holiday, and the traffic is practically bumper-to-bumper.

"So, where are we going?" I ask.

Cooper shrugs. "You'll see."

I laugh. "You're not going to tell me?"

"No. It's a surprise."

I settle back in my seat. "Okay, fine. Be that way."

He lays his left hand on my thigh, and I lay my hand over top of his, stroking the back of his long fingers. I can't get over the change in him since we came back from Sweetwater. He's so much more comfortable in his own skin now—much more comfortable owning his sexuality. As traumatic as the trip was—and the ensuing aftermath—I'm grateful that it happened. I'm grateful he was willing to confront his past and begin to let go of the horror he experienced.

I'm so focused on him that I'm not paying attention to where we're going until the taxi comes to a stop. I glance out the window and am surprised to see we're parked in front of Rowdy's—a neighborhood bar that's popular with the McIntyre Security crowd. I can see through the front windows that the place is packed tonight. That's not surprising as it's St. Patrick's Day. Tonight all of the bars are bound to be filled to capacity.

Cooper takes care of the fare, and then we hop out. When we reach the entrance, he opens the door for me—the perfect gentleman—and motions for me to step inside. Sure enough, it's standing room only. That's no surprise, given the holiday. It seems like everyone's out to party tonight. But that's okay. I'm just excited to be out with my guy.

Cooper follows me inside, and as the door closes behind him, there's a sudden hush in the room as everyone turns to look at us.

"Surprise!" Everyone in the bar jumps to their feet and shouts, "Happy birthday!"

That's when I start to pick out all the familiar faces in the crowd. Beth, Shane, Lia, Jonah, Erin, Mack, Mateo, Philip, Liam, Miguel, Gabrielle, Jake, and so many more friends and colleagues I can't even begin to count them all. Everyone's here. I swear, half of the Chicago office is here tonight. I'm floored that he would do this for me... something so public.

I glance back at Cooper, who has a big smile on his face. "Did you do this?" I ask him.

He nods, then he stuns me even more when he reaches for my hand, linking our fingers. "Isn't this what boyfriends do?"

My eyes tear up, and I wrap my arms around Cooper, squeezing him tight. He hugs me back, fiercely and completely, without reservation, and everyone in the joint starts cheering. My throat closes up so tightly I can't even speak. I just bury my face in the crook of his neck and hold on for dear life as I struggle not to bawl like a baby. I knew he was *trying*, but *this?* This is insane. I never dreamed he'd put himself—put *us*—out here like this.

When I lift my head to look at him through tear-filled eyes, he smiles and brushes his thumb across my cheek catching a tear. His expression—part terrified, part exhilarated—says it all. This is what I needed from him. This is everything. It's beyond anything I ever dreamed possible. I'm so his for the rest of my life.

Cooper takes my hand and leads me up to the bar where the bartender has two glasses of champagne ready for us. He hands Cooper a microphone.

Holy shit! Now what?

Cooper turns to face the crowd and clears his throat. He hesitates for a moment, taking a deep breath as if he's trying to psych himself up, then clears his throat again. "Thank you, everyone, for coming tonight to help me celebrate Sam's twenty-ninth birthday."

The place erupts in cheers again, and I reach for Cooper's free hand, squeezing it tightly. My heart's pounding, and all I can think is that I hope I don't have to say anything, because I don't think I can speak right now.

Cooper hands me a glass of champagne and picks up the other one for himself. "I'd like to make a toast," he says into the mic. "To Sam Harrison. Happy twenty-ninth birthday, Sam. May you have many, many more."

That's when I notice that everyone is holding a glass of champagne, and they all raise their glasses and drink to Cooper's toast. Beth smiles at me over the rim of her glass of orange juice.

After taking a sip of his champagne, Cooper sets his glass on the bar and takes my hand. Then he turns to face the crowd. "As some of you know, Sam is my better half. And in case there are any of you who don't know...news flash, I'm gay, and I love this guy right here."

He raises our joined hands above our heads, and the crowd erupts in more cheers accompanied with some hoots and hollers.

Beth launches herself into my arms and squeezes the breath right out of me. "Happy birthday, Sam!" she says, releasing me just long enough to pull Cooper into a group hug. "Two of my favorite guys. I couldn't be happier."

Shane moves in behind Beth and claps Cooper on the back, nodding with approval. "Well done, my friend." Then he claps me on the back as well. "I'm happy for you both."

For the next half hour, we're bombarded with well-wishers coming up to shake our hands and wish me happy birthday. Cooper takes it all in stride, never straying from my side.

"Hey, red!" Lia says, making her way up to the bar. She bumps me with her hip. "Happy birthday."

"Thanks, shorty."

"Hey, be nice," she says. "My boyfriend's providing the entertainment tonight. Show some respect."

At her gesture, I spot Jonah setting up a microphone stand and a stool on the small stage off to the side of the bar.

"Jonah's playing tonight?" I say, rather unnecessarily as the guy's sitting on the barstool now and tuning his acoustic guitar. After fiddling with the microphone stand, Jonah nods to someone off stage, and the lights go down in the bar. A spotlight shines on Jonah, and the crowd goes quiet with anticipation.

"Good evening, everyone. I'm Jonah Locke."

Applause and cheers fill the air, and Jonah smiles.

"Thank you. I'm going to start with a special request," Jonah says, looking our way.

Cooper lifts our joined hands and kisses the back of mine. "Sam, will you do me the honor of dancing with me?"

The room starts spinning, and I feel light-headed. And fuck, now I have even more tears obscuring my vision. He's going to make me cry in front of a room full of people.

"I'll take that as a 'yes,'" Cooper says, and everyone laughs.

Jonah starts strumming a few opening chords, and then he starts singing one of our favorite songs, *Somewhere Only We Know*. This song is our anthem.

Cooper leads me to the small dance floor, which is currently vacant and surrounded by a ring of people standing several deep. He pulls me into the middle of the open space and holds my hand and my waist and leads me in a slow, shuffling dance. Everyone moves to surround the dance floor, couples with their arms around each other, holding hands. I can't help noticing that I'm not the only one who's tearing up.

"This isn't so bad, is it?" I ask him.

He nods, giving me a rueful smile. "I think I can get used to this."

Cooper pulls me close and leans in to whisper. "I love you, Sam. I don't deserve you, but I'm yours for the rest of my life, if you'll have me."

I pull back to stare at him, honestly more shaken than I've ever been in my life.

He pulls me close once more, bringing his lips to my ear. "Sam, will you marry me?"

Shocked, I pull back and search his gaze as if I'm afraid this is all a big prank. But his gaze is earnest, if a little wary as if he's not sure of my answer. Swallowing a choked cry, I throw my arms around him and bury my face in the crook of his neck. I just can't deal right now. He draws me close, his big hand gripping the back of my head, holding me securely against his strong body. "Is that a yes?" he says, chuckling.

"Yes," I manage to get out, holding him tightly. "God, yes."

Someone taps me on the shoulder, and I look down into Beth's teary-eyed face. "Can I cut in?" she says, her voice wavering as she reaches for me.

Cooper smiles as he hands me over to Beth, and she wraps her arms around my waist.

"He asked me to marry him," I tell her.

"I know," she says, her voice breaking as she rubs my back. "He asked for our permission. Shane's and mine."

"Really?"

"Yeah, really. What did you say?"

"I said 'yes,' of course! What did you expect?"

Beth and I dance for about half a minute before Cooper cuts back in.

"I want to dance with my fiancé," he says, pulling me into his arms. "That's what fiancés do, right?"

I smile at him through tear-filled eyes. "Right."

The end... for now.
But it's just the beginning for Sam and Cooper.

Books by April Wilson

McIntyre Security Bodyguard Series:

Vulnerable

Fearless

Shane (a novella)

Broken

Shattered

Imperfect

Ruined

Hostage

Redeemed

Marry Me (a novella)

Snowbound (a novella)

Regret

With This Ring (a novella)

Collateral Damage

Special Delivery

The Tyler Jamison Series:

Somebody to Love

Somebody to Hold

The British Billionaire Romance Series:

Charmed

For a list of my audiobooks, visit my website:

www.aprilwilsonauthor.com/audiobooks

Please Leave a Review on Amazon

I hope you'll take a moment to leave a review for me on Amazon. It doesn't have to be long... just a brief comment saying whether you liked the book or not. How did it make you feel? Reviews are vitally important to authors and they're so hard to get because not many readers leave them! I'd be incredibly grateful to you if you'd leave one for me.

Stay in Touch

Follow me on Facebook or subscribe to my newsletter for up-to-date information on the schedule for new releases. I'm active daily on Facebook, and I love to interact with my readers. Come talk to me on Facebook by leaving me a message or a comment, or share my book posts with your friends. I also have a very active fan group on Facebook (just search for "Author April Wilson's Fan Group" on Facebook) where I post weekly excerpts and run lots of giveaway contests. Come join us! We're a super fun bunch!

Acknowledgements

So many wonderful people supported me on this journey.

As always, I owe a huge debt of gratitude to my sister, Lori, for being there with me every step of the way. She's read *Ruined* so many times, she must surely be sick of it by now. Her support and encouragement are priceless.

I want to thank Rebecca Morean, my dear friend and writing buddy, and author extraordinaire, for finding Sam for me. She found my cover model after I'd spent countless hours searching and came up empty-handed. Thank you, Becky, for your amazing friendship and camaraderie.

I want to thank fellow author Damien Benoit-Ledoux for his invaluable feedback and kind support. His generous guidance helped make *Ruined* a better book—plus, he's just an all-around awesome guy!

I want to thank Sue Vaughn Boudreaux for taking pity on me and volunteering her many excellent skills in support of my work. You've quickly become a trusted and valued confidant.

I want to thank my awesome beta reader team for all of their love and support: Sue Boudreaux, Julie Collier, Sarah Louise Frost, Lori Holmes, Keely Knutton, Tiffany Mann, Becky Morean, and Brooke Smith.

Finally, I want to thank all of my readers around the globe and the members of my fan group on Facebook. I am so incredibly blessed to have you. Your love and support and enthusiasm feed my soul on a daily basis. Many of my readers have become familiar names and faces greeting me daily on Facebook, and I feel so blessed to have made so many new friends. I thank you all, from the bottom of my heart, for every Facebook like, share, and comment. You have no idea how thrilled I am to read your comments each day. I wouldn't be able to do the thing that I love to do most—share my characters and their stories—without your amazing support. Every day, I wake up and thank my lucky stars for you all!

With much love to you all... April

Made in United States
North Haven, CT
28 April 2022

18693945R00198